THE FOOLISH GENTLEWOMAN

BOOKS BY

Margery Sharp

RHODODENDRON PIE

FANFARE FOR TIN TRUMPETS

THE FLOWERING THORN

FOUR GARDENS

THE NUTMEG TREE

HARLEQUIN HOUSE

THE STONE OF CHASTITY

THREE COMPANION PIECES

CLUNY BROWN

BRITANNIA MEWS

THE FOOLISH GENTLEWOMAN

THE FOOLISH GENTLEWOMAN

Margery Sharp

Little, Brown and Company · Boston
1948

PRINTED IN THE UNITED STATES OF AMERICA
BY H. WOLFF, NEW YORK

TO

GEOFFREY CASTLE

PART ONE

Chapter 1

Chipping Lodge is the oldest house on Chipping Hill, and the least typical: for being so high and airy, and only eight miles from Charing Cross, the district early attracted commercial or professional wealth, and the resulting villa-residences (each a monument to Victorian success) are as remarkable for exuberance of design as solidity of construction. Some resemble enormous cuckoo clocks, others miniature railway stations; Chipping Priory crosses cathedral with *chalet;* but the Lodge shows a plain white façade topped by a flat cornice, with for all ornament the fan-shaped pediments to the long rows of windows, and a pair of stucco goddesses, antique but decent, on the terrace behind.

Forty years ago it belonged to a family named Massey. There were two daughters, Ruth and Isabel, both very pretty girls with twenty-inch waists and quantities of fluffy hair — enough to go up in a dozen little puffs by day, or eighteen (bound with ribbon, like a charlotte russe) for an evening party; they played tennis rather well (Ruth could serve overhand), and sang duets. These gifts and accomplishments, their own good-nature and their parents' hospitality, made them universally popular, but their closest allies were the two Brocken boys from the Priory, whom they had known all their lives. Mark and Simon Brocken partnered the Massey girls at tennis, and squired them to dances—Mark with alacrity, Simon out of affection for his brother, and because they formed so natural and accepted a quartette. It was a surprise to neither family when in 1912 Mark and Isabel became engaged. Twelve months later they were married; and this was the root-reason why Simon Brocken, on the last Saturday in June 1946, found himself once more a guest upon the terrace of Chipping Lodge.

He was not a very eager one. He liked the big white house, and always had done; he had a taste for plainness, and its architecture pleased him; but the very fact that it was still his sister-in-law's property, open to whomever she chose to invite, aroused a whole train of infuriating memories.

The sequence of events was this.

When old Mr. Massey died a widower he left the house to Isabel and the money to Ruth—a reasonable act enough, since Ruth had married a New Zealander and gone to live in Wellington. Isabel and Mark, however, were already settled at the Priory, inherited by Mark from old Mr. Brocken: the reasonable act for Isabel was obviously to sell the Lodge. If its size was now a disadvantage, its grounds, as building land, had become extremely valuable, and attached as she was to the whole district of Chipping Hill, Isabel could hardly want two houses on it.

But it turned out that Isabel did. Both Mark and Simon reasoned with her in vain: she was very fond of the Priory, genuinely admiring its rabid architecture, and at the same time disliked the idea of selling the Lodge. She said it was such a dear old house, and they had all had such happy times there, and moreover she was sure her father had meant her to keep it. The problem was solved, or rather shelved, by the appearance of the Wakes, a family of returned Anglo-Indians who offered to take the place furnished while they tested the amenities of the neighbourhood. To this Isabel agreed because she knew a very nice woman who had been at the same boarding-school as Mrs. Wake, and actually in the same House (St. Patrick's), though not at the same time.

Again Mark and Simon reasoned, pointing out the endless troubles to be expected from a succession of tenants; Isabel was confident that once the Wakes were in they would stay. Her confidence was justified. This was no doubt partly because she set a very low rent; she avoided telling Simon what it was, and Mark loyally held his tongue, merely observing (when he saw the first cheque) that it would be more picturesque, and about equally profitable, if Mr. Wake appeared in person with a bag of peppercorns. In any case the Wakes stayed on, year after year, actually until the 1940 blitz; at the same period Isabel evacuated herself to Bath; and a month later — how undeservedly! — was justified afresh when a direct hit reduced the Priory to ruins. She had now not two Chipping Hill houses, but one. If she had not held on to the

Lodge, she would have had no Chipping Hill house at all.

Simon had now to find a caretaker. For Mark Brocken never saw the destruction of his home; his death twelve months earlier spared him that, as it spared him much else very distressing to so kindly a man; Simon, feeling the greatest loss of his life, nevertheless knew himself far the better equipped to carry on, literally through fire and water, the business and traditions of the family firm. (Brockens had been solicitors since solicitors were attorneys: during the night of the twenty-ninth December, 1940, Simon Brocken personally carried fifteen deed boxes out into Red Lion Place and stood guard over them till morning.) Isabel's affairs had devolved upon him as a matter of course, and he was actually seeking a caretaker for the Priory, as well as for the Lodge, when the bomb halved his pains.

They were still considerable. Even one caretaker was hard enough to come by: for months Mr. Brocken looked hopefully for the Lodge to be requisitioned. But Chipping Hill abounded in large empty houses: Food Office, A.R.P., Red Cross and Ack-Ack — all were easily accommodated, elsewhere. In the end he engaged a Mrs. Poole. She was recommended by the local news-agent, she appeared clean, quiet and civil, had a small daughter who would not only keep her company, but also postpone her call-up; the size of the house did not alarm her, and Mr. Brocken stifled his qualms. These indeed were due to no more than her extreme smallness and slightness; she didn't look big enough for the job. But a subsequent visit of inspection showed that she could keep the place clean, and the news-agent, upon whom Simon also paid a call, assured him that the Pooles lived quietly and decorously—"snug as mice in a wedding-cake"; a flight of fancy, with its reference to the great white house and the diminutive Pooles, by no means inapt.

For nearly six years this arrangement continued satisfactorily, and when the war ended Mr. Brocken on his own initiative advertised the property for sale. Owing to numerous and complex building regulations the land was now less attractive, but the proprietors of a commercial college made a very fair bid for the whole. Mr. Brocken communicated their offer to his sister-in-law at Bath, and received a reply from Chipping Hill. Isabel had just returned, and was living at the Lodge herself. She had not told him in advance because she wanted to give him a surprise.

She failed. Mr. Brocken was merely infuriated. Their long connection had established only one point in his sister-in-law's favour, but it was this: he knew where he was with her. Her behaviour was consistent. If she now returned, a childless widow, to a house so large it couldn't possibly be run; if she casually rejected the best offer she was ever likely to get for it; if she simply closed her eyes to the inevitable and exasperating consequences—at least Mr. Brocken had not to seek a reason for her conduct. Being idiotic, it explained itself. The whole long imbroglio merely reaffirmed two convictions: that no woman could be trusted with property, and that Mark had married a fool.

For the immediate present, however, while the bomb-damage to his own house was being repaired, her hospitality was convenient, and Simon Brocken had arrived resolute to forbear. This resolve was at once put to the test, since Isabel was not at home to receive him.

She was out with the dog. A Miss Brown who let him in offered to show him his room; Mr. Brocken characteristically stood on the point of etiquette and said he would await his hostess on the terrace. Since then half an hour had passed; the unusual heat of the June sun brought him out in a light sweat; he was wearing City clothes and wished to change; that he could still take pleasure in the beauties of architecture struck Simon Brocken, quite simply, as admirable.

"Admirable!" he said aloud—passing the compliment on, as it were, to the scene before him. Scene was the right word: it now struck him that in the strong light, against a blue sky, the white façade resembled a stage set. There were no shadows, save for the twin silhouettes cast by the two statues, and these fell so boldly and precisely that they might have been painted, *pour tromper l'oeil,* on the two planes of wall and pavement. But if the effect were theatrical, it was also classic: the theatre (the French phrase carried its overtones) that of Racine: suggesting unity of time, place, action: strict logic and no nonsense. Such fancies came rarely to Mr. Brocken, but this one pleased him, he admitted it as acceptable; at least, he thought, whatever happens here will be rational; and familiar, and undisturbing. He even began to regret that he had not accepted his sister-in-law's hospitality sooner. She had telephoned him, during the past month, at least three times.

At this moment Miss Brown emerged from the house carrying a small tray.

2

"I've brought you some tea," she said. "Do you like gingerbread?"

"Very much," replied Mr. Brocken. He looked at the neat brown squares appreciatively; he had not tasted gingerbread for years. As Miss Brown set down the tray on a small iron table he looked at her too: of medium height, compactly built, fair-haired and clear-skinned, she struck him as healthier-looking than most of Isabel's companions, and moderately sensible.

Miss Brown, frankly returning the scrutiny, saw a man of sixty, small and spare, and neat with the neatness of a bachelor whose housekeeper looks after his clothes. His linen was fresh, his waistcoat unspotted; some wives let their husbands go about like scarecrows; but any woman could tell at a glance that Mr. Brocken was unmarried. There were only two things noticeable about him. One was his iron-grey moustache: uncommonly thick, and clipped uncommonly close, the resultant texture something between moleskin and badger, it exactly filled the whole of his upper lip like a strip of fur neatly applied. The other thing was a scar across his forehead made by a German trench dagger in 1917. Mr. (then Captain) Brocken had killed the German with a revolver, thought nothing much of the episode at the time, and rarely thought of it since: it was a mishap incident to his age and nationality. These parallel lines of scar and moustache, barring his narrow face, made it easy for him to appear formidable. The companion said hastily,

"I'm sure Mrs. Brocken won't be long, because after the first hill Bogey always has to be carried."

"That creature!" said Mr. Brocken. The only dogs he respected, and therefore liked, were Airedales; Bogey was a Sealyham. "Isn't he dead yet?"

Miss Brown in some surprise answered that Bogey had in fact seen the vet on Tuesday, but the vet only prescribed exercise — which was no doubt why Mrs. Brocken had not liked to forgo their usual walk.

"She'll find the heat too much for her," prophesied Mr. Brocken. "How is she?"

Miss Brown hesitated.

"Very well . . ."

"You seem to be in some doubt," said Mr. Brocken. "My sister-in-law's health is usually excellent."

"Oh, it is. It is now. Well, you'll see for yourself," said Miss Brown; and withdrew into the house.

Evidently less sensible than she looked, reflected Mr. Brocken — but without surprise. He was used to being disappointed. It didn't surprise him that the gingerbread into which he now bit failed to come up to his recollections of it: Camembert cheese hadn't either. . . . Simon chewed and chewed, producing a sort of rubbery paste that stuck to his palate, insoluble even by tea; he kneaded it with his tongue till his tongue ached, and at last almost choked in swallowing it. "I shall do myself some injury," thought Mr. Brocken morosely; the gingerbread was undoubtedly below par.

Quite a large piece, however, remained on his plate. He did not want it, he did not like to leave it; he determined to commit the economic crime of throwing it away. Below the southern end of the terrace, if memory served, the lawn dropped so steeply as to form a little dell of long grass, impossible to mow: towards this natural oubliette Mr. Brocken carefuly bore the crumby wedge. He reached the end wall, he looked over; the dell was still there, and in it, face downwards, lay a naked young man.

3

The moment of anxiety was brief. The lean brown body showed no wound — or no fresh wound; one shoulder bore a dimpled scar — the fair head lay comfortably pillowed on a towel. Sun-bathing was not a practice Mr. Brocken actively disapproved, trespassing was; but the knowledge that his sister-in-law might appear at any moment, and possibly look over the wall too, impelled him to deal with the lesser point first. He coughed loudly, and the young man stirred.

"I think you should know," said Mr. Brocken, "that there may be ladies present at any moment."

The young man rolled over and reached for a pair of sun-glasses; and in the second before he put them on Mr. Brocken recognized him. He was Humphrey Garrett, the son of Isabel's sister Ruth, and at one time Mr. Brocken saw a good deal of him; for though the Garretts lived in New Zealand the boy Humphrey had his schooling in England and spent holidays with his Aunt Isabel and Uncle Mark. That was of course several years ago, but Mr. Brocken felt no hesitation in resuming an old authority.

"Good afternoon, Humphrey," he said severely. "Put that towel round you at once. Are you staying here?"

"For the moment," replied Humphrey. "Are you?"

"For some weeks. Didn't your aunt mention it?"

Humphrey shook his head.

"Nor did she mention you to me," said Mr. Brocken.

"I reckon," said Humphrey, after a moment's thought, "she wanted us to be a surprise for each other."

"Humph," said Mr. Brocken. The explanation was undoubtedly correct; he might have discovered it for himself. "How's your mother?"

"In the pink of health."

"I'm glad to hear it. Does she still like New Zealand?"

"In Mamma's opinion, Down Under remains tops."

Mr. Brocken was at once pricked by a familiar irritation. That ridiculous turn of speech, that mixture of slang and preciseness, had always annoyed him; and he would have been annoyed still more to know that the preciseness was in origin a mimicry of himself. However, he strove to look amiable: the lad had by all accounts done very well in the war, this was their first meeting since it ended, it was a moment for cordiality.

"Well, we've all been very proud of you," said Mr. Brocken.

"How nice," said Humphrey.

"I suppose you're demobilized?"

"Last month. Don't you like your gingerbread?"

"I am particularly fond of it," said Mr. Brocken. He took a demonstration bite. "Why should you think otherwise?"

"I thought perhaps you were coming to chuck it away," explained Humphrey. "Aunt Isabel tells me she often used to get rid of seed-cake here. As a child, of course. I thought perhaps you had the same idea."

There was a short silence while Mr. Brocken masticated. The prospect of this young man's company was not exactly disagreeable, but he felt it had been sprung on him. To conceal a slight resentment he said encouragingly,

"So you are here to take a well-earned rest. Excellent. I wish I could do the same. How is your aunt?"

"Very well," said Humphrey; and removing the glasses turned back upon his face.

Mr. Brocken retraced his steps in a distinctly worse humour. He felt he had been trifled with; he had certainly been foiled; he was far too much put out to sit and wait any longer like a pumpkin ripening in the sun. Annoyance carried him past his tea-tray, past the goddesses, and off the terrace altogether.

From its other end a path masked by laurel led to the back entrance of the stables: a mere doorless slit between coach-house and harness room, so dark and narrow that any child at once recognized it for a secret passage; as all secret passages should, it opened (at least when the sun shone) upon splendour. For stables are built of brick, whatever mode a house follows, and weathered brick, in sun, holds all the colours of a zinnia; moreover the roofs were blue slate, and the doors and sills painted green; and wherever mortar had dropped, or paint flaked away, a yellowish lichen spread rich as velvet. To the right rose the end wall of the house, to the left stables for three horses with a hayloft above; directly opposite wide gates opened on the drive. The space thus enclosed, when Mr. Brocken entered, was filled with stillness as a cistern is filled with water: not even his own footfall sounded, the cobbles were so overgrown.

He entered, accompanied by ghosts.

All places we have known in youth are haunted, but not all ghosts wring their hands; as many play cat's-cradle, or strum "The Merry Peasant," or slip a first ball dress over bright hair. The party pressing close on Mr. Brocken's heels was an extremely cheerful one. There was his brother Mark, a young man as lanky and elegant and high-collared as had been, thirty-five years ago, Mr. Brocken himself; the two girls were there, Ruth and Isabel, smart in white piqué; and a third man, a stranger, someone the Brockens had staying with them . . . a subaltern in the Gunners, called Macgregor. They all trooped through the narrow passage, talking and laughing and carrying Mr. Brocken along with them; and there in the centre of the yard a girl in a big apron, her head tied up in a pink handkerchief, clasped a wet Maltese poodle in her streaming arms. Every detail of the scene was noon-day clear.

4

"There's Tilly washing Puck," said Isabel.

"Mind your skirts, girls," said Mark. Puck had leapt from the tin bath; the three men gallantly formed a protective screen. But Tilly caught the animal in time and held him struggling against her bib; she bent her head this way and that to avoid Puck's dripping ears, her sallow cheeks for once as pink as carnations—as pink as her head-kerchief; still she held on, so tightly that streams of soapy water ran over her thin arms and down her apron to the ground.

"I say, can't I lend a hand?" offered Mr. Macgregor.

But Isabel said Tilly would manage, and they would show him the stables later, and the party beat a retreat. No one ever paid much attention to Tilly Cuff; she was the Masseys' poor relation, some sort of second cousin, who lived with them and made herself useful. But when some nights later the Masseys gave a dance, both Mark and Simon, after their duty turn with Tilly, found in Puck a valuable topic of conversation. "He was quite good as soon as you went," said Tilly, in her flat colourless voice. Evening dress didn't suit her, she was too skinny, whereas the Massey girls in their new Liberty satins bloomed and sparkled and outshone everyone else. Isabel especially was in good looks; Simon began to watch his brother anxiously, for Simon had a low opinion of girls in general, made no exception in favour of the Masseys, and considered Isabel in particular a fluffy-headed nincompoop. He was twenty-four, and Mark a year older; but Mark was dashing, Simon cautious. By careful chaperonage (by making a third, for instance, at their *tête-à-tête* in the conservatory) he prevented Mark from taking, that evening, any irrevocable step. But all in vain; next morning, as the two Brockens prepared to walk up with their guest for his farewell call at the Lodge, Mark privately announced his intention of asking Isabel to marry him.

Was it this that accounted for the curious flatness, the discomfort almost, of that visit? Simon was certainly distressed, Mark probably nervous; but the girls too seemed out of sorts. They were all gathered in the morning-room; it was a moment (before the elder Masseys appeared) for a last bout of the chaff and friendliness that had been a feature of Macgregor's visit. But a constraint hung over the party; only Ruth had anything to say for herself; Isabel was silent, and Tilly, most astonishingly, rude. She turned her back on every one, clattered among the flower-pots in the bow-window, and when Macgregor politely approached, with a word of praise for the hyacinths, replied tartly that she found their scent overpowering and left the room.

"What's the matter with Tilly?" asked Mark.

"Oh, I expect she's offended about something," said Isabel carelessly. "She often is. Mr. Macgregor, come and see the hyacinths in the hall."

They went out; they came back. With the appearance of Mr. and Mrs. Massey conversation became general and uninteresting. As the three young men walked back down the drive Simon felt a slight resurgence of hope. He said he had always heard that women were short-tempered before lunch.

"Oh, rot," said Mark (the incurable). "One just shouldn't call on girls the morning after a dance. They're tired out, poor kittens. If it hadn't been for Macgregor, they'd all be having breakfast in bed."

There was no saving him. His goose was cooked. He proposed to Isabel a week later, and went on proposing till she accepted him. She took an uncommonly long time about it, but the issue was never (in the opinion of either family) seriously in doubt.

5

Mr. Brocken took a step forward over the grass-grown cobbles: the ghosts vanished. For a moment he was left suspended between past and present, and well he knew which way his heart yearned. It was not his youth he so much regretted, nor even the old familiar faces; his emotion was far more general. What he longed to return to was an orderly world. No one, in Mr. Brocken's opinion, had tasted the sweetness of life who had not lived before 1914. What years those were for solid comfort! What servants, what meals, what excellent claret! Simon meditated nostalgically upon this theme for some minutes; but even dearer to his recollection was the general atmosphere of order and decorum. One did not then meet young men lying naked on lawns: they appeared decently erect, high-collared on the hottest day. Laxity was unknown, at any rate upon Chipping Hill: the parent Brockens, like the parent Masseys, brought up their offspring to count their blessings, do their duty, and respect their elders. Yet the régime was not oppressive, it produced cheerful households, full of plans and pleasures; able to bear misfortune when it came (usually in the form of some one's death) all the more stoutly because disaster no less than prosperity was the Will of God. In those days, as often as not, a death meant a legacy.

Such was the picture revived, and perhaps a little gilded, by Simon Brocken; but gilded or not, where now could one find a picture to match it? The general lowering of standards, affecting manners and morals no less than gingerbread and cheese, afflicted him so severely that he often talked of retiring altogether from active life. Where now was the old-fashioned integrity, the old-fashioned conscientiousness? In his own office his own chief clerk had suddenly demanded a working day of nine to five instead of nine to six: as for domestic servants, tradesmen and public officials, in Mr. Brocken's view they simply did no work at all; and since the spare tyre had been stolen from his car he had begun to look doubtfully even upon the police. The wider scene was in a worse state still: one could only quote Oxenstiern: *Nescis, mi fili,* do you not know, my son, *quantilla prudentia,* with how little wisdom, *mundus regatur,* the world is governed? Mr. Brocken repeated the phrase frequently; he did so now; and thus found himself talking Latin to his sister-in-law, who at that moment walked towards him through the great gate.

Chapter 2

At fifty-five Isabel Brocken was still a nice-looking woman. She dated, of course, all her female friends said so — poor Isabel certainly dated; she was rather plump, and wore her faded hair in a kind of neat bird's-nest, but her complexion was pretty and the blue of her eyes scarcely faded at all. The most striking thing about her was her expression, for she nearly always looked pleased; and though this, in 1946, was really but a final proof of her thorough foolishness, some people found her appearance refreshing.

Mr. Brocken did not. "*Quantilla prudentia!*" he thought, as she advanced towards him (looking pleased) with outstretched hands. She kissed him warmly on both cheeks, leaving a faint smell of violet powder, stood back a pace to look at him, and kissed him again.

"My dear Simon, how lovely to see you! But what on earth are you doing here? I've looked for you everywhere!"

"I have been in this spot," said Mr. Brocken, "ten minutes at the most. Before that — "

"But they told me you were on the terrace. Then I

looked upstairs, and I looked in the dining-room, it's only by the merest chance I've found you at all. But I *am* sorry I was out when you came; I didn't expect you so soon."

"I said I should be here at three, and I was," stated Simon.

"I know, dear, but you might have missed your train."

"Do I usually miss my train?"

"No, Simon, I must admit you don't. You're like the pitcher to the well. But they are often *late,* of their own accord."

Mr. Brocken let the matter drop; his sister-in-law's anthropomorphic view of trains was familiar to him. Isabel, still regarding him fondly, suggested that they should return to the terrace for more tea, and as he followed her back through the passage Simon, not for the first time, reflected with surprise that she really appeared to have a genuine affection for him. He couldn't for the life of him think why. In all their dealings his was the disagreeable rôle of mentor; whatever plan Isabel advanced, his duty was inevitably to thwart it; and Mr. Brocken was not conceited enough to perceive in himself any compensating charms. To be loved without reason did not flatter him. He put up with Isabel's affection, as he put up with Isabel, because he had to.

They regained the terrace, where a fresh tea-tray had been placed on the iron table. In the round of shadow beneath sat a large Sealyham. His shaggy eyebrows and meditative gaze gave him an old-gentleman look; he sat there like a retired colonel, newspaper laid aside, contemplating Socialism. The sight of Mr. Brocken, however, produced a startling change; without the slightest warning the animal went into transports. His years fell from him, he rushed forth, he leapt up and down, hurled himself at Mr. Brocken's knees, fell over backwards, waltzed after his own tail, all the while barking furious protestations of love and admiration. Simon was not impressed. He knew that a tramp would have received the same welcome; in his view such extreme sociableness amounted to a form of canine lunacy.

"See how Bogey remembers you!" exclaimed Isabel fondly.

"I am not taken in," said Mr. Brocken. He felt Bogey's demonstrativeness an uncomfortably close parody of Isabel's; it was a relief when the animal, after one last shout of praise, returned with cynical abruptness to his rôle of old gentleman. He ceased to leap, indeed could hardly stand; tottered back into the shade and there, panting feebly, collapsed.

Mrs. Brocken meanwhile poured out. She did so with a certain conscious elegance; in her youth the nice conduct of a tea-table had been a minor feminine accomplishment, and even behind a clothless iron tripod her gestures referred to immaculate linen, thin china, and silver spoons.

"By the way," said Simon, "how do you get on with the Pooles?"

"Very well, dear," said Isabel. "Very well indeed. In fact, we never see them."

"But they make themselves useful?"

"Very. Jacky — that's Miss Brown — worked it all out, and we all do our share." Isabel paused. "Mrs. Poole tells me you gave them the use of the winter garden."

Mr. Brocken remembered that this was so. When he offered them the kitchen, the maids' sitting-room and two attics, Mrs. Poole had said they would like the winter garden as well. It abutted on the southern end of the house, the end opposite from the stables, and since it could be reached by a door from the service quarters, as well as from the drawing-room, he had raised no objection.

"I believe I did," he admitted. "Do you mind?"

"Not in the least, dear. I just can't think why they want it. You were wonderfully clever to find them — but then of course you *are*." Isabel beamed. She always longed to show gratitude to her kind brother-in-law, and now she could. She was going to give him a treat. "My dear Simon," she said, "I've such a surprise!"

"If you mean young Humphrey, I've seen him," said Mr. Brocken.

Isabel's face fell.

"Oh, dear, have I missed your meeting?"

"It was not," said Mr. Brocken, "particularly moving."

"But you must have been pleased to see each other. Don't you think he's grown wonderfully handsome?"

"He seems a nice-looking boy. I have also encountered Miss Brown. You had better tell me about her."

Isabel sighed. Ever since she had accidentally engaged a young woman wanted by the police (though for no more, as Isabel pointed out, than receiving stolen goods) Simon required the dossier of each fresh companion. Isabel vaguely suspected a reflection on her judgment, but had learnt not to argue. She folded her hands, crossed her ankles in front of her, and said patiently,

"Her name is Jacqueline Brown, she's just out of the ATS, and I gave her a lift in my car between Bath and Wells."

"One of these days you'll pick up a thug," prophesied Mr. Brocken.

"She was then *in* the ATS, dear. In uniform. I must say I'm so glad the papers have started to put 'a man wearing uniform' instead of 'a soldier'—when they do anything wrong." Mrs. Brocken reflected a moment, and added, "Though perhaps that destroys my point. However, we made great friends. She's going to be a painter, and doesn't mind being a companion while she starts, which I think is most brave and sensible. Her father—you'll like this, Simon—is a bank manager at Iron Newton, near Wolverhampton, Staffs."

"It must be a potty little branch," said Simon unkindly. "Have you seen him?"

"As a matter of fact, dear, I have. He came to London to be X-rayed, and we all had lunch together, and as a matter of fact I gave him *you* as a reference for *me*."

Mr. Brocken felt this was going too far. His sister-in-law, whatever her shortcomings, was obviously a gentlewoman; moreover it was going to be a great nuisance if every few months he was called on to provide her with a character.

"Hasn't he taken it up?" enquired Isabel anxiously.

"He apparently felt it unnecessary."

"I did so want to know what you'd say about me. I meant to find out from Jacqueline. But at least it shows I made a good impression."

A faint cloud crossed Mrs. Brocken's brow—only briefly, however, for her attention was really occupied by her brother-in-law, and she had still a treat in reserve for him which it was now (the examination over) time to produce. The Humphrey-treat had fallen a little flat; but that was more of a surprise, and Simon did not care for surprises—though Isabel never remembered this until just after she had given him one. It was with complete confidence, however, that she now gently spoke.

"And now, dear, we'll go to the Priory," said Isabel. "We won't take Bogey; we'll go just by ourselves."

2

Sentimental, affectionate, uncritical, Mrs. Brocken so easily attached herself to persons, places, and even objects that after no more than two days in an hotel she had a favourite waiter, a favourite ornament, a favourite view. She had adored her husband, and was very fond of her French pepper-mill. An old watering-can was dear to her because she remembered seeing the gardener use it on her mother's rose-beds, and a new alarm-clock, because it was so nice and bright. She had thus many small sources of pleasure, inoperative perhaps on deeper intellects, which,

again. A certain character endured, and in the big drawing-room, through which they entered, even a certain pride. It was a fine conventional saloon running the whole length of the house — lofty, well-proportioned, panelled in white and gold; though the paint had deepened to primrose, and the gilt faded, though the three chandeliers hung like gigantic wasps' nests in their holland bags, still one could visualize an old brilliance. Twenty couples had danced there, to a piano and two violins; and afterwards sat out on the stairs eating strawberry ice. . . .

"Do you remember our dances?" asked Isabel, over her shoulder.

Mr. Brocken nodded. They went on into the hall, where a big grandfather clock, its gold face incised with the signs of the Zodiac, emitted a steady, opinionated tick; on up the stairs, past the four coaching scenes, the two steel engravings, "Wellington and Blücher" and "Gordon at Khartoum"; the landing displayed more engravings, after Winterhalter, and a large oil copy of "Dignity and Impudence." Simon looked at them approvingly, for these were the sort of pictures he liked. In the room that had been Ruth's, and that was now to be his, the walls were bare: Ruth took her own pictures with her to New Zealand, and any substitutes put up by the Wakes had vanished with them; but Simon liked this too. The plainness and airiness of the big room were remarkably restful; its windows, facing east, admitted a cooler air. His suitcase stood at the foot of the bed, and clean towels muffled a can of hot water.

"This looks very pleasant," said Mr. Brocken.

"Doesn't it, dear? And the bathroom's just at the end of the passage." Isabel paused, lingering in the doorway. "Have you everything you want?"

"Everything, thank you."

"You know dinner's at seven, if you'd like to rest first."

"I believe I may take a short nap."

Still Isabel lingered. It was in her view a very agreeable conversation; she was loath to break it off.

"I've put a lot of good books on that shelf, in case you want to read. . . ."

Simon glanced at the row of calf bindings, and said that at the moment he could doze unaided.

"Then I expect you'd like to be left in peace," said Isabel regretfully.

Mr. Brocken did not deny it; at last Isabel closed the door. She closed it very quietly and gently, as though Mr. Brocken were an invalid; or as though he were some shy animal, newly captured, which she did not wish to alarm.

Chapter 3

A shipwrecked mariner, riding his hen-coop through the surf of an unfamiliar lagoon and observing islanders gathered on the beach, does not, in his eagerness to observe the colour of their skins, forget the colour of his own. They may be brown, black, yellow; himself white: it is important that a difference in pigmentation should not preclude sympathy. The case is extreme.—A girl coming new to her holiday camp scans the camp-pigmentation of slacks, play-suits or summer frocks; and before she reaches her *chalet* has mentally reviewed the contents of her suitcase. A wrong outfit might wreck her holiday. But it is the curious fact that Mr. Brocken, a man of far higher mental capacity than either girl or mariner, regarded his arrival at Chipping Lodge as a purely one-sided event. He knew how the house struck him, and how young Humphrey struck him, and Isabel and Miss Brown: it never entered his head to wonder how he struck them.

As far as Isabel was concerned this was reasonable; her welcome could be taken for granted. The knowledge that both Jacqueline Brown and Humphrey Garrett had resented his coming, disliked him in advance, and so far seen no ground for changing their opinion, would have surprised him considerably.

In the first place, they desired no change of any kind in the life at Chipping Lodge. As a rule it is the old who fear changes; but the circumstances of Jacqueline and Humphrey were peculiar — or peculiar to their generation. Both had got through the war years well enough: warfare, even civilized warfare, is not, to a thoroughly healthy young male, unmitigated purgatory; Jacqueline had suffered chiefly from the curtailment of her liberty and the enforced company of too many women, and on the other hand been glad to escape from a dull home. The enjoyment they were now tasting, however, was one of which the war had peculiarly deprived them: they were able to fall in love at leisure. During the war one met a man (or a girl) at a dance, on a course, discovered a sympathetic attraction, a promise of something more: before it had time to develop he (or she) was posted to Berwick or to Burma, and that (unless one were a faster and less fastidious worker than either Humphrey or Miss Brown) was the end of that. But now Humphrey could not be posted to Egypt, nor Jacqueline to Newcastle; they were sure of seeing each other to-morrow, and the day after that; and so rediscovered the delights of a leisured courtship. They had even, in Mrs. Brocken, a chaperon. When Simon later saw them sun-bathing side by side, half-naked in the dell, he certainly never thought of Jane Austen; but it was — comparatively speaking — at Miss Austen's tempo that their courtship proceeded.

They were enjoying every moment of it. Humphrey, at work in the garden, often let Jacqueline set down his mid-morning beer without attempting to detain her. Jacqueline could see Humphrey alone on the terrace without abandoning whatever task she was engaged on, and without resenting the task because it kept her from him. They were not only happy, but tranquil; and tranquillity was almost as precious to them as happiness, because they were both tired.

This was the second reason why Humphrey and Jacqueline desired no change. They were both tired after the war. By a piece of enormous good fortune they had found, in the gentle atmosphere of Chipping Lodge, an ideal climate in which to rest and recruit their spirits. This, they could say, is Peace, this is it; and asked no better than to live each day over again, unaltered, for at least a year.

Thus they felt the arrival of Mr. Brocken to be nearly as bad as a posting. Humphrey remembered him as dictatorial; both had had enough of being ordered about. Isabel spoke of him with affection, but also with uneasiness. The night before he came she made Jacqueline construct a detailed account of their expenses for the last two months, a thing they had never done before. It would have taken a far more amiable address than Mr. Brocken's to turn this current in his favour; and he in his obtuseness did not even suspect that any current flowed.

He took a short nap, awoke refreshed about six o'clock, and decided after all to go for a walk. He had no thought of revisiting the scenes of his youth, he simply wanted exercise. Nor did he think of inviting Isabel to accompany him. He simply walked out of the house.

2

Chipping Hill is by no means homogeneous. Its characteristic villa-residences occupy the Hill itself, and particularly the mile-long avenue known as the Ridge, but there is also a newer suburb below, centring round the railway station. Station Road is very different from the Ridge; its small houses, and shops with flats over them, are not exactly jerry-built, but they are not handsome. They are attractive chiefly because their owners take a pride in them, and put stucco dwarfs in the front garden, and invent names like Gladbert or Mibillet to paint on the gate. Row upon row of such dwellings rise from either side of Station Road, until checked on the south by the Ridge, and on the north by the outskirts of Broxbury: they house a population of small tradesmen, clerks, artisans, and their families: highly respectable, at a pinch heroic. Men had come back to Station Road from the stratosphere, from the ocean bed, from adventure unimagined by Jules Verne; while their much-bombed wives continued to wash on Mondays, mow the front lawn, and stick together, whenever possible, the fragments of their stucco dwarfs.

For so large a community there are very few big shops; these are found in Broxbury, the local metropolis. Broxbury also boasts a Palais de Danse and an Odeon. In Station Road the three centres of gaiety and sophistication are the

Cameo Cinema, Bob's Café, and Madame Esmé's Beauty Parlour.

Mr. Brocken, out for exercise, which was why he had walked down the hill, in order to walk up again, instead of going along the Ridge, paid little attention to the objects of interest in his path. He was neither distressed, as Isabel would have been, by the evidences of bombing, nor pleased by the bright paint of Bob's. He did not anticipate having to patronize a café. Since he never went to the cinema, the Cameo's posters were wasted on him. If he paused outside the Beauty Parlour it was not that the gay little window had caught his eye, nor even the waxen head, pink and white as the beauties of his youth. He paused because some one inside appeared to be making a speech, in a voice so high, clear and arbitrary that it pulled him up short like an electric ray.

"You are not, I believe—" the voice rose a tone, as though to bear down some opposition—"one of our regular clients? I thought not. I agree that your appearance is lamentable; but you still look considerably better than you did when you came in. I noticed you particularly. A course of six treatments (at slightly reduced rate) would do wonders; but if Madame Esmé does not care to undertake them—and really we are very busy—I should advise her to return your money."

Mr. Brocken peered through the window. Across a screen of lotion bottles, powder boxes and *bijouterie* he perceived three persons: a young woman with a remarkably frizzled head, Madame Esmé (unmistakable) and an old acquaintance, Dora Tremayne. It was she who had just spoken: she was standing behind the counter, evidently in the post of receptionist, which at Madame Esmé's appeared to double that of umpire. As Simon watched she deliberately sat down and opened a large appointment book; Madame silently and disdainfully tendered a handful of silver. To Simon's admiration (but not to his surprise) the young woman did not accept it. On her small stupid face anger was giving place to uneasiness; she would probably argue some minutes more, but the issue was not in doubt.

As soon as he saw that he had not been observed, Mr. Brocken walked quietly on. Dora Tremayne's history was an unusually interesting one; her new avatar completely unexpected; Mr. Brocken did not dislike her; but he walked on. It was his habit to avoid people whenever possible, in case they became a nuisance. For Simon was profoundly convinced that all people became a nuisance sooner or later: logic, and arithmetic, informed him that the fewer people one became involved with, the less danger one ran of being annoyed. Carrying his inviolability like a cup of precious water, Mr. Brocken returned up the hill to Chipping Lodge.

3

The meal served in the mahogany dining-room consisted of tinned soup, corned beef and salad, and for sweet a concoction of macaroni inadequately laced with treacle.

The table, in short, was not bare, just as Humphrey Garrett, in flannel trousers and a check shirt, was no longer naked. Jacqueline Brown changed the plates. She had put on a different dress, full-skirted, ankle-length, made of flowered cotton; very artistic. Isabel wore what was actually a house-coat, but which Mr. Brocken took to be a dressing-gown; his own alpaca jacket completed the sartorial confusion.

They were a rum-looking party.

"Humphrey," observed Mrs. Brocken, "has been putting the seat up. It's a swing seat, Simon, a new one, for the terrace. They've just come in again, and I got one last week."

"I've no doubt you paid a pretty penny for it," said Mr. Brocken.

"It has a cover, dear."

"For which Jacqueline is to be responsible," said Humphrey.

"Nonsense." Simon fixed the young man with a disapproving eye. "That's much more a job for you. If you take my advice you will write 'Back' in large letters on the back, and 'Front' on the front."

"Surely one or other would be sufficient, sir?"

"On the inside of the front," amended Mr. Brocken, who was not a lawyer for nothing.

Jacqueline slipped from her place to remove the sweet plates, and substituted a large cut-glass dish containing a very small piece of cheese. They all looked at it with concern.

"Oh, dear!" said Isabel. "The men had better divide it . . ."

The men did so. "What claret!" thought Simon, as the meal ended. "What food, what servants!"—and wished that he had been, while opportunity offered, a greedier man.

4

It was only half-past seven, or half-past five by the sun; they took coffee outside, to use the new seat. This was so large, and so boldly striped in green and orange, that it completely altered the aspect of the terrace; but it was undeniably comfortable. The four of them could sit on it in a row, and for a few minutes, urged by Mrs. Brocken, actually did so; then Jacky went off to wash up, and Humphrey followed her, and their two elders were left to swing alone. Quite considerable movement could be produced by pulling on a rope; Mr. Brocken soon found he preferred an iron chair. The evening was remarkably warm, and so still that he could hear the trains pass through Chipping Station at the bottom of the hill; pleasant odours of grass and foliage rose from the cooling garden. To return to such peace, after a day in the City, would be really agreeable, and Simon determined that starting from Monday (it was then Saturday evening) he would stake out a claim to one end of the terrace—the end farthest from the swing—and let it be known that he expected to read or write there undisturbed. Only good manners prevented his putting this plan into action at once; for the first evening at least his sister-in-law had a claim to his conversation.

Mr. Brocken conscientiously sought an agreeable topic. It was not easy to find one: Isabel had very little general information, and that gained chiefly from doing cross-words. As a rule, Simon realized, she chattered away spontaneously; so long a silence was unusual; and as he now considered her it struck him that she in turn was seeking a topic agreeable to him. The last time he stayed at the Priory she had read, as advance preparation, a whole book on Company Law: there were her initials at the end of each chapter, and towards the end of the volume at the bottom of each page, to prove it. They were also the only proof.

Isabel caught his eye. Putting on a very earnest expression, she prepared to speak. Mr. Brocken waited with some interest.

"Have you heard any good sermons lately?" asked Isabel.

"No," said Mr. Brocken at once. "All very poor."

"Surely not *all,* Simon?"

"All," repeated Mr. Brocken.

"How very tiresome for you." There was a slight, not unnatural pause; but Isabel was dauntless. She said, "I heard a sermon myself three weeks ago."

"Aha!" thought Mr. Brocken. "Advance preparation!"—for Isabel never went inside a church except for weddings, and liked to tell people she worshipped nature;

a backsliding all the more remarkable when one remembered how regularly, in the old days, Masseys and Brockens met every Sunday, wet or fine, at St. Peter's-on-the-Hill. Isabel herself seemed to feel a need of explanation.

"I'm not a church-goer, as you know, dear, I just worship nature. Sunday mornings were always so nice—at the Priory we used to go and give the horses their apples, and then have Pimms before lunch—and though that was in summer, in winter it so often rained. And Mark didn't go either."

"I regretted it," said Mr. Brocken.

"Though he lived a *very* good life," put in Isabel stoutly. "However, when Jacky was going last month, I thought I would too. I just thought it. So I went; and there was a sermon."

"There usually is," said Mr. Brocken, beginning to be bored. He recovered himself, however, and asked what it was about.

"I'm afraid I can't quite tell you, dear. You remember how as a child one got into the habit of not listening? I wasn't really listening to this one, I was thinking about food; but I did suddenly, right at the end, hear him say something." Mrs. Brocken broke off, evidently concentrating all her powers in an unusual attempt at accuracy. "He said, Simon, *it was a common error to suppose that the passage of time made a base action any less bad.*"

Her brother-in-law, who from all this preamble had expected something rather more striking, merely nodded. Isabel looked at him impatiently.

"He meant, don't you see, that because a thing happened a long time ago, it doesn't make it any less base if it was base at the time. He meant that however long ago—"

"I take the meaning perfectly," said Mr. Brocken. "It is not so revolutionary an idea as you seem to think."

"But I never *had* thought . . . Do you think it's true?"

Under her earnest gaze Mr. Brocken allowed the platitude a moment's consideration.

"My dear Isabel, of course it's true."

Isabel uttered a long sigh. The intellectual conversation was creditably over, but it was remarkable, thought Mr. Brocken dispassionately, how the slightest mental effort exhausted her. She really looked quite distressed. What was it one used to say to women? "Don't bother your pretty head about it. . . ." No doubt Mark had used the phrase a good deal, it must have been a life-saver to him. Simon did not employ it now, but ended the conversation by observing that it was time to cover the seat.

"Oh, must we?" asked Isabel. "It won't take a minute."

"More like twenty," said Mr. Brocken gloomily; and went off to find young Garrett.

5

Once out of his sister-in-law's reach, however, the notion took him to complete his inspection of the house. He had visited the stables; now he would visit the winter garden. Finding the door which led into it from the drawing-room locked, and masked, moreover, on the winter-garden side by a Venetian blind, Simon went out through the hall and turned right in order to approach from without: the winter garden abutted on the southern end of the house, and because of the fall of the ground was reached by a flight of steps on the hither side of the dell. Here weeds grew as thickly as in the stables, and wild mint that under Simon's foot gave out a warm fragrance; the dell too was full of it, still bearing the imprint of a body. Mr. Brocken remembered having noticed the same warm scent in the vicinity of young Humphrey, and concluded with distaste that the lad had sat down to dinner unwashed.

The steps led directly to a glass door (the winter garden being in fact built over that part of the terrace) and glass panes stretched on either hand; Mr. Brocken had a perfect view of the interior. In the centre of the tiled floor rose an Italian fountain, incongruously circled by whitewashed conch shells; the rear wall was covered with cork, now very much dilapidated, and pierced by two doors — that leading to the drawing-room, double-leaved and glazed behind its Venetian blind, and another, smaller, to the service passage. The place was of course empty of plants, and much of the glass had been broken; but Simon was most favourably struck by its general cleanliness. He felt that the Pooles (his *protégées*) deserved a word of praise; and since this door too was locked, he went back to the front of the house and thence made his way to the kitchen.

"May I come in?" asked Mr. Brocken.

A small murmur answered him. Mrs. Poole was not there herself, but only the child. She was seated at the table, pen in hand: a scrap of a thing, not pretty, with straw-coloured hair scraped back from a high forehead and eyes too large for her pale pointed face. As Mr. Brocken entered she slipped from her seat and stood before him in a very respectful manner.

"Good evening," said Simon. "Do you know who I am?"

"You're Mr. Brocken," said the child.

"Yes. And your name is — ?"

"Greta."

It was very appropriate, though Mr. Brocken wondered how her mother had hit on it; with her fair skin, and almost colourless hair, Greta could well have passed for a little Scandinavian. Only her eyes were out of keeping: large, brown, curiously tilted at the outer corners, they were like the eyes of a squirrel.

"Is your mother here?" asked Mr. Brocken.

"She's in, but she's just going out."

"Ah," said Mr. Brocken. He reminded himself that it was barely half-past eight. Advancing further into the kitchen, he said formally, "No doubt I shall see her to-morrow; but you must tell her from me that I am very pleased with the way the house has been kept."

The child looked gratified. She was about fourteen; her manner, in its mixture of shyness and composure, made her seem at once older and younger. She did not speak, however; no doubt the company of the elderly was strange to her, as the company of the young was strange to Mr. Brocken. They were still regarding each other with a sort of dumb politeness when at a light step in the passage Greta's head swiftly turned.

"Greta!" called a voice gently. "I'm just going!"

Gently the child called back.

"Okay, Mum. I'll hold the fort!"

The footsteps withdrew. Owing to the angle of the half-open door Mr. Brocken had not seen Mrs. Poole, nor she him. He had not seen mother and daughter together. But this exchange, though so brief, and on Greta's side so slangy, nevertheless left upon Mr. Brocken an oddly distinct impression: that the Pooles were very fond of each other.

"I didn't say you were here," explained Greta courteously, "because it would've held her up."

Mr. Brocken felt a moment's uneasiness. Was the child to be left alone for long? The kitchen, though comfortable and well-kept, was so large that Greta looked like a midget in it; in relation to the whole house, no bigger indeed than a mouse in a wedding-cake. But she seemed perfectly at ease. More than that: her eye kept straying to the papers on the table, as though in eagerness to resume her interrupted occupation. What was it—some puzzle? A mixture of crossword and noughts-and-crosses? Whatever the game, Greta was evidently content to go on playing it by herself.

"That's a good child," said Mr. Brocken vaguely; and left her to it.

Chapter 4

Among natives well-disposed, in a well-run camp, mariner and girl quickly settle down, not to a new life, but to a period of life detached from the common run of their experience, and complete in itself. A diet of calipee and cocoanuts, of spam and ice-cream, is not accepted as permanent: the mariner looks for a trading vessel, the girl knows the exact hour of the station bus; in the meantime they settle down, often with enjoyment. Mr. Brocken, after a week at Chipping Lodge, was not precisely enjoying himself, but he had settled.

He was not precisely enjoying himself but he was suffering less than he had anticipated. He had found a routine. Each morning he caught the nine-twenty to town, and each evening the five-twenty back: the walk to and from the station supplied regular exercise. In the evenings he read, or strolled in the garden, really very little annoyed by the rest of the household. Miss Brown and Humphrey left him alone (they in fact avoided him like the plague), and though Isabel at first came trotting after him down the lawn, or brought her knitting beside his chair, Mr. Brocken easily quenched her mild attempts at conversation. It struck him, indeed, that his sister-in-law had become less talkative altogether: she often sat for quite long periods in rational silence.—This was no doubt paying Isabel's silence too high a compliment: Mr. Brocken did not know what she was thinking about: but at least she looked fairly sensible. Altogether, apart from the food, he felt himself fortunate, and during the second week so far relaxed as to remark to Humphrey Garrett that the Lodge was architecturally a pleasant house.

"Also atmospherically," observed Humphrey — as usual with a faint parody of his uncle's manner.

After a moment of reflection, Mr. Brocken acknowledged this also: the atmosphere of Chipping Lodge was pleasant.

"Or perhaps I should say morally," added Humphrey.

"You may say so, certainly," agreed Mr. Brocken, "if you know what you mean."

"Well, there's no fiddling. Aunt Isabel doesn't pop off to buy eggs under the counter, and Jacky doesn't buy clothing coupons, and under their virtuous influence I have ceased to buy Black Market gin. It makes a nice change."

"It makes no change to me," said Mr. Brocken severely.

This was quite true. Simon Brocken was a very honest man. He would indeed have gone to the Tower rather than pay a penny more Income Tax than was legally due from him, but he never attempted to pay a penny less, and dealt with Isabel's income in the same spirit, and took her co-operation for granted. But Simon's honesty was censorious, and Isabel's was not. When she read in the paper of young men prosecuted for selling stockings without coupons, she hoped, and was generally able to believe, that they had just returned from being Commandos, or frogmen, or midget-submariners, so that their initiative had been (in the best of causes) almost over-developed. But as far as she herself was concerned, she felt it would be wrong to buy their stockings, and simply refrained. Simon's virtue had the effect of making him extremely irritable. He paid up, but he complained. He too shunned the Black Market, but complainingly. He also complained about the currency regulations and the electricity cuts—considering it indeed a duty thus to register his protest against the tyranny of the state. Most of his acquaintances complained also. Isabel did not, and her foolish cheerfulness set the tone of her household. Mr. Brocken found it quite restful to cease, for a few weeks, to kick against the pricks.

He did not realize any of this immediately. It was only weeks later, when everything at the Lodge was so changed, that he realized how very pleasant the atmosphere had been. Nor did he realize, even while unconsciously appreciating the result, how remarkable a feat, on the purely material side, was the smooth running of such a house as Chipping Lodge. Here indeed Isabel's chief virtue was the negative one of non-interference, but few mistresses of households would have so abdicated all authority, and so cheerfully taken orders from a companion, in the interest of domestic peace.

2

The running of Chipping Lodge, a large house inhabited by six persons, was greatly complicated by the peculiar standing and characteristics of the Pooles.

They had been engaged not by Mrs. Brocken, but by Simon, and not as domestics, but as caretakers. The letter from Isabel announcing her return had been followed, in the next post, by a letter from Mrs. Poole demanding a definition of her status. Mrs. Poole put it rather more tersely — "Do we go on caretaking, or What?" The capital *W* struck Simon as ominous; he at once telephoned his sister-in-law, then spoke to Mrs. Poole and informed her that she was indeed still a caretaker, but should accept some slight readjustment of her duties. The Pooles stayed on; but there was no doubt who commanded their allegiance. Simon Brocken's signature on their monthly cheque convinced them that he was their actual employer. The sum was in fact monthly paid back through Isabel's account, and the whole arrangement originally one of war-time convenience; but though Simon believed he had explained this, the misconception persisted.

The Pooles were also clearly determined to preserve their personal independence. Polite, soft-spoken, they nevertheless rejected all attempts at sociability. They were extraordinarily quiet; no one ever heard them shouting to each other, or banging about; they possessed a wireless, but kept it turned down very low. Their looks matched their manners. Mrs. Poole's diminutive figure, in a drab overall, hair covered by a duster, was so inconspicuous as to be almost invisible; Greta's occasional flittings through the garden left no more impression on the eye than the passage of a moth. All they asked was to live their own life, apart and unobserved.

A household thus divided, not exactly into two camps, but certainly into two communities, might have been very uncomfortable; but Jacqueline Brown had come straight from Admin. She at once grasped the situation in all its aspects, and evolved a controlling scheme. Functions were redistributed: Mrs. Poole, originally responsible for the whole house, now cleaned only the kitchen and her own and Greta's room, but in addition cooked all hot dishes, which she then handed to Jacqueline at the kitchen door. Jacqueline and Mrs. Brocken did the rest of the rooms and prepared all cold food, using for the purpose a large pantry where they also kept and washed up their own tableware. Thus they never needed to set foot in Poole territory, nor had the Pooles to leave it: a ten-minute interview each morning, on the neutral ground of the service passage, settled the menus of the day. Isabel at first gave trouble by neglecting to replace furniture polish; Jacqueline promptly laid on duplicate sets of cleaning material. It was in short a fine feat of organization, for which great credit was due; and Jacqueline was almost disappointed to realize that the C. O.'s inspection, which she had subconsciously been anticipating, would never take place.

"Have you got used to it yet?" Humphrey once asked her.

They were lying in the dell, their favourite place for conversation. Like the conversation of children, it consisted largely of questions and answers; for they still had a great deal to find out about each other.

"Used to what?" asked Jacqueline.

"To peace. To not being at war. To having a future."

She reflected.

"Yes, when I don't think about it. Day by day it seems quite natural. But when I look ahead—I suppose there's still at the back of my mind the idea that some one will tell me to do something. You know?"

"I'm only just getting used to it myself. What do you want to do? Paint?"

"Oh, dear!" Jacqueline buried her face deeper in the grass, divided between mirth and remorse. "That's what I told your aunt," she said, in a muffled voice. "She's so good, she doesn't feel justified in having a companion unless they *do* something; then she feels she's helping art. One of her companions wrote poetry, and one wrote a book on numerology, and one made lino-cuts—but they all did something. So I told her I wanted to paint. . . ."

"Can you paint?"

"I used to copy puppies in boots for Dad's birthday. He had them framed."

"How loathsome."

"They were. I can't do anything, really. Before the war

I just messed about, and in the war I suppose I made an effort . . . and now I'm just messing about again. . . . I was born," said Jacqueline thoughtfully, "to be the hanger-on of a great house."

"That's a rum ambition for an ex-sergeant."

"Usen't they to keep lodges?" asked Jacqueline vaguely. "I shouldn't a bit mind popping out to open the gate. . . ."

"With a clutch of apple-cheeked children clinging to your skirts."

"In sun-bonnets," agreed Jacqueline.

She turned her face away from him, pressing her cheek close to the grass. As so often when their conversation reached one of these exquisitely interesting points, both fell silent; Mr. Brocken, glancing down from the terrace overhead, thought them asleep.

Simon had never forgotten his first encounter with young Garrett, and whenever he came out on the terrace at once made a swift reconnaissance in the interests of modesty. He was now glad to observe that Humphrey had on a pair of shorts; Miss Brown wore a backless cotton garment, a sort of bibbed skirt, the colour of lavender. This lavender against the green, and the bronze and cream of their young skins, made a rather pleasing picture; Simon paused to examine it a moment before turning away. The word "idyllic" occurred to him; the notion that so had lain the nymphs and shepherds of Arcady, weary from goat tending. A classical education made it easy for him to supply the details: Jacqueline's slim pink heels, half-buried in wild mint, suggested the process of grape treading, and for the first time he understood why the poets made so much of it. Had all feet, in Arcady, been as clean and pink as Miss Brown's? Probably not: only ideally, to the poets. Mr. Brocken, in fact, was momentarily a poet himself—but fortunately without realizing it, for had he done so he would have felt disturbed. And indeed it was a moment as isolated in his existence as were the four lines of verse in the pages of the day's *Times,* to which he now returned.

Neither Jacqueline nor Humphrey had noticed him. Presently they began to talk again.

"This house," said Jacqueline, "is it weak-minded of me to love being here, just because it's so beautiful? I always hated our house at home, it was such a poky little place, we fell over each other's bicycles in the hall, I hadn't even a room to myself . . . and then in the ATS it was Nissens, and they were hideous. I'd like to stay here all my life."

"I reckon winter might be pretty grim."

"In *our* Nissen the snow came in. We were so damn' hardy we jammed all the windows open for fresh air. That was when I was on searchlights."

"It's nice we can bore each other," said Humphrey. "In the desert I used to shave with sand instead of soap." He pulled out a stem of grass and began to chew its pale, succulent end. Jacqueline reached for a stalk of her own; they chewed, thoughtfully and pleasurably, like a couple of young animals.

"Aunt Isabel," said Humphrey, "is going to leave me a

packet of money. I dare say if I asked her, she'd leave me the house instead."

"But you're going back to New Zealand."

"Not necessarily. I might get a job here. I like this house too."

"What on earth would you do in it?"

"Rear a clutch of apple-cheeked brats," said Humphrey cheerfully.

They burrowed again in the sweet grass; and when they next spoke it was of a man they had each encountered, at different times, by the hazard of war, and always with a different blonde.

3

Oddly enough, it was Mr. Brocken, far less naturally sociable than either Isabel, Humphrey or Jacqueline, who made the first real contact with the Pooles. He was not unaware of their esteem for him: Mrs. Poole, complimented in person on the state of the house, had replied that so long as Mr. Brocken was satisfied, so was she; all the same, he would have made no move towards furthering the acquaintance had not his socks needed mending. His housekeeper, who usually mended them, was taking a prolonged holiday with her family in North Wales. After some reflection Simon determined to approach Mrs. Poole, or Greta, with an offer of threepence per pair. This was to be a flat rate, one hole in one sock and upwards, and he considered it generous.

"May I come in?" asked Mr. Brocken, at the kitchen door.

The Pooles were seated at the table, busy with the same puzzle, or crossword, that had occupied Greta: Mrs. Poole as usual with her head tied up in a handkerchief, Greta with her strawy hair scraped back from her forehead: except for the colour of the eyes—Greta's were brown, her mother's grey—their two small pale faces, turning upon Mr. Brocken the same gently startled look, were remarkably like. They might have been the same age, or with no more than a year or two between them; evidently they shared the same taste for puzzles.

"I am wondering," said Mr. Brocken, "whether you would care to undertake the mending of my socks. For a consideration, of course: threepence a pair. I am not, as you will see, what is known as hard on them."

In demonstration he thrust his hand into one of the pair he had brought with him; there was but a single hole, and that minute, in the toe. He thrust his hand into the fellow, and displayed a slightly larger aperture in the heel; but all in all, he thought, an easy threepennyworth.

The Pooles, however, looked at each other doubtfully.

"Well, I don't know, I'm sure," murmured Mrs. Poole. "It depends whether we've the time . . ."

Her voice was as soft as her daughter's; indeed a peculiar gentleness of demeanour, in both the Pooles, amounted to a physical characteristic. Mr. Brocken considered it a great point in their favour. He also approved their inconspicuous appearance. But he thought they might have shown more enthusiasm over his really generous offer. It depended on whether they had time — ! Mr. Brocken glanced pointedly at the puzzle, or crossword.

"If you have not leisure yourself," he suggested, "perhaps Greta has. I'm sure Greta darns very nicely."

Greta wriggled her legs further under the table. Her mother looked at her enquiringly.

"Okay," said Greta.

"I *could* do 'em myself . . ."

"You got enough already. Okay; I'll have a stab at it."

So Mr. Brocken left his socks behind him, and two days later they reappeared on his dressing-table. The small hole had been simply stitched up, the larger disguised by a sketchy trellis-work, tight at the edges and loose in the middle, through which his investigating finger was plainly visible. When Greta had said she would have a stab at it, she was evidently employing a precisely descriptive term.

Mr. Brocken groaned. He had been prepared to think well of the Pooles, and the state of his socks proved Mrs. Poole completely negligent of at least one maternal duty. She had not taught Greta to mend. As for Greta, ignorance might be an excuse, but the child had evidently no notion of earning an honest threepence. Where now, Mr. Brocken's soul lamented, was the old-fashioned conscientiousness? — for he had a distinct recollection of the aged sewing-woman, employed by his mother at a few shillings a day and her lunch, under whose hands the family hose, miracles of neat darning, endured from year to year. . . . He placed a threepenny bit on the dressing-table, and subsequently dispatched all mending to North Wales. It was a great nuisance; caution led him to register each packet; in addition, his housekeeper's family lived at Penrhyndendraeth, a name extremely difficult to transcribe.

He could of course have asked Isabel to mend for him, and she would certainly have done so, but she would have made too much fuss about it.—Yet Isabel did not usually fuss; this was Mr. Brocken's first, as yet unconscious acknowledgment that his sister-in-law was not quite, was not altogether and imperturbably, her usual placid self.

Chapter 5

Simon had noticed that Isabel was talking less, and been glad of it: she never said anything worth listening to. A certain subduedness of manner he also noticed, and gratefully, though half-incredulously, attributed it to the sobering effect of middle age. Towards a subdued and silent Isabel he could feel almost tolerant. But when Isabel emerged from her silence to fuss — as she fussed one night when Humphrey was late for dinner, and as she fussed when Simon left the light on in the hall, and as she fussed over the dog Bogey's paws — when Isabel began to fuss from morning till night, then Simon bleakly admitted to himself that he actually preferred her amiable chatter.

Had he not been thoroughly conversant with all his sister-in-law's affairs, and known her to be as blameless as solvent, he would have said that Isabel had something on her mind.

The first really noticeable incident occurred at the Sunday lunch table, and arose from a moment of great good humour. Humphrey praised (with justice) a fine savoury stew, and Isabel, looking pleased, and directing her approbation particularly at Simon, observed that now that they had four ration-books instead of three, the cook had more scope.

"And soon we'll have five," added Jacqueline—also very cheerfully.

Mr. Brocken glanced suspiciously round the table.

"Five?" he repeated. "Is any one else coming?"

"Well, yes, dear," said Isabel. "I've asked Tilly Cuff. Humphrey, do you like pancakes?"

"Tilly Cuff!" Simon stared at his sister-in-law in natural astonishment. "Why on earth should you invite Tilly Cuff? You can't have seen her for years!"

"I haven't, dear; not since she left us in 1912. But we always sent Christmas cards, and I've written to her last address."

"But why on earth—"

"Because I chose to," snapped Isabel.

Mr. Brocken's astonishment increased. As a rule Isabel's self-confidence, however unjustified, was reflected in manners of great ease and gentleness; for her to snap, as she had just snapped at Mr. Brocken, was as startling as if she had thrown a plate at him. However, Jacqueline and Humphrey began to discuss a new film (Swedish, apparently, and horrible) from which it was but a step (at least for Isabel) to the regretted talents of Shirley Temple. The awkward moment passed; Simon himself said a good word for *Desert Victory;* the meal ended in decent amity. But he remained offended. He hoped Isabel was not becoming irritable; an irritable man himself, Simon naturally reprobated the quality in any one else.

When later in the day Isabel invited him to play piquet with her, he curtly replied that he considered piquet a particularly poor way of wasting time.

"Mark didn't think so," said Isabel. "Mark and I used to play two games of piquet, after dinner, every night of our lives."

This was a palpable over-statement; Mark and Isabel had not played piquet, for instance, while Simon was staying with them. He refrained, however, from pointing this out; and for all reward saw Isabel wipe her eyes and hurry from the room.

2

What the younger people, what Jacqueline and Humphrey noticed, about this time, was not irritability, but pathos. Jacqueline, accepting the post of companion, had been chiefly attracted by its absence. "She's an ass, darling, but she *is* cheerful," said Jacqueline, reporting on her new employer to a fellow ex-sergeant. "She's cosy. She doesn't moan; which at her age don't you think is creditable?" It was to Miss Brown's credit that when this cosiness began to disintegrate, and when pathos, so naturally disliked by the young, began to take its place, she answered with sympathy. Jacqueline was particularly patient with Mrs. Brocken at this time, and refrained from scolding her about the furniture polish.

Humphrey Garrett's apprehension was slower, pathos

being more readily perceptible to the female than the masculine eye; the first time he really noticed it was on the Tuesday after the incident at the lunch table, and he noticed it not in Isabel alone, but in Isabel and Bogey together, as they set out before dinner — the small plump woman and the grizzled old dog — for their usual promenade. They struck him, most unexpectedly, as a pathetic pair. Humphrey's good heart made him offer to join them; Isabel gratefully accepted; and as they walked along the Ridge her nephew, with discreet sidelong looks, tried to discover what it was that had made him feel so sorry, and so suddenly sorry, for her. Isabel trotted energetically at his side, plump but trim, well-dressed, really expensively shod; Bogey careered before or limped behind, as pampered a dog as drew breath; yet about them both — or about the pair in conjunction — this curious air of pathos. "They've been left behind," thought Humphrey. "They're both of them fifty years out of date . . ." — and felt vaguely uneasy before such evidence that time does indeed pass.

"I used to run along here in short frocks," said Isabel, unconsciously meeting his thought. "When I was a little girl. And in my first long skirts too, with Ruth and — and Tilly. I do *hope,* dear, you were a happy boy?"

"Perfectly, Aunt Isabel; so far as I remember."

"Then probably you were. I mean, when these psychoanalysts get at one, it's always the dreadful memories they dig out. I once read a book on it," said Isabel, "before

Mark had a very clever friend to stay with us. And I was very glad, because all *I* remembered were things like long frocks and garden-parties."

Humphrey forbore to point out that there are memories which memory itself suppresses; if his aunt had found the theory in her book, it evidently left no impression on her. But again she unexpectedly met him.

"Of course there are always things one would rather forget; but if one can't, don't you think the best way is to do something about them?"

"Undoubtedly," said Humphrey. "If it's possible."

"That's just the point. Of course I haven't any children—which I always felt such a *great* grief, and I can't tell you what a comfort your letters were, Humphrey dear, when I was living in that hotel. *All* the other women had letters, from sons or from husbands, and of course they read bits out in the lounge, and without yours I should have felt so dreadfully out of it. I know that's trivial of me; but if you'd been there yourself you'd understand."

Her nephew, uneasily remembering the brevity with which he had acknowledged her parcels, asked whether that meant she had read bits out of his.

"Of course, dear. They were from *Africa.* And you were so funny about shaving, every one said you ought to write a book. Of course you wrote much *longer* letters to your mother, which was quite right; but Ruth used to send bits to me, and I read them out too."

This was a side-light on the war which Humphrey had never before considered: letters, "bits," circumnavigating the globe, to lend prestige to one's female relations. Again he felt the soft, the mournful breath of pathos; glimpsed an affection, also, between two middle-aged women, his mother and his aunt, to which he had never given a thought. They quite possibly missed each other. However, the party had by this time reached the site of the Priory, and here was so interesting a study in contrasts, so perfect a landscape in the modern style, that his thoughts were (not unwillingly) diverted. The area nearest the road was filled by the foundations of a great house, in a brick-strewn jungle of abandoned garden; the farther part of the grounds by a neat row of prefabricated bungalows, each in its well-tended plot.

"I *think* Simon sold the Council the ground," said Isabel vaguely, as she contemplated this picture. "Or else they just took it; but anyway I'm very glad, because people must live somewhere; and some of them have put up hanging baskets. Do look, Humphrey; that used to be my sitting-room."

They picked their way over the rough ground to where in the shell of a wide bay great masses of purple flowers swayed and nodded before the wind. The shape of the room, and beyond it the ground-plan of the whole house, was delimited by the butts of party-walls: here and there a block of stouter masonry marked the root of a chimney or the base of a staircase; a few fragments of ironmongery still littered the ground.

"And that's rose-bay-willow-herb," pointed out Mrs. Brocken. "It's a weed, but isn't it pretty? I often wonder who decided which were weeds and which weren't . . . Quite a lot of the house was left, but it had to be pulled down. You remember it, don't you, dear?"

"I remember every room," said Humphrey, not quite truthfully. In boyhood the Priory had been a sort of second home, but he had spent only his holidays there, and not all of them; boylike, he took the house for granted. When he was about fifteen an aesthetic school-friend pointed out some of its more startling incidents—the Gothic turret housing a water-closet, the built-in cosy corners, one Turkish and one Art-Nouveau, that effectually destroyed the proportions of the drawing-room. These were the features he now remembered best. But he was fond of his aunt, and wished to give her pleasure. "It was a beautiful house," said Humphrey stoutly.

"Still, I've got the Lodge," proceeded Isabel, more cheerfully. "How glad I am I didn't sell it! Now I shall finish my days there, because people do so hate you to die in their hotels. I believe they used to make you redecorate the whole room, though now of course you wouldn't get a license. I've been adding us up, Humphrey: with you and Jacky and Simon and the Pooles, that makes six, and with Tilly that's seven; but do you think I ought to take in lodgers as well? I mean, what *can* the Pooles want with the winter garden?"

"I doubt whether lodgers would care for it either," said Humphrey. "But I think you have a very nice mind."

Isabel turned her back on the purple flowers to look at him earnestly.

"Do you really, dear? I was so unkind to poor Simon—

not in deed, you know, but in thought, which is supposed to be just as bad. Though I don't believe it," added Mrs. Brocken, with unusual independence, "for if you think of doing some one an injury, and don't do it, they aren't injured. But of course if one hadn't had the thought, there wouldn't be any risk. Do remember that, dear. Write it down somewhere: it may save you so much trouble." Isabel sighed. "Poor Simon!"

"What did you do to him?" asked Humphrey, rather callously.

"My dear, the very first evening, I asked him to come *here.* And of course he wouldn't. He feels so deeply, he can't bear even to see it; and I never guessed." Isabel sighed again. "I've been thoughtless about Jacky too; she ought to have more time for her painting. She hasn't even started yet, which must fret her very much."

"I shouldn't worry," said Humphrey.

"I don't even know whether she paints indoors or out. But if it's *out,* don't you think — " Mrs. Brocken indicated the mass of purple loosestrife, indeed picturesque within the broken walls — "don't you think she might make something of this?"

Humphrey, remembering a recent conversation with Jacqueline, did not know quite what to answer; but fortunately the dog Bogey, who had found his way into the cellar, at that moment discovered that he could not find the way out. His infuriated cries put an end to the conversation. Humphrey, by lying flat on his stomach and reaching down between two sheets of corrugated iron, managed to haul the animal forth. Bogey at once attempted to bite him. Humphrey scratched himself rather badly. They returned home at a brisk pace, to apply iodine; Isabel scolding her dog, and commiserating her nephew, but so much more cheerful than when she set out that Humphrey temporarily forgot his solicitude for her. If he immediately sought out Jacqueline, who was mixing salad in the pantry, it was not because he was worried about his aunt, but because he was worried about Jacky.

"Pull yourself together, my girl," said he, "you're going to paint a picture of the Priory ruins, complete with rose-bay-willow-herb."

"Oh, dear!" said Jacqueline. "That's purple, isn't it?"

"And when it's done," continued Humphrey, with relish, "Aunt Isabel will no doubt have it framed and pop it into Uncle Simon's room for a lovely surprise. I reckon he'll tear it down and stamp on it."

"*I* think he's very unkind to her," said Jacqueline severely. "I think he's a very bad-tempered old man. He's out on the terrace now, waiting for his dinner, and he won't speak till he's had it, and then he won't say anything agreeable. If he were a stone image, he'd turn his nose up at the offerings. . . ."

This vigorous character sketch, however, was not justified by the facts, Mr. Brocken having been neither alone nor silent for the last half-hour; for scarcely had he settled to the enjoyment of solitude when the child Greta appeared round the corner of the winter garden carrying a cardboard box. She carried it in both arms; it sagged under a weight of metal.

3

"I suppose you don't want any bits of bomb?" enquired Greta politely.

"No, thank you," said Mr. Brocken.

"I don't either. I used to collect them; it's funny," said Greta tolerantly, "what you'll do when you're a kid. Now I'm just going to chuck them away."

She suited the action to the word, choosing as mark a flower-pot on top of a dahlia stick. But she was not a good shot; the pot remained intact, a dozen fragments of iron-mongery strewed the edge of the lawn, where Greta was evidently prepared to leave them; she had no notion of outdoor tidiness. When Mr. Brocken instructed her to gather them up, she protested reasonably that she had just thrown them away—as no doubt she threw away paper bags, orange peel, banana skins and every sort of litter. However, she humoured him; and built a neat cairn in the middle of the flower bed.

"Some of 'em had the dates on," remarked Greta, returning. "It was Mum's idea; we thought they'd make nice souvenirs, but they got too common."

She appeared to have lost, quite suddenly, all shyness; as she now sat down on the terrace steps, ready to continue the conversation, an old formal phrase crossed Mr. Brocken's mind: she proposed herself the pleasure of his company. He did not wish to encourage her, however; he made no comment.

"Did you know we were the fourth worst place in London?" asked Greta. "Croydon was top, and I forget who came next, but we were fourth. Our bomb-chart looked like the measles."

"Then you ought to have been evacuated," said Mr. Brocken—quite forgetting that a child living with her had at the time constituted, in his own eyes, one of Mrs. Poole's advantages.

"Not me," said Greta. "I stayed with Mum. A lady did come after me once, but I cried and cried, and Mum cried, till she went away again; and the next time she came I hid in the attic and Mum told her I'd gone to Scotland." Greta giggled. "O' course, she saw me about again in a day or two, and *I* told her I'd come back because the other kids were infectious; so she finally gave up."

Mr. Brocken, whose sympathies were always on the side of authority (except where it incommoded himself), observed severely that no doubt the lady meant well.

"I dare say; but she shouldn't have said Mum was keeping me to dodge the call-up. Mum wanted ever so to be a Wren, she'd have looked smashing in those little caps; she just couldn't bear to leave me. But she joined the A.R.P. She was Outgoing Messages."

Mr. Brocken felt this to be very proper: he himself had been a Warden, and a ferociously efficient one. But at the same time he wondered how Mrs. Poole's duties had been combined. Was the house left empty at night, or Greta left to guard it alone? He very much hoped not; and though the defection, if any, lay in the past, felt impelled to ask which shift Mrs. Poole had been on.

"Oh, the day ones," said Greta at once. "Mum told the Chief Warden she had a little girl, and he agreed straight away I oughtn't to be left. So I was a real advantage to her. And we made ever such a nice place in the cellar, like a nest it was, with mattresses all round — " She paused uneasily. "We took mattresses off all the beds. We didn't think you'd mind."

"Indeed, no," said Mr. Brocken.

"It was lovely. We used to creep in whenever the bombs got close, and Mum used to tell me the stories of all the movies she'd seen. She remembered the dialogue and everything." Greta sighed gently, like one who indulges in pleasant reminiscence. "She went on at six, sometimes, and then we'd make tea first, and sometimes the moon was still up when the sky was getting blue, and if there was snow the air was all cold and silvery, and much thinner than usual air, and the snow crunched under our feet — "

"But surely your mother didn't take you *with* her?" protested Mr. Brocken.

"Didn't she?" said Greta vaguely. "No, 'course not . . ." She looked at Mr. Brocken kindly but impatiently, as though he were a rather stupid child. "But she told me about it," said Greta.

The sound of voices in the drawing-room announced Humphrey's and Mrs. Brocken's return. Greta jumped up and scooted away.

Chapter 6

When Isabel lamented the changes on the Ridge, she was not thinking only of bricks and mortar: the loss of her old neighbours was a far deeper grief. All were gone, all save Dora Tremayne, in her three rooms over the ironmonger's; and with Dora Tremayne Isabel had immediately and enthusiastically resumed relations. A night later, on the Wednesday, Dora came to dinner.

Simon had never referred to the scene in Madame Esmé's. He did not refer to it now. Isabel reintroduced him; Simon, with reserved courtesy, and Dora, with loud astonishment, acknowledged their old acquaintance.

"Well, *you*'ve aged," said Dora (always noted for her frankness). "I suppose it's living among all those deed boxes. My poor Simon!"

Mr. Brocken, slightly nettled, replied that they were none of them as young as they used to be.

"True enough," said Dora. "I am fifty-six; but I hope I'm not petrified. And Isabel's as plump as ever; I always said plump women had the best of it. Still, you've these youngsters — " she nodded affably at Humphrey and Miss

Brown — "to rejuvenate you. My word, they've their work cut out."

Mr. Brocken found himself remembering several disobliging facts about Dora Tremayne. She had been the perennial wallflower of the Chipping Hill dances. Lanky, freckled, with a remarkably long neck and a remarkably small head, her nickname was inevitable: the Giraffe. In addition, she had shown herself criminally reckless with money, and brazen in her acceptance of the consequences. . . .

Isabel looked at her friend with loving eyes.

"Do you know what Dora does now, Simon? She's the receptionist at Madame Esmé's Beauty Parlour. And Madame Esmé told me — she told me the last time I went in, Dora — that you're absolutely invaluable. Simon, don't you think that's marvellous?"

"Astounding," murmured Simon.

"Certainly I'm invaluable," agreed Miss Tremayne complacently. "I am the woman who never had a facial. I sit there in all my natural decrepitude, and after one look at me our clients hasten to enroll themselves for a course of tinting and massage. Madame Esmé is nobody's fool."

Simon offered no comment; the conversation became general. But Miss Tremayne had not finished with him, and about an hour later, alleging a sudden headache, demanded that he should escort her home. Though Simon could not believe this to be coquetry, he was pretty sure Dora meant in some way to annoy him; but he could not refuse. His suspicions were justified; they had just turned from the Ridge into Chipping Hill, which would presently lead into Station Road, when Dora Tremayne halted.

"Simon . . ."

"Well?" said Mr. Brocken discouragingly.

"Does it strike you that Isabel has something on her mind?"

"No," said Mr. Brocken at once. "Isabel has nothing on her mind. She is merely a rather short-tempered woman."

"Nonsense," said Miss Tremayne. "Isabel has a disposition like a saucer of milk. She's nervous. I noticed it when she came in for a shampoo and set; for I naturally went in to chat with her — " ("What an establishment!" thought Mr. Brocken) — "and I thought then, Isabel has something on her mind."

Simon reflected: remembered a certain ambiguity in Miss Brown's reply to his first formal enquiry after Isabel's health; a moment when Isabel, most unusually, had snapped at him. . . .

"So I'm very glad you've come," said Dora, beginning to walk on, "for if ever a woman needed a man to look after her, that woman is Isabel."

Simon did not feel glad at all. With the last part of Dora's remarks he thoroughly agreed; but he resented being the man. It was precisely the prospect of some such situation which had kept him away from Chipping Lodge; now that he was there, and fairly comfortable, the idea was even more annoying. For the repairs to his house were going to take far longer than originally anticipated. The roof, and part of one outer wall, had been pronounced dangerous, and removed. This was done rather promptly, as soon as Mr. Brocken moved out, and effectually prevented his moving in again. Since then, except for the stretching of some tarpaulins, nothing had been done at all. The workmen were waiting for timber. A tart note to each relevant authority produced only the barren satisfaction of catching them out in contradictory statements. Mr. Brocken drew attention to this all round, recommended the planting of fir cones, received polite acknowledgments and wisely stopped wasting his energy. He felt a certain confidence in the foreman, a middle-aged Yorkshireman whose disposition rather resembled his own. They agreed that things were in a mess; Mr. Brocken blamed the Socialists, Mr. Ison the Tories; still, they agreed, and the latter promised to keep an eye on the tarpaulins.

For the time being, therefore, Mr. Brocken was fixed at Chipping Lodge, and it was important to him that he should be worried as little as possible. What could Isabel have to worry him about? She had snapped, but why had she snapped? Mr. Brocken, lengthening his pace to keep up with Dora, said dubiously,

"Women can be very trivial. Isabel has asked Tilly Cuff, if you remember the female, to come and stay at the Lodge. I thought it a mistake at the time; I dare say she is now regretting it."

"Of course I remember Tilly." Dora halted again. "I am rapidly reaching the age when thirty years ago is rather more vivid than yesterday." She reflected a moment, and added casually, "I remember Tilly's mother."

Simon was taken by surprise. In his eyes Tilly Cuff had always been a connection of the Masseys, and nothing more; he had never speculated as to her exact parentage; at the same time it slightly displeased him to find Dora Tremayne better informed than himself.

"My dear Dora," he said jealously, "Tilly was an orphan."

"My dear Simon, even orphans have had parents at some stage. Tilly's mother was George Cuff's housekeeper, and George Cuff was Mrs. Massey's cousin, which accounts for the relationship, and he lived at Bournemouth for the sake of his health. When I was a girl we spent every summer there: we used to see him on the promenade in a bath-chair, with Tilly's mother pushing it. She'd been his housekeeper for years, and when he was about sixty he married her."

"It's the first *I've* heard of it," said Mr. Brocken suspiciously.

"Naturally the Masseys didn't cry it abroad; *we* only knew because of Bournemouth. But Tilly was born, and George Cuff died, and they found that all his money was in an annuity; and I believe Mrs. Cuff took lodgers. At any rate, when *she* died Tilly was about sixteen; and that was when the Masseys sent for her. Isabel must have very strong family feeling."

"She has," admitted Mr. Brocken. "Though it has lain dormant a considerable time. Isabel tells me she hasn't seen the woman since before the last war."

"When Tilly was packed off to Switzerland." Miss Tremayne nodded sagely. "No doubt they'd had enough of her. But she was a quiet, useful little thing; and I don't see why Isabel should be in a fantod over the prospect of seeing her again."

Nor did Simon. Looking at the matter in this reasonable light, he could not understand it at all. Dora Tremayne's description was just; Tilly Cuff was quiet and useful; he did not expect to see much of her; yet the fact remained that he himself strongly disliked the idea of her coming.

"We're very well off as we are," he said resentfully. "I've been put out less than I'd thought possible. Why not let well alone?"

Miss Tremayne cackled.

"The fact is, Simon, you're an old crab. I hope Tilly turns up frail and forlorn and charming; and I hope you lose your heart to her; and I hope," finished Miss Tremayne relishingly, "she breaks it. It would do you a power of good."

They walked on, united only by the conventions: Simon had undertaken to see Miss Tremayne to her door, and he did so. He looked up at her three windows over the ironmonger's, decided she must live in a potty little place, and turned back towards the Ridge. The very absurdity of Dora's last squib had shown the foolishness of his own (momentary) apprehension. He must have caught an infection from Isabel; for how could Tilly Cuff (quiet and useful) really disturb his peace? It was not as though she were some siren, like—Mr. Brocken cast back his mind, and had to cast it back a good many years—like that woman he had once met at a dinner-party, tall and dark and elegant, who turned out to be a divorcée. Then Simon had felt himself to be in danger; he actually called on her once or twice; and saved himself only just in time by taking on the very tricky business of *Bolitho Estates* versus *The Treasury*. He would not care to go through such a time again; at least he ran no risk of doing so in the company of Tilly Cuff—or Dora Tremayne.

Still, he was not quite easy. It was in the effect of Tilly upon Isabel, not upon himself, that the danger lay. If the mere prospect of Tilly Cuff was enough to make Isabel nervous, what might her presence not produce in the way of irritability and snappishness? Why his sister-in-law should be so affected by Tilly Mr. Brocken had no idea; nor why, if she disliked Tilly, she had invited her to the Lodge: all women being unreasonable, and Isabel egregiously so, Simon wasted no time on speculation. He merely noted the uncomfortable omens. He felt the need to reflect; he did not wish immediately to encounter his sister-in-law. After entering the drive, instead of going straight into the house, he paced on towards the winter garden.

The front- and back-doors of Chipping Lodge are, unusually, on the same side of the house, but concealed from each other by a wide tongue of shrubbery; as Mr. Brocken rounded this he received a shock. Just outside the back-door, thrown into strong relief by background of brick and laurel, stood the figure of a strange woman in full evening dress.

2

Mr. Brocken could not but stare; her appearance, in both senses of the word, was amazing. For her gown, the colour of tomato soup, detracted nothing from the brilliancy of her complexion; her lips were a scarlet bow, her eyelashes, black, an inch long; a remarkable wealth of auburn curls, profuse yet disciplined, supported two gardenias and a black velvet bow. "God bless my soul!" thought Simon; and was just about to offer his services, no doubt in a matter of redirection, when a gentle step approached the back-door. It was Greta, beaming with pleasure, which the sight of Mr. Brocken evidently increased. She gave him one of her widest smiles.

"Doesn't Mum look smashing?" asked Greta fondly.

"Mr. Brocken doesn't know me," said Mrs. Poole.

Indeed he did not. Mrs. Poole's habitual uniform of overall and head-kerchief rendered her practically invisible; he could not for the life of him have described her, beyond saying that she resembled Greta — and now they stood side by side like a mouse and a macaw, a leveret and a peacock, a May-fly and a Painted Lady. By this time it had become absolutely necessary for Mr. Brocken to say something, and something complimentary; but the longer he looked at Mrs. Poole, the more strongly he felt that the only thing to be said for her appearance was its candour. There was no deception. Nature alone could never have produced such an astounding effect, and to nature Mrs. Poole owed, candidly, nothing.

He found he could do no better than echo the child. "Smashing," he repeated courteously.

Both Pooles looked pleased. Mrs. Poole indifferently, like a mannequin, let slip the piece of fur round her shoulders to reveal her bodice, which was strapless.

"She's going dancing at the Palais, with her friend," explained Greta. "Off you go, Mum; I'll hold the fort."

"Can I get you a taxi?" enquired Mr. Brocken.

This pleased them too; they exchanged a gratified glance, a signal *en clair* acknowledging a perfect gentleman. But before the offer could be discussed (and quite possibly accepted, the Pooles being easily carried away by the dramatic moment) a new figure appeared moving swiftly, yet somehow unobtrusively, up the path from the back-gate. Mr. Brocken would have withdrawn, but Greta's eye held him: her pride in her mother evidently extended to her mother's escort. They all waited till he came up.

"This is Mr. Simmonds, my friend," said Mrs. Poole.

Mr. Simmonds bowed. He was a large man, very smartly dressed, in a blue suit and lighter blue shirt; his tie and handkerchief matched each other, his thinning hair shone with oil, and he carried a pearl-grey Homburg hat.

"Mr. Simmonds is a wonder at the *rumba,*" said Mrs. Poole.

"Last month they got second prize," added Greta. "It was bath-salts."

Mr. Simmonds now spoke. His voice was deep, rich and melancholy.

"I do it for my health," he stated. "I believe in opening the pores. Mrs. Poole here is kind enough to lend a hand. I have my car," said Mr. Simmonds, "at the gate."

At this Greta gave an involuntary leap of pleasure—the puppyish jump of a child receiving a toy. Mr. Simmonds offered Mrs. Poole his arm; Greta waved good-bye until they reached the gate. There Mrs. Poole paused and waved too, and Mr. Simmonds elevated his hat; and thus they departed.

3

Simon looked at the child. She had inevitably the air of being left behind; but without regret, certainly without rancour. He said,

"And what shall you do now?"

"Oh, I've plenty to do," said Greta absently. "*Did*n't Mum look smashing?"

"Very striking indeed," said Mr. Brocken.

"Like someone on the movies. That was a joke you not knowing her—but that was like the movies too. . . ."

"Or like Cinderella." Mr. Brocken was rather pleased with this fancy; but Greta brushed it aside.

"Like Bette Davis. . . . I *do* think Mum's smashing!"

"You are not, I hope, going to sit up for her?"

"Oh, no," said Greta, still absently. "She's kissed me good-night already, before she did her face. . . . But I'll hear all about it in the morning — and next year, as soon as I'm fifteen, I'm going too. That's where my mum's so wonderful," said Greta earnestly, "she never leaves me out. When Mr. Simmonds takes her to the movies, she always makes him buy me a seat downstairs."

Mr. Brocken walked on round the house in some confusion of mind. While he could not approve Mrs. Poole's appearance, choice of friends or view of maternal duties, he was at the same time forced to admit that mother and daughter were undoubtedly united by a strong tie of affection. He had observed it before. But — "*She's kissed me good-night already, before she did her face.*" What a comment that was, to be sure, upon what a change of manners! In Mr. Brocken's youth a woman who painted her face was at once placed among the unvirtuous; was any virtuous mother more beloved and admired than Mrs. Poole? Casting his mind back into the past, reviewing the mothers and daughters (all virtuous) of his acquaintance, Mr. Brocken doubted it. He thought of Mrs. Massey — agreeable, just, sensible; of his own mother, equally sensible, agreeable and just: each in character immeasurably superior to Mrs. Poole. Their families loved and appreciated them; but had he ever seen, on the face of Isabel or Ruth, the look of rapt adoration with which Greta watched Mrs. Poole set off to *rumba* with the wonder?

He had not.

It appeared that a flashy and highly unmaternal appearance, allied to irresponsible indulgence, produced just as good results, in the way of filial affection, as character and anxious care.

Here Mr. Brocken approached several famous truisms — that the heart has its reasons which reason does not know, that kissing goes by favour, that virtue is its own reward. He did not explore them, however; they were too alien to his own cast of mind. All he could bring himself to admit was that times change; and in his opinion they changed for the worse.

This encounter, and these reflections, while temporarily driving Tilly Cuff from his mind, reinforced the apprehensions of which Tilly was the root cause. Mr. Brocken began to feel, in short, that in spite of every effort to the contrary, he was becoming involved with a great many people. Dora Tremayne allowed herself the liberties of an old acquaintance: the Pooles were beginning — Mr. Brocken could find no less vulgar an expression — to take to him. Isabel, in any fuss or fantod whatsoever, would undoubtedly attempt his sympathies. Mr. Brocken determined that on Saturday morning, instead of going to Red Lion Place, he would go to Kensington, and have another look at his house, and see whether he could not make do in the cellar.

Chapter 7

From this point — from the Wednesday evening till the Saturday afternoon — events moved steadily, yet at the time unremarkably, to what Simon Brocken ever afterwards thought of as the show-down. It was a word he had picked up from Humphrey, or Jacqueline — even his vocabulary becoming infected by his sojourn at the Lodge; still, it was fairly appropriate.

The first incident was very trivial. Simon returned from Town on the Thursday night, after a trying day, in a bad temper. Isabel at once met him in the hall with the news that they were all to dine at Bob's, because the fishmonger had no fish.

"Then I for one shall not dine at all," said Mr. Brocken disagreeably. "I come home tired, after a hard day, and I shall not immediately turn out again."

No sooner had he spoken than he noticed an odd slip. "Come home," he had said; but Chipping Lodge wasn't his home, his home was in Kensington, or, more truly, among the deed boxes of Red Lion Place. It was the merest slip of the tongue, quite unnoticed by Isabel, but he resented it. Again he felt, and more strongly, that he was being got hold of, becoming involved; the house itself had grown familiar: even homelike. Well, at least he could make a stand; he would not troop off to Bob's.

"I suppose some one can produce a cup of Bovril?" said Mr. Brocken. "Thank you. I will have it, if I may, in Ruth's room."

2

He thus missed a very pleasant party, for Dora Tremayne was also at Bob's, and joined Isabel and Humphrey and Jacqueline at the large centre table. It was a cheerful place, the walls salmon-coloured, the cloths gaily patterned, and such tables as had no cloths covered with blue-and-white linoleum. Behind the counter complicated devices for making milk-shakes or ice-cream shone silver-bright, and the walls were covered with calendars and advertisements. When Miss Tremayne first went there (she was now an habitué) these last surprised her by their uniformity: the same subject—a young woman in a negligée, by firelight—appeared again and again, associated so indiscriminately with liquids or cigarettes, or even insurance companies, that Miss Tremayne really wondered whether all these different firms had made a gentleman's agreement not to steal a march on each other. Bob informed her, however, that the subject was simply supremely popular.

Bob himself waited upon them, and lingered to indulge in military reminiscences with Humphrey. Possibly some of his remarks were directed at the ladies; he himself had come out of the army, said Bob, with nothing but a pair of flat feet, which he got at the Battle of the Fallen Arch, in Tripoli. For Humphrey he produced beer, with a large wink and the observation that milkless tea required no license. All laughed appreciatively; the ladies turned a blind eye, and Miss Tremayne stood a female round of orange squash. In one sense the absence of Mr. Brocken was an advantage: they could discuss him, and did so, freely.

"Still the same old crab," cried Miss Tremayne jovially. "What's he like at the breakfast table?"

"We don't see him," said Jacqueline. "We only see the back pages of *The Times.*"

"But he lunches out," said Isabel. "And I must say I'm very glad, because though he doesn't say anything he eats his food as though — as though it were offal."

"I only wish it were," said Jacqueline. "We haven't seen liver for months."

The discussion of Mr. Brocken's character was suspended while they developed this passionate topic; but at last Dora returned to it.

"By the way, I twitted Simon last night about Tilly Cuff. He's annoyed with you, Isabel, for inviting her; and I must say I think it's unnecessarily kind-hearted. I didn't think you liked the woman."

"I don't," admitted Isabel uncomfortably. "At least, I used not to. But she can't have had a very easy life."

"Companions rarely do. I suppose the most successful

are those who run off with their employers' husbands—and we've never heard of Tilly doing that." Miss Tremayne's bright intelligent glance flickered from Jacqueline to Humphrey: Miss Tremayne was a very observant woman. But she was also, towards one special class of persons, kind. She was kind to the young. Her own girlhood had been unsuccessful; even Simon remembered her as a wallflower—but not so clearly as Dora remembered herself, lanky and plain and freckled, trying desperately to appear interested in the conversation of dowagers. She remembered the dances at Chipping Lodge: Mrs. Massey's glance, shooting arrowlike across the room to rouse one or other of her daughters to hospitable action; Ruth or Isabel kindly rounding up a stray male. The Chipping Lodge dances had not been the worst of Dora's ordeals, at least she always got taken in to supper. But these unhappy experiences had planted in Miss Tremayne a great sympathy with all young persons: she could enter into the feelings of even so pretty a girl as Jacqueline Brown. "Has any one," asked Miss Tremayne, "ordered our sweet?"

As the meal ended, however, she could not resist one last aside to Isabel.

"Do you know what I told Simon?" murmured Dora. "I told him I hoped he'd fall headlong in love with Tilly Cuff."

"*Oh!*" breathed Isabel. "Oh, Dora, if he only would!"

3

They stayed till the Café closed, and then left Humphrey behind them: Bob had more milkless tea in his back room. Jacqueline and Isabel saw Miss Tremayne to her door, and then escorted each other up the hill. It was an agreeable night, not very warm, but still; they lingered a moment in the drive.

"I wonder if Dora ever wanted to marry Simon herself?" mused Isabel.

"I shouldn't think so," said Jacqueline thoughtfully. "She seems to me the perfect happy spinster."

"She *is* happy, isn't she? And she lost all her money, you know, every penny, except about a hundred a year. . . ."

"How did she lose it?" asked Jacqueline curiously.

"My dear, she speculated. Her parents left her quite well off, they used to live at the Cedars, and Dora put every penny into gold-mines, and it turned out afterwards they were the wrong sort. She even had to sell the house. And of course every one thought she'd leave Chipping Hill altogether; but Dora," stated Mrs. Brocken admiringly, "thought otherwise. She said every one was so kind to her, she'd stay on as a universal poor relation, and we could all give her our winter coats."

It was at this point that Mr. Brocken, from his bedroom window, heard their voices in the drive and put out his head.

"The front-door," he observed pointedly, "is still unlatched. Perhaps you will be good enough to lock and bolt it. I am in my pyjamas."

"But Humphrey isn't here!" called up Isabel. "He's still at Bob's!"

"Am I expected to sit up for him?" called Mr. Brocken —really very unreasonably.

"No, of course not, dear. He'll lock up when he comes in. Jacky and I are going to bed."

"Then I shall keep my light on," announced Mr. Brocken. "A dark house, and an open front-door, in these days, is simply an invitation to burglars."

It is hard to say why this episode so irritated him. Chipping Hill is not a particularly burglar-prone neighbourhood, and there were five people in the house. Perhaps it was because, as the senior male on the premises, he felt like the householder, and yet had none of a householder's authority. In any case, he was irritated; and more irritated still when Humphrey, coming in some hours later, and perceiving a line of light under his uncle's door, thoughtfully rapped on the panel and asked whether Mr. Brocken knew his light was on.

4

On the Friday morning Mr. Brocken was subjected to really serious annoyance.

Travelling up to town on the nine-twenty, first class, in a non-smoker, he was often fortunate enough to have the compartment to himself. He did not deny the right of other passengers to share it with him, provided they also had first-class tickets, and did not smoke. ("Do you mind — ?" asked, now and then, some rash optimist. "I do," snapped Mr. Brocken.) He merely preferred their absence. Until the train moved out he sat with his legs across the doorway, and his dispatch-case on the seat opposite; and was thus often, as has been said, fortunate enough to travel alone.

On this particular morning, however, someone entered the carriage so closely upon his heels that Mr. Brocken had no time to erect these defences. The seat opposite was taken. To make matters worse, it was taken by someone Mr. Brocken recognized. In short, it was Mr. Simmonds, handsomely turned out in light brown tweed, and exuding a strong smell of hair oil.

"Good morning, sir," said Mr. Simmonds.

Simon grunted, and opened his newspaper. His manner was more than usually forbidding; he detested being talked to in trains, and hoped that Mr. Simmonds could take a hint. But if the latter did not immediately speak again, neither did he produce any reading matter of his own. He simply sat, a large majestic presence, gazing directly before him, and therefore directly at the back of Mr. Brocken's *Times*. The barrier was not insubstantial, but it was insufficient: as the minutes passed (the train now in motion) Simon began to feel as though he were leaning the sheets against some invisible pressure, palpable as a current of air. The leader page bulged. Mr. Brocken, who had been holding the paper wide open, was forced to lower and double it back. At once his eye was caught.

"Nice morning," said Mr. Simmonds.

"Muggy," said Simon. "May I offer you the *Economist?*"

"Thank you, no," said Mr. Simmonds. "I find reading in trains tiring to the eyes. I trust all are well at the Lodge?"

Simon grunted.

"It's a healthy situation," pursued Mr. Simmonds dauntlessly. "In fact, I would back Chipping Hill, and particularly the Ridge, against any situation in Middlesex. Yet not for all."

"No?" said Simon, pointedly returning to the editorial.

"No," said Mr. Simmonds. "Mrs. Simmonds, for example, finds it lowering. Mrs. Simmonds lives at Torquay, with her parents, for the benefit of her health."

Now why, thought Mr. Brocken, is he telling me that? His attention was caught in spite of himself. Experience had given him a keen ear for what might be called conversation with intent: conversation aimed at the extracting of a little free legal advice. This note he now detected in the voice of Mr. Simmonds — and yet with a difference. He felt that what Mr. Simmonds desired was to make a statement; and he was right.

"We go, as you may say," continued Mr. Simmonds, "each our own way: but always on the best of terms: Mrs. Simmonds being of very delicate constitution. I invariably pass the Christmas season at Torquay, also two weeks in August, thus giving no cause for talk, and each autumn Mrs. Simmonds, accompanied by her mother, passes a week in London. Being great theatre-goers, and also great shoppers, they find it more convenient to put up at the Great Western Hotel."

"Very natural," said Simon. He also felt it perhaps natural that Mr. Simmonds should prefer to keep them away from Chipping Hill. However, the Simmonds ménage seemed well able to settle its own affairs. "Very agreeable," said Simon.

"I put up there myself," added Mr. Simmonds, "in order to escort them about; we have, I may say, a very pleasant time. On the other hand — " he paused, evidently arranging his next phrase with some care — "on the other hand, being used to female society, and in particular fond of dancing, I find the companionship of such a lady as Mrs. Poole extremely welcome."

Simon replied that he could well imagine it.

"We get on," said Mr. Simmonds, with unusual simplicity. "She's quiet. She's a credit to take about, but she's quiet. I like her, and she likes me. I've grown fond of the kid. I've none of my own. You might say we have formed a real friendship. But nothing — " and here he suddenly fixed Mr. Brocken with an eye almost as formidable as Simon's own — "but nothing, mark you, out of line."

Mr. Brocken believed it. He believed himself able to recognize a truthful witness. He also understood perfectly why the statement had been made. What irritated him was a sense that he was being dragged into Mr. Simmonds's, or rather Mrs. Poole's, affairs. He realized that the latter, regarding him as her employer, was naturally anxious to stand well with him; could comprehend that Mr. Simmonds prized highly a good name that echoed as far as Torquay; each, in Mr. Brocken, had apparently recognized a sort of censor before whom the position needed to be made clear. "But what the deuce is it to do with me?" thought Simon angrily. "Am I to give this fellow a character, if his wife suspects an intrigue? Am I supposed to stand up for Mrs. Poole, if Isabel hears gossip? Why should I be so involved?" While he was thus reflecting, Mr. Simmonds said slowly,

"I mention the matter, and I may be speaking out of turn, Mrs. P. having mentioned that Mrs. Brocken spoke shortly to Greta. Ladies being what they are—" Simon felt a momentary sympathy—"one never knows what is in their minds; I merely wish to assure you that Mrs. Brocken has no cause to come down on Mrs. P."

On this point at least Simon could assure Mr. Simmonds. His knowledge of Isabel convinced him that she would never enter on a quarrel with Mrs. Poole by way of the child. He was certain that if Isabel, who spoke sharply to no one, had spoken sharply to Greta, it was simply out of her new nervousness. (In this Mr. Brocken was right: Greta, appearing quietly on the terrace, made Isabel jump, and Isabel had snapped. It was no more than that. But the Pooles had not much more sense than Isabel.) Mr. Brocken said precisely,

"I employ Mrs. Poole, through my sister-in-law Mrs. Brocken. Had I not every confidence in her behaviour, I should have ceased to do so."

"I thank you," said Mr. Simmonds; and at once closed his eyes. Mr. Brocken returned to *The Times,* and read it undisturbed until the train drew in at London Bridge. The two men got out, and Mr. Simmonds, with no more than a courteous elevation of his hat, at once disappeared.

Mr. Brocken very much wondered what business, if any, had brought him up to town.

5

That same day Bogey precipitated a small crisis. It was Bogey's fate to live chiefly upon fish, and of fish chiefly upon cods' heads; unlike cats, he had not the secret of discreet digestion; his powerful breath proclaimed his country's shortages. But the fishmonger, who had no fish the day before, had still no fish on Friday; Isabel recklessly purchased and gave Bogey a whole liver-sausage. The unusual richness was too much for him; he withdrew from the public view, unfortunately into Mr. Brocken's room, where he was very sick. It was Humphrey who cleared up the horrid mess, but not until Simon had discovered it; and when the latter very naturally expressed his displeasure to Isabel, she burst into tears.

Simon had said nothing to make his sister-in-law cry. He was sure of it; he had merely stated his opinion that Bogey ought to be shot. That Isabel should weep for half an hour indicated something radically wrong with her nerves. Simon reviewed his own exemplary behaviour, the extreme considerateness (he willingly acknowledged it) of Humphrey and Miss Brown, and recollected his conversation with Dora.

On the Saturday morning, according to plan, he visited his house in Kensington. No progress had been made. He was lucky enough to encounter Mr. Ison on the spot, also making a tour of inspection. They greeted each other with something like cordiality; but the foreman, though sympathetic, would raise no foolish hopes.

"I know how it is," said Mr. Ison. "The missus and me, after we were bombed out, lived fifteen months with her sister. *I* know how it is. When you get to our age, a chap wants a place of his own."

"I could live very well in a couple of rooms," suggested Mr. Brocken.

"*We* hadn't but one," said Mr. Ison.

"One, then," said Simon.

"There's no gas," said Mr. Ison.

He put the earliest date of reoccupation at September; and in the idiom of an earlier war advised Mr. Brocken, if he knew of a better hole, to stick to it. From Red Lion Place Mr. Brocken telephoned every hotel he could think of, and learnt that they were all full. The only flat available was a luxury apartment in Park Lane (with sunken bath) at twenty guineas a week. There was no alternative to Chipping Lodge. This being so, the logical step was to remove, or attempt to remove, what he believed to be the threat to his comfort there; Mr. Brocken determined to tackle his sister-in-law at once.

Isabel was alone, when he returned, on the terrace; he at once walked out to join her. He walked out quite confidently, not anticipating any serious trouble. He passed through the drawing-room, under the three chandeliers in their holland bags, without noticing their resemblance to wasps' nests. Even had he done so, he was not a man to read omens in the ceiling. He went out with a smooth brow, prepared only with patience.

Chapter 8

That morning rain had fallen, but stone flags dry quickly; Isabel was encouraging Bogey to promenade unmuddied. He suffered from blisters between his toes, and while any one was watching walked so to speak with a stick. When the appearance of Mr. Brocken diverted his mistress's attention, he nipped down the steps and made quietly for long grass.

"The sky is clearing," said Mr. Brocken affably. "The sun is quite warm."

Isabel received these trite remarks with unsuspicious pleasure, and hopefully added that the iron chairs were quite dry. It sounded like a conversation in a French primer. Mr. Brocken nearly offered to uncover the seat for her, but the waterproof top, slightly concave, probably held puddles, and he refrained. Isabel sat down on iron; Simon leant against the terrace wall; and since he had nothing else to say to her, at once opened his case.

"Last Sunday, if you remember, you mentioned having written to Tilly Cuff."

Mrs. Brocken instinctively folded her hands in her lap.

"Yes, I did, dear. I mean I did mention it, and I had written. I wrote to her the day after you came."

"Then I gather there has been no reply."

"Yes, dear, there has," said Isabel, surprisingly. As a rule she could not keep even a circular to herself. "It came on Tuesday. She's in Birmingham, but she's coming as soon as her notice is up. I didn't tell you before because I was waiting to see if we could get a chicken."

Simon ignored this implication, which was indeed not flattering, to concentrate on the phrase which preceded it.

"You say 'her notice,' from which I assume that she is in some sort of post, and also that she intends to relinquish it, on your representations. This is news to me. May I ask how long you expect her to stay here?"

"As long as she likes, dear."

All this was far worse than Mr. Brocken had anticipated, but he kept himself in hand. Perhaps some uncontrollable movement betrayed him, for Isabel suddenly closed her eyes, like a person expecting a douche of water. But Simon had himself in hand, and after no more than a quick turn up and down the terrace came back to address her in still kindly tones.

"My dear Isabel," he said, "you have a most creditably warm heart; but in this case it has led you astray. You are making a mistake. If Tilly Cuff takes you at your word, she may stay for months. It will mean more work for Miss Brown, who must have her hands full already; it will possibly upset the Pooles. I should be loath to see our happy party disturbed: why not write a tactful letter and put the woman off?"

"I couldn't do that, dear."

"Of course you could. What beats me — " Mr. Brocken's grip on himself was loosening — "is why you ever looked her up at all."

Isabel was silent.

"No one was ever particularly fond of her," continued Mr. Brocken. "I can remember no tears when she went off to Switzerland. Your own behaviour, I have observed it, is apprehensive. No one wants her here — and I must say, where I'm concerned, I think you have been very inconsiderate."

Still Isabel did not speak; and scrutinizing her more closely, Mr. Brocken perceived that she was unable to. Tears — good heavens! — brimmed her eyes, her mouth was set, her chin quivered, she was already in a fantod.

"Good heavens!" exclaimed Mr. Brocken loudly. "What is it? What's wrong now? I make a perfectly reasonable suggestion — "

She shook her head. Two tears, released by the movement, trickled slowly down her cheeks. She wiped them away and two more at once followed. It was fantastic!

"I merely make an observation — !" cried Mr. Brocken.

"It's not that," whispered Isabel. "It's not that at all . . ."

"Then what the deuce is it?"

Thus braced and buffeted, she found a certain spirit.

"I shall be glad to tell you, Simon, if you will stop walking about, and sit down and don't shout at me."

Mr. Brocken sat. He took the other iron chair, placing it directly opposite his sister-in-law's, so that he could fix her with his eye; Isabel sat bolt upright, her hands clasped in her lap. She was so short, however, that her neatly crossed ankles swung to and fro an inch from the ground; during the silence that followed Mr. Brocken perceived that she was swinging them deliberately, taking (even while her cheeks were wet with tears) an absent pleasure in the motion. Incurable, ineradicable frivolity! But her distress was undoubtedly genuine, she was finding it very difficult to begin; and when at last she spoke her voice was not quite under control.

"You—you know, Simon, I've always tried to do my duty?"

Upon reflection, and rather to his surprise, Mr. Brocken found himself forced to agree. As the childless wife of a wealthy and amiable husband, as a well-dowered widow, Isabel had no doubt found her duty easy enough; but she did it. She had made Mark Brocken very happy. She was very charitable. And when a harder duty was placed squarely in her way, she did that too. In 1914 she was a V.A.D. In 1940, at Bath, she at once volunteered again for the same arduous work. . . .

"You had a sound upbringing," explained Mr. Brocken.

"Thank you, dear." Isabel looked gratified. "And so had you; and you've kept it up so. That's why I wanted to ask you about the sermon."

"What sermon?"

"The one about the passage of time. The passage of time not making a base action any less base. I asked you about it as soon as you came."

Mr. Brocken had to agree that this was so; and his uneasiness increased. That Isabel had carried a conversation in her head over a period of weeks was remarkable enough; if, in addition, a topic he had believed chosen from pure politeness — a tribute to his own superior intelligence — should now prove to have been of real moment to her, and if she were actually going to proceed from it to some logically connected proposition — then Isabel's brain had been almost dangerously stimulated. But by what?

"And it was that convinced me," continued Isabel earnestly. "I didn't *want* to be convinced. I hoped you'd say it was just a catchword." (Mr. Brocken winced, recognizing a favourite term.) "Because you see, Simon, I did once, a long time ago, do a base act."

In the pause that followed Mr. Brocken was visited by a most unusual sensation. Facing his sister-in-law, he also faced the house: on that same spot, the day he arrived, he had fancifully invoked the theatre of Racine. It now struck him, with one of those superstitious twinges by which the most rational men are sometimes embarrassed, that the theatre of Racine is tragic. Had his fancy been an unlucky one? "Bah!" thought Mr. Brocken. "Let in imagination, and see what follows! Sheer nonsense!" Shaking himself free of such cobwebs, and considering Isabel's words by the light of reason, he saw no cause for alarm.

Whatever Isabel's wicked deed—and with all her faults he could not believe her guilty of anything really criminal—the point was that it had happened a long time ago; was over and done with; needed no action of his. Her present remorse (which no doubt preceded confession) was characteristically tiresome, but would carry no consequences; and seeing the tears start again in his sister-in-law's eyes, he leant forward and quite kindly patted her hand.

"Thank you, dear," said Isabel gratefully. "Now I can go on. Do you remember, just before the last war, a Mr. Macgregor?"

2

At once Mr. Brocken was back in the stables—back with his brother and the girls, and Tilly washing Puck, and a gunner subaltern. . . .

"Oddly enough, I remember him quite well," said Mr. Brocken. "He was a subaltern in the Gunners, who stayed with us on one of his leaves, and came to one of your dances."

"And he was wonderfully good-looking."

"I don't remember that," said Mr. Brocken.

"Perhaps not, but he was. He was like Lewis Waller. He stayed with you a week, it was in the spring of 1912, and we saw him nearly every day."

Simon raised his eyebrows.

"You sound as though you were in love with the fellow."

"I was," said Isabel gently. "That's my only excuse. I was twenty, and I fell in love with him, and I thought he was in love with me. I dare say I was very vain in those days, but I *was* pretty, wasn't I?"

Simon nodded. The Isabel Massey of 1912, whose image he had just revived, was as pretty as a buttercup.

"And when he came to see us almost every day," continued Isabel, watching the toe of her swinging shoe, "and really paid me a great deal of attention, I don't think I was so unreasonable. The only thing was, the time was so short, and he was so shy, and we were so well brought up, I thought he might be afraid of Papa; I thought he couldn't screw himself up."

"He probably hadn't a penny," said Simon practically.

"Yes, he had, dear; his father was Macgregor's Oatmeal Biscuits. So I knew it wasn't that. Well, on the Friday, which was the day of our dance, and he was leaving on Saturday, one of the maids told me that he'd been over before breakfast and waited about half an hour in the stables, looking at the horses, and then gone off again. Of course I remembered telling him I often went out early, though that day I hadn't—and you can imagine how furious I was! But there was our dance that night, so I hoped he might speak to me then. It was the most *dreadful* dance," said Isabel earnestly, "the most dreadful evening, I've ever endured."

"You appeared," said Mr. Brocken sceptically, "to be enjoying yourself."

"Of course. Girls have to. But I hardly *saw* Mr. Macgregor. There were all our guests to look after, and then I simply could *not* get rid of you and Mark. . . . I'm telling you this, Simon, to try and make you understand, because no one ever had a better husband than Mark was, I loved him with all my heart; but just for that evening I suppose I was infatuated. I had only one dance with Mr. Macgregor, and we didn't even sit out afterwards because I had to go and be nice to Dora Tremayne. And of course he left with you and Mark. So I had just one hope. I was up next morning at half-past six."

Isabel's shoe had stopped swinging. She sat perfectly still, looking down at her clasped hands.

"It was a beautiful morning," she said softly. "The maids were all in the kitchen, but they'd pulled up the blinds, and the hall was full of sunshine. We grew lots of hyacinths, and the scent and the sunlight together seemed to go to my head. I felt absolutely certain he was coming, and coming to ask me to marry him. I went to open the front door, and there in the box was a letter."

"At half-past six?"

"Of course it hadn't come through the post, Simon. It had been left by hand. Mr. Macgregor *had* come, even earlier than I'd expected. I knew the writing would be his, he'd written in our albums, and it was; only the letter wasn't addressed to me."

Isabel paused, her face crumpled in an expression not only of distress, but also of disbelief: she had been reliving those moments so completely that the shock struck her afresh. How long had she stood there, in the sunlight, in the smell of hyacinths? By intensity, an hour; and in fact the emotions now in an instant recapitulated had held her powerless for many minutes. Behind her a clock ticked, a flower dropped; and still Isabel Massey stood incredulous, staring at the envelope in her hand. . . .

"It was addressed to Tilly," said Isabel Brocken. "*Miss Tilly Cuff*. I couldn't believe it. And at last — without meaning to, just as though I were a marionette and some one had pulled the strings — I found myself opening the front door and walking out and round to the stables. The envelope was one of your very stiff blue ones, and the flap only just held. I opened it and I read the letter."

Mr. Brocken stirred uneasily; on his narrow face the parallel lines of moustache and scar had become very noticeable. For though his sister-in-law's misdeed did not so far appear very black, it was . . . unexpectedly vulgar. However much, in the past, he had reprobated her silliness, he had always relied on her breeding; she was a gentlewoman, if a foolish one. His face reflected his thoughts; Mrs. Brocken looked away, and said rapidly,

"It was a proposal of marriage. He asked her to marry him. It began, 'My dearest Miss Cuff.' "

"Is there any point in repeating it?" asked Simon.

"You'll see. He said that only doubt of her sentiments had kept him silent; and if when he came to say good-bye after breakfast, she could offer him the least encouragement by word or look, he would at once speak to Papa; but if she couldn't, he would take it as a definite rejection, and spare her all further embarrassment. I couldn't believe it."

"I can't believe it either," said Mr. Brocken, after a moment's thought. "He'd hardly seen the girl."

"I suppose he saw her nearly every time he saw *us*. She was always so mum. But I couldn't believe it, it seemed too improbable, no one ever fell in love with Tilly, not even curates; and at last I made up my mind — I made up my mind it was nothing but a cruel joke."

"My dear Isabel!"

"Yes, I did. I thought perhaps you and Mark together — "

"Rubbish!" ejaculated Mr. Brocken sharply. "Neither Mark nor I would ever have been party to such a thing, and you must have known it. Moreover, if your memory is at all accurate, it was the letter of a perfectly serious and honourable man."

"A moment ago you didn't believe he could have written it."

"I am still perplexed," admitted Mr. Brocken. "But the evidence is certainly stronger in favour of Macgregor's falling in love with Miss Cuff than of Mark and myself behaving like cads. However, you persuaded yourself that the letter was a cruel joke; and I imagine you are now going to tell me that you suppressed it."

Isabel nodded miserably.

"Well, what happened?"

"I went back into the house," said Isabel meticulously, "and there was Tilly coming downstairs. She always came down early, to dust the drawing-room. She looked quite pretty, for Tilly; she had that pink handkerchief round her head. And I thought, how dreadful it would be if she made a fool of herself — accidentally, you know — by putting herself forward in any way, when Mr. Macgregor came. I thought you and Mark might make fun of her."

Mr. Brocken snorted.

"Yes, I know, dear; but that's what I thought. Or rather," admitted Isabel painfully, "what I *made* myself think. I said, 'Oh, by the way, Tilly, Mr. Macgregor's coming after breakfast, to say good-bye; you must give him a last chance to flirt with you too.' Then I went upstairs."

For some minutes Mr. Brocken sat without speaking; he was shocked into silence by this revelation of the devilishness of nice women. For he understood enough of the situation, of Tilly's position in that household, to appreciate the full force and skill of such a seemingly playful phrase. It was a warning to Tilly to keep off the grass. She would not dare to ignore it. Her existence depended too utterly on the Masseys' goodwill. Moreover, he at last had the clue to the peculiar flatness, the ill-feeling almost, of Macgregor's parting visit. . . .

"*What's the matter with Tilly?*"

"*Oh, I expect she's offended about something. She often is . . .*"

After thirty-four years Mr. Brocken found himself able to recall, quite clearly, that scrap of dialogue; as though the intensity of the emotions which must have played like lightning about his unconscious head had printed the words upon his unconscious brain. The devilishness of women!

"You behaved very badly," said Mr. Brocken.

"Yes, dear. I know."

"What did you hope to gain by it?"

"I thought, after Tilly had gone away — and she did go very soon, to Switzerland — I thought perhaps Mr. Macgregor would come back and stay with you again, and — and really fall in love with *me*."

"Well, he didn't," said Mr. Brocken. "So you had probably made no impression on him whatever. You merely deprived poor Tilly of a possible husband. I agree that it was indeed a base act. However," finished Mr. Brocken distastefully, "you have now relieved your mind, and you had better forget the whole business."

"But I can't," said Isabel pitifully. "Not since I heard that sermon. And I don't *only* want to relieve my mind, I want to do something about it. That's why I've asked Tilly."

"So I now realize. I still think it a mistake. The damage is done, my dear Isabel. It was done thirty-five years ago."

"But, dear, *the passage of time* — "

"I know, I know," cut in Mr. Brocken irritably. "And I've said I agree with you. The point is, there is now no action you can take."

At this moment, and before she could reply, the cover of the seat bulged; a foot thrust from beneath it, feeling for the ground; between two folds of waterproof Humphrey Garrett stuck out his head.

3

It was an enormous relief to Mr. Brocken to be able to lose his temper.

"If you have been there all the time, listening to our conversation," he shouted, "I am thoroughly ashamed of you! You have been eavesdropping, sir! Your conduct is disgraceful! Isabel, do you realize that this nephew of yours has probably heard every word you have said?"

"Well, I don't mind," said Isabel mildly. "It saves me telling it twice. *Did* you hear, darling?"

"I did, Aunt Isabel. I didn't listen, but I heard."

"About the passage of time? And don't you think I'm right?"

"There can be no argument."

"You see?" said Isabel, turning in modest triumph to her brother-in-law.

Mr. Brocken, still furious, exclaimed that if one were already sure of one's ethical ground any outside opinion was merely irrelevant.

"But young people to-day are so much cleverer than we are," said Isabel.

"Then you had better consult Miss Brown as well!"

She had the grace to flush.

"As a matter of fact, dear, I told Jacky this morning. I was feeling so very dreadful about it all—and as you weren't here—I—I just told Jacky . . ."

Mr. Brocken was beside himself. And naturally: after

listening, with the greatest patience and sympathy, to a tedious and distasteful story, he was now informed that his sister-in-law not only ranked young Humphrey's opinion above his own, but had already confided in a paid companion.

"Had I known, my dear Isabel," he said bitterly, "that you were merely seeking a wider audience, I should not have wasted my time listening to you. However, as I have done so, I will repeat what I said earlier: though your conduct towards Tilly Cuff was indeed base, and the whole story extremely discreditable, there is now nothing you can do. To offer her a month's holiday as amends for a frustrated life is simply insulting and a damned nuisance, so for heaven's sake let us hear no more of it."

The dog Bogey, covered with wet mud, staggered up the terrace steps and collapsed across Mr. Brocken's feet. Mr. Brocken leapt up, Humphrey seized Bogey by the collar, Isabel cried out for Jacqueline, who came running from the house, received Bogey from Humphrey and dragged him off towards the stables. As soon as peace was restored Isabel said cheerfully,

"Of course a month's holiday won't be enough, Simon. What I'm afraid I'll have to do, only you wouldn't let me tell you, is to give Tilly my money. I *think* I'll keep the house."

Chapter 9

Now it was serious. Both Mr. Brocken and Humphrey believed that they had been giving their full attention already, but now the quality of that attention changed. Money talks. A romantic dream of restitution is one thing, the making over of cash quite another.

It took some little time for Isabel to make herself perfectly understood; both men interrupted a good deal; yet her position was really quite simple. She had (she now, belatedly, realized) ruined Tilly Cuff's life: her own life, so easy and happy, was the pattern of what Tilly's might have been. What could she do but try and give up, so to speak, her place to Tilly? To Isabel it was as simple as that.—As simple as though, a child at a party, she had slipped into another child's seat at the supper table; now the feast was nearly over, but all the same the other child should have her place. The satisfaction of having been a wife, of now being a widow, Isabel was not able to transfer (the child had finished the chicken salad) but she could transfer an income. She could give Tilly independence. She could enable Tilly to go to Jamaica. Isabel had no idea whether Tilly wanted to go to Jamaica, but as she had contemplated doing so herself, it seemed possible. She was certain Tilly would like a fur coat; and since a fur coat and a trip to the West Indies were things a widow might very well comfort herself with, Tilly, enjoying them, would feel almost like a widow.

Simon, faced by this mixture of irrational sentiment and practical detail, hardly knew which point to tackle first. However, there was one most obvious problem.

"And what," he asked, "after you have given away your income, do you propose to live on yourself?"

With an air of cheerful competence, Isabel replied that should she retain Chipping Lodge, she would take boarders. She would run Chipping Lodge as a guest house, like the Cedars and the Towers. "Heaven help the guests," thought Mr. Brocken, and paid the project no further attention. "Or should I keep *some?*" asked Isabel diffidently. "Dora I believe has about a hundred a year . . ."

"She is also," pointed out Humphrey, "paid by Madame Esmé to advertise her decrepitude."

"Dear, you know she isn't. That's just Dora's way of talking. Dora *enjoys* herself there."

"Whether Dora enjoys herself or not," said Mr. Brocken, rather loudly, "is beside the point. Isabel, listen to me: you have an income of roughly a thousand a year, representing a capital of about forty thousand. I cannot imagine it is the capital you are intending to give away — "

"Yes, it is," said Isabel.

"Nonsense," said Mr. Brocken.

It was all he could say, at the moment; his thoughts

were too busy, there were too many implications to be explored. For Mrs. Mark Brocken, as has been said, was childless; the money was Brocken money; and though childless himself, Simon Brocken had a very strong sense of property. The money should come back to him — to be left probably to charity, but in any case to be left in his name; the only other claim he admitted was that of Humphrey, down for five thousand. Mr. Brocken was perfectly familiar with his sister-in-law's will: she left five thousand to Humphrey, her jewellery to her sister, one thousand to Dr. Barnardo's, and the residue to himself: after death duties, by no means a fortune. . . .

"You know, Simon," said Mrs. Brocken, rather appositely, "you *are* older than I am."

Since the idea that he might die first, or even die at all, was one Simon always refused to contemplate, the remark failed to placate him. He said roughly,

"You can't do it."

"Yes, I can," said Isabel. "It's my money. Mark explained all about it."

"You still can't do it."

"Wouldn't it be legal?"

Mr. Brocken paused. Certainly it would be legal, but he felt it ought not to be. He felt no woman ought legally to be able to make such a fool of herself. And the damnable part was that he himself was not a trustee, but merely an executor. What had induced Mark — what sudden aberration had permitted him — to leave such property so unsecured? It was insane, it was outrageous—but it was undoubtedly legal.

"Yes," he admitted heavily. "It's legal."

"Then there is really nothing to discuss," said Isabel cheerfully. "I shall tell Tilly when she comes, and you must arrange it for us. Don't stay here to be cold, my dears; I think I'll go in."

2

For a while the two men sat in silence. Rain once more threatened, but neither felt inclined to move; the act of getting up and going in would put too definite a period to a debate which, so long as they refused to budge, might still be presumed to continue; the mental attitude often reflects, or is even influenced by, the physical. Moreover, if any joint measure were possible, now was the moment to combine. Mr. Brocken looked at his young companion doubtfully; at that age, twenty-six or so, the instinct for property was often quite reprehensibly undeveloped; but surely Humphrey had some plan, some thought for the future, in which his aunt's money played a part? How did one approach the young? Mr. Brocken knew no persuasive arts; he said flatly,

"If this mad scheme went through, you'd lose your legacy. You're down for five thousand. Does it matter to you?"

"Not in the least," said Humphrey.

This was not true; he simply and instinctively gave the answer most likely to annoy old Brocken. It did.

"Then you are a very unusual young man," said Simon sourly.

"I have developed, sir, into a prig."

"So I perceive. Yet you do not seem wholly enthusiastic. Personally I make no claim to quixotry, I consider your aunt's project imbecile, and I shall endeavour to combat it; but I am surprised that it does not appeal to so noble a youth as yourself."

Humphrey's countenance relaxed into a perfectly natural expression of uncertainty.

"They're all such silly types," he said thoughtfully.

Simon frowned. Though he agreed in his heart with this judgment of his sister-in-law, he disapproved of so young a person giving voice to it.

"I don't know what you mean," he said severely. "Macgregor was a very capable officer, and Miss Cuff a sensible young woman who earned her own living." (For the life of him he could think of nothing in favour of Isabel.)

"She lived on her rich relations. A pure parasite. Mind you, I'm not blaming her," said Humphrey magnanimously, "in 1912 I reckon there was damn' little else for her to do; but the fact remains. She was a pure parasite."

"Are you a Communist, by any chance?" asked Mr. Brocken.

"I don't know," admitted Humphrey honestly. "I've certainly no use for the social system of 1912—"

"It was the best system that ever existed," retorted Mr.

Brocken. "I look back to 1912 as the highest point of civilization, from which we have been steadily retrogressing ever since. But that is beside the point. The point we have to deal with is your aunt's extraordinary aberration."

"Why do you call it that?" asked Jacqueline Brown.

3

She had returned so quietly that her voice took both men by surprise. She was standing behind them, the Sealyham, rinsed and towelled, in her arms: in a moment of hallucination Mr. Brocken saw not Miss Brown and Bogey, but Tilly and Puck. The moment passed; but it was strange, he thought, how the type, the combination, persisted. Companion and lap-dog, the first casualties (wouldn't one have thought?) of war and revolution . . . and yet up they popped again wherever a dwindling pocket of wealth afforded broken biscuits and an office boy's wage. . . . Mr. Brocken glanced sharply at young Garrett, as though conscious of having taken some mental infection.

"Why," repeated Jacqueline, "do you call it an aberration?"

"Because it plainly is," replied Mr. Brocken.

"Because the whole thing's crackers," said Humphrey.

Jacqueline gave Bogey a final rub and set him down.

"But it isn't, you know. You both talk as though it were, and I can see why: it—it's all so mixed up. I think myself that Mr. Macgregor was a muff and Tilly a rabbit.

But it was a tragedy for her all the same, and what Mrs. Brocken's trying to do now isn't crackers at all." She paused, and added, almost diffidently, "The thing is, it's a heroic story, but Mrs. Brocken isn't a heroic person."

"Too right," said Humphrey.

"But if you . . . translated it," went on Miss Brown painstakingly, "you'd see. Suppose it was a — a political prisoner in Siberia, who all that time ago got released by impersonating someone else: it would be heroic if he went back and gave himself up again. I'm trying to think of something with the passage of time in it. But suppose a man was going to be repatriated, and another man stole his papers — it would be heroic of the other man to go back."

"Not at all," said Mr. Brocken. "It would be common honesty."

Miss Brown took no notice of him. Her argument was now addressed to Humphrey alone.

"And she's going to tell, you know. She's going to tell Tilly what she did. How would you like to own up to a thing like that?"

Humphrey shrugged.

"If you want my opinion, it was a damn' silly business when it happened, and it's a damn' silly business still." He paused; his conscience — the remorseless conscience of youth — pricked him. "I admit it may have been a tragedy for the Tilly girl, but beside all that's happened since it's a flea-bite, it doesn't exist. Tragedy's been rife in the world. All over Europe, and Russia and China — add up the tragedies there and tell me what's to be done about *them*. . . ."

"That does not," said Jacqueline stubbornly, "alter the principle. Because you can't put everything right, that's no reason for not doing what you can. It's a matter of integrity. It couldn't be more or less important now or a hundred years ago, or a hundred years hence, and it doesn't make the least difference to the principle that your aunt's a silly ass. In fact," concluded Miss Brown, "it isolates it."

She went in; once again the two men were left alone.

"God bless my soul!" ejaculated Mr. Brocken. "What an extremely opinionated young woman!"

But he spoke without conviction, being in truth more struck than he liked to admit. Integrity! — she was right there: come down to brass tacks, and it was the only thing that mattered, the only virtue (for it embraced courage), the only salt of the earth. No man valued it more highly; and while he resented its turning up in a form so peculiarly troublesome to himself, still he could not deny it. He was in fact so shaken that he did a very unusual thing: he asked the opinion of a person younger than himself.

"Humphrey," said Mr. Brocken dubiously, "do you think it possible that the women may be right?"

"In theory, undoubtedly, sir. We seem to have landed in company beyond our moral station."

"Something should, perhaps, be done for Miss Cuff. Isabel might even make her a small allowance. But as for giving up her income — ! It's insane."

Humphrey said nothing.

"Tilly wouldn't take it!" cried Mr. Brocken.

"Has she a high moral character too?"

Mr. Brocken didn't know. He knew practically nothing about Tilly Cuff. He began to wonder whether he really knew much about Isabel. Jacqueline Brown had just surprised him considerably. . . .

"I bet the padre would have been pleased," said Humphrey suddenly.

"Padre? What padre?"

"The parson, sir. The bloke who preached. It can't be often that a sermon produces such a striking effect."

"And very fortunately," said Mr. Brocken.

"But they should, you know. Personally I think that's the most remarkable feature of the whole affair — that Aunt Isabel went to church, and heard what the parson told her, and then went home and did it."

Mr. Brocken snorted.

"She heard nothing. She wasn't even listening. It was simply that one phrase — "

" — struck home to her heart. I had an Irish nursemaid who brought me up on the lives of the saints; the situation seems vaguely familiar."

Mr. Brocken pushed back his chair with such violence that it rolled clanging over the flags. He said forcibly,

"If you're going to make your aunt out a saint as well as a heroine, I can only assume that you're as mad as she is. I've heard enough nonsense for one afternoon. I shall now go for a walk."

But before he left the terrace he paused a moment to

look at the white façade, the classic statues, the severe lines of roof and wall. "Rational!" he thought sardonically. "Familiar! Undisturbing! Theatre of Racine be damned!"— For it wasn't tragedy he had fallen into, it was farce; and his sister-in-law was neither a saint nor a heroine, she was a fool; and to crown all Mr. Brocken felt a deepening suspicion that he had somehow been made a fool of himself. His own favourite question, so often repeated, over so many years, echoed back to him: where now, Mr. Brocken had demanded, was the old-fashioned conscientiousness, the old-fashioned integrity? And now pat came the answer: pat, positive, and accompanied by every circumstance most apt to infuriate a reasonable man. . . .

If from Isabel the spirit of tragedy instinctively averted its gaze, the spirit of irony undoubtedly had an eye on Mr. Brocken.

Chapter 10

Jacqueline and Humphrey took a kinder view. In their eyes the silliness of the affair was worse than the vulgarity (which had so upset Mr. Brocken) and the silliness distributed. They were more severe upon Tilly and Macgregor than upon Isabel: two people in love, with nothing on earth between them but tongue-tied diffidence. Unlike Simon, they could not realize the difficulties of Tilly's position in the Massey household; and where Macgregor was concerned were perhaps right in labelling him a muff. But he had been an extremely shy young man, and Tilly had given him no visible encouragement: it was one thing to fall in love with a girl at sight — to be pierced to the heart by her pluck and fragility and pink kerchief — and quite another to cut her out from a couple of brilliant and talkative cousins. Another young man might have done so; not Macgregor. The Misses Massey commanded his attention; manners compelled him to give it, and though his eye sought Tilly Cuff in the background, her eye had never sought his. His letter, in fact, was an act of extreme daring; and it would have been hard to say whether relief or chagrin predominated when Tilly took no notice of it. He did not subsequently pine. He knew there would have been great opposition from his parents. Yet he had loved Tilly Cuff for a week; he might very well have married her, for if he was shy, he was also stubborn.

Humphrey and Jacqueline, both peculiarly detached from their parents, set him down a muff.

"I dare say she's been far better off without him," remarked Jacqueline sagely. "At least she's had her independence."

"Do women still want their independence?" asked Humphrey.

(So quickly do times change. Women had fought for their independence for generations: had so briefly enjoyed it that Jacqueline's mother used her vote with a sense of almost terrifying responsibility: yet Jacqueline saw nothing odd in young Garrett's question.)

"They prefer it to being dependent on a muff," said she; and even this was forced to qualify. "Of course, if a woman can earn a good living, if she's a real success, and has no one but herself to think of, she's very well off; but it's surprising how often really successful women have people dependent on *them*. So it works both ways."

"In fact," said Humphrey, "there's still a lot to be said for a really successful husband. What could I be a success at?"

Jacqueline looked at him seriously.

"I don't know. I don't think you'd ever make a lot of money, you don't care about it enough. But you might turn out steady. . . . In the ATS, you know, when we had Brains Trusts, someone always put that in—"What is the most desirable quality in a husband?"—and all the girls agreed on the same answer. They wanted their husbands to be steady. It may have been the war . . . weren't you going to be anything in New Zealand?"

"Certainly I was. I was going to be a schoolmaster."

"*That's* steady."

"Though not particularly lucrative."

"And greatly in demand. There's a prep school at Broxbury."

"I wonder," said Humphrey, "what the deuce is going to happen to this house?"

That was their last oblique reference, in this absorbing conversation, to Tilly Cuff.

2

How the Pooles formed their opinion of her was a mystery. Isabel as a matter of course told them that another guest was expected, adding some cheerful comment about an extra ration-book; but why should Mrs. Poole have immediately given notice? Mrs. Poole really couldn't say; she just thought they might not get on so well. "But you won't *see* Miss Cuff!" protested Isabel. "She won't come into the kitchen, there'll be no extra work: you won't know she's here!" Mrs. Poole replied oracularly that one never knew; one couldn't tell; changes were not always for the better. She appeared, said Humphrey later, to have the same instinct that warns a cat of wet weather: she was washing behind her ears.

In this juncture Isabel turned to Simon. (The first swallow, thought Simon dourly.) But there was no doubt that the Pooles regarded him as their patron; he had originally engaged them, by him they might be influenced. Simon made his way to the kitchen with honey on his tongue.

"My dear Mrs. Poole," he said, "my sister-in-law tells me, to our great regret, that you think of leaving us, simply because there is to be another person at the Lodge. Now, why should you want to do a thing like that?"

"Well, you don't know," said Mrs. Poole uneasily. She and Greta were seated at the table, still engaged on their eternal puzzle.

"You don't know what?" asked Simon, controlling a natural impatience.

"You can't tell," explained Mrs. Poole. "Another lady in the place . . . well, you never know."

"Have Mrs. Brocken and Miss Brown ever been other than helpful?"

Mrs. Poole admitted that they had not.

"Then a third lady," said Mr. Brocken, "will probably lighten your work still further. From my own point of view I may say that I have found you extremely satisfactory, and that I should be very sorry to see you go."

He had struck, albeit unwittingly, the right note. Like all human beings the Pooles desired, above everything else, to be appreciated. Mother and daughter exchanged a complicated glance.

"You never," observed Mrs. Poole, "said nothing about your socks."

Mr. Brocken found himself in something of a quandary.

The darning of his socks had been abominable. Any truthful observation on them would undoubtedly give offence. There are occasions when a lie is so expedient as to be almost moral.

"Greta mended them very nicely," said he. "I hope she found her threepence on the dressing-table."

"Yes, she did," admitted Mrs. Poole. "But as you didn't say nothing, we thought perhaps you weren't satisfied."

"I was more than satisfied," declared Mr. Brocken.

"Well, there've been none since — now, have there?" demanded Mrs. Poole.

"I am not (as I think I told you at the time) hard on them. But if Greta looks in my room to-morrow, she will find two pairs for her to mend."

This was a considerable sacrifice on his part, for Mrs. Evans in North Wales darned extremely well. But it produced its effect. Greta smiled widely.

"I'll do your underthings too," she offered.

"Not if you are going to leave," countered Mr. Brocken swiftly. "And — good heavens! — why should you? Aren't you comfortable here?"

Again mother and daughter exchanged one of their long looks.

"It's been like heaven to us," said Mrs. Poole simply. "It's just that we don't want it changed. But if you say stay, we'll stay."

Mr. Brocken was flattered. In spite of himself, he was flattered. There is always something agreeable, to a solicitor, in the confidence of the widow and orphan. If he had had any of his sweet-ration with him, he would have given it to Greta. But they parted, even without this *douceur,* on the most friendly terms.

So friendly, indeed, that before he left the kitchen Mr. Brocken frankly demanded the secret of the game, or puzzle, which apparently absorbed so much of the Poole leisure.

It was Greta who answered him, in accents of sheerest astonishment.

"Why, don't you know?" breathed Greta. "It's our football pool!"

3

When he informed himself upon the subject (from his chief clerk, of all people) Simon could not give football pools his approbation; but this was a side issue. His intervention had been successful, he had done what was required of him. He even made a couple of holes in a couple of perfectly sound socks, for Greta to darn; those socks which needed darning being already in the post. He therefore felt all the more injured when Isabel calmly proposed that he should turn out of his room to make way for Tilly Cuff.

"But—good heavens!" protested Mr. Brocken—"she *has* a room here! She must have slept somewhere!"

"Yes, of course, dear," said Isabel. "But it wasn't a very *nice* room. At least, it wasn't one of the best. And anyway, Humphrey is in it now, and Jacky has my old one, and I moved into Mamma's, because I didn't like to think of any one else there; so really, Simon, I know it's a great nuisance to you, but what can we do?"

"Shift Miss Brown."

"But Jacky's got all her things here; she *needs* a big room . . ."

From this Simon gathered that the room allotted to himself was certainly small and probably inconvenient. It was in fact both: it was the old sewing-room, situated at the end of the passage farthest from the bath, and facing north. For once, however, Isabel was firm; she was the mistress of the house; and so long as he accepted her hospitality, Simon was obliged also to accept her domestic rulings.

He had also, for the moment, had enough of arguing with Isabel. She was beyond reason. To Mr. Brocken money, and especially family money, his brother Mark's money, was something almost sacred: the notion of giving it all away, of throwing it into the lap of a stranger, something so profane that he could hardly connect the two ideas together. His mind rejected the unnatural conjunction. Isabel's mind accepted it with ease. Mr. Brocken's mind rejected even the possibility of such an act: to give away all one's money was unheard-of — and why was it unheard-of? Because it didn't happen. Isabel blandly replied that it was going to. More irrationally still, she appeared to have no fears for the future: and when Simon enquired how she proposed to live without money, immediately retorted with Dora Tremayne.

"Of course I shall manage," said Isabel placidly. "How did Dora manage, when she lost all *her* money?"

"In the first place, she took a post as schoolmistress," said Simon. "And as I remember, she didn't keep it long."

"The girls had such squeaky voices, dear. And when the Merchant of Venice came up for the third time, and Shylock squeaked worse than ever—What I mean is, Dora left of her own accord."

"Bah!" said Mr. Brocken loudly. "And where is she now? Behind a counter in one shop, living in three rooms over another."

Isabel's face brightened.

"Perhaps I could live there too," she suggested hopefully. "I shouldn't at all mind living with Dora, she's so cheerful. If I kept just a hundred a year, and two can live as cheaply as one—or is that a horse and a sparrow? Dora *is* rather horselike—we might do very well. I've finished my life," said Isabel earnestly. "What becomes of *me* doesn't matter!"

"It does to me," said Simon bleakly. "I could hardly see you, for example, in the workhouse."

Isabel looked at him. For once her glance was both shrewd and sad.

"I know what you mean, my dear; because my name is the same as your own. I've always known, really, that was why you felt you had to look after me. I'm your brother's widow. Mark—" her voice shook—"Mark would have looked after me, I mean if I hadn't been married to him, just because we were all young together. You're very different, Simon: I don't believe you've ever cared for any one, except Mark, in all your life."

"And why should I?" returned Mr. Brocken. "Who cares for me? You behave as though you do, but I can't for the life of me see why."

"Why?" cried Isabel, suddenly amused again. "Of course I care for you! If I didn't, who would?"

No one else attempted to argue with Isabel. Completely recovered from what now turned out to have been simply a bad conscience — as disastrous to her, and for the same reason, as measles to a South Sea Islander — Isabel went about innocently happy, absolved and gay, full of hopeful and idiotic plans. Should she live with Dora Tremayne, should she take guests at the Lodge, should she start a tea shop — she made excellent cream-buns, only now there was no cream — should she undertake the care of very young children? In every newspaper Isabel opened women were exhorted to work; if women had been invited into coal mines, down a coal mine Isabel was ready to trot.

"My gum, she's never worked in her life!" Humphrey once exclaimed.

"She was a V.A.D.," said Jacqueline. "She told me. *That* was work."

"But with a glamour to it. All for the sake of our brave boys."

"V.A.D.'s didn't get near the brave boys. They ran about for the nurses.

Jacqueline was Mrs. Brocken's ally. She alone — and it was her word — saw the older woman as heroic. She alone saw tragedy — a woman's tragedy — in the fate of Tilly

Cuff. For Jacqueline wished to marry herself, and deep in her heart, despite all she said about muffs, believed that a woman had better take her chance with a husband, than cherish her independence alone.

On one single point Mr. Brocken determined to make a stand, and succeeded. He persuaded Isabel to make no confession to Miss Cuff, and to say nothing of the golden shower that awaited her, until Tilly had been some little time at the Lodge.

"But why, Simon?" asked Isabel, in evident disappointment.

Simon's true object was simply to postpone an evil hour; perhaps he also remembered that spoken words are our masters. However, what he told Isabel was that Tilly Cuff would hardly be flattered to find her invitation merely a new way to pay old debts.

"I see what you mean," said Isabel doubtfully. "But I *shouldn't* have asked her, you know, if she hadn't been on my conscience."

"Are you sure?" asked Simon. "If you had thought of her, and guessed she needed a holiday?"

"Well, I might have, dear. I hope I should." Isabel looked rueful. "I remember how good Mamma was about our governesses: she sent one of them for two weeks to Llandudno. I'm sure *she*'d have thought of Tilly Cuff. . . ."

"Then let Tilly Cuff come here, as she would have done in your mother's day, for a pleasant vacation. My dear Isabel, when you tell Miss Cuff, as I know you are determined to do, of your really very reprehensible act, let there be a friendly atmosphere to soften the blow. I'm not thinking so much of yourself," said Simon shrewdly, "as of Tilly. Let her feel, first, that we are all friendly to her."

So Isabel agreed; and what Simon hoped to gain by this was, as has been said, merely time. He hoped that Tilly Cuff might have turned into a reasonable woman. He hoped, not to threaten her, but to establish himself in her eyes as guardian of the Brocken money before she saw it easy to gather as blackberries. He saw, as always, only his own point of view.

The interval of waiting was shorter than had been expected: a telegram from Tilly Cuff announced that she would arrive on the following Saturday. Both Isabel and Simon read between the lines, but with this difference: where Simon saw an unusual readiness, on the part of Tilly's employers, to lose her services, Isabel saw only an affectionate alacrity on the part of Tilly. Her spirits rose: she meant to love Tilly, as well as do her duty by her, and looked forward to being loved by Tilly in return.

Simon moved his belongings into the sewing-room. In his old apartment pictures appeared on the walls—a flower-piece of Isabel's, a landscape from the dining-room, an engraving after Watts from the upper staircase. China adorned the mantelshelf, knick-knacks the bureau. A nightdress case in the form of a crinolined doll, purchased by Isabel at a pre-war bazaar, completed (to Simon's eye) the travesty. The days, the peaceful days, passed all too swiftly: it was Saturday morning.

Chapter 11

Isabel hired a car and went to the station alone: they were all agreed that the first meeting would be easier, for both women, without spectators. The others, including Mr. Brocken, who had been persuaded to take the morning off, promised to be waiting, in attitudes of welcome, upon the terrace. The train was due at eleven-twenty: they would all have a glass of sherry, and then lunch at one, to allow Miss Cuff time to refresh, if necessary, her costume.

There was a military precision about the scheme which aroused, said Humphrey, unpleasant memories.

Isabel set off at eleven. The trip to the station took about five minutes, but she wished to be in good time; moreover, whatever lip service she paid to reason, her view of trains remained secretly anthropomorphic; she felt that Tilly's train might get in early out of wilfulness, so to speak, and it was a risk she dared not run.

At eleven-fifteen Jacqueline carried out the tray of sherry and set it on the iron table. Mr. Brocken and Humphrey were removing the cover from the seat. The weather was warm but overcast, and Simon, who by this time hated the cover bitterly, observed that he couldn't for the life of him understand why they weren't to wait comfortably indoors.

"It's the *alfresco* touch," explained Humphrey. "Open air notoriously promotes gaiety. Why do people give garden-parties?"

"To save the mess indoors," said Mr. Brocken. "Where did that sherry come from?"

"South Africa, sir. A Commonwealth wine. I did suggest cocktails, but Jacky thought sherry more appropriate."

Jacqueline smiled, but said nothing. She was more than usually silent, she was grave. Alone of the three she was altogether on Mrs. Brocken's side; she was a great upholder of feminine solidarity.

Mr. Brocken glanced at his watch. Humphrey glanced at his.

"Zero hour," said Humphrey, "approaches. Where are the movie-men?"

They did indeed look and feel rather as though they were about to have their photographs taken. Mr. Brocken in particular, drifting uneasily past one of the stucco goddesses, offered a fine satiric subject. Jacqueline sat down composedly on an iron chair, Humphrey leant against the terrace wall. A moment later footsteps sounded in the drawing-room; Mrs. Brocken emerged, followed by Tilly Cuff.

2

It is by no means uncommon for elderly women to wear old-fashioned clothes: often such garments suit them; give character, and dignity; proclaim a becoming indifference to millinery opinion. As a rule the chosen style is that of the wearer's prime; women go on dressing as they dressed when they liked their clothes. The unfortunate thing about Tilly Cuff was that this sartorial turning-point, or rather sticking-point, marked a period not of complacency but of fear. In 1928 Tilly Cuff was forty; it was the period of all others when a youthful appearance was most prized, when all women tried to look like little girls if they could not look like little boys; for six months Tilly was out of employment. She knew then that if she was to survive she must stay young. All advertisements demanded young, bright companions. Young and bright therefore she became; she had been young and bright ever since; and she still clung to the fashions that had helped her to seem so.

Her dress, of boldly patterned silk, round-necked and short-sleeved, came about an inch below her knees. Her jet-black hair was shingled, brushed straight back save for a half-moon curl in front of either ear. She wore long jade earrings, a necklace to match, and several large green bangles. Her shoes had extremely high heels. If one glanced quickly a little to one side of her (as one glances at a distant clock, the better to tell the time) one received the impression of a fashion-plate of the 'twenties.

"Here's Tilly," said Isabel, rather breathlessly. "Here's Miss Cuff. This is my nephew Humphrey, Ruth's boy, and Miss Brown, who—who helps us all, and Simon, whom of course you know."

There was a moment's pause; then Miss Cuff pounced. She pounced upon Mr. Brocken.

"Simon!" she cried. "After all these years! How perfectly ripping to see you!"

She grasped his hand with such vivacity that for a moment Mr. Brocken feared she was going to kiss him as well. And indeed Tilly wanted only the slightest encouragement to do so. She was used to making such entrances. She was used to being the perpetual newcomer; and experience had taught her the importance of getting off on the right foot. (*Never carry your bag up yourself, if there is a servant to do it for you: begin as you mean to go on.*) Now she was instinctively establishing herself as an old friend. Since Mr. Brocken's expression, though perfectly courteous, put kissing out of the question, she merely retained his hand.

"It's a great pleasure," said Simon politely, "after, as you say, a long time."

"Let me give you a sherry," said Humphrey.

Miss Cuff replied that she would adore one. Her shrewd black glance flickered from him to Jacqueline; in two seconds she had formed a first rough-and-ready appraisal of their position, including importance and/or security of tenure, in the household. This also was instinctive; she was always alert for the presence of hangers-on, possible rivals to herself. (*Men always more dangerous than women.*) Humphrey at least she put down as being almost impregnably entrenched. She smiled at him engagingly, and released Mr. Brocken's hand to take the glass.

"Ruth's boy!" she exclaimed wonderingly. "It doesn't seem possible!—and yet I believe I should have known you. How good-looking she was!"

"And still is," murmured Humphrey.

"And she lives in New Zealand! Issy has been giving me all the news, for I'm so dreadfully bad at writing letters, that no one *ever* writes to me."

"I know I wrote to you about Ruth's wedding," said Mrs. Brocken.

Tilly laughed. She had a curious laugh, high-pitched and very abrupt, like the barking of a Pomeranian.

"You mean you sent me a piece of cake, dear. It followed me half round Europe, and when it arrived I thought it was insect-powder."

Mr. Brocken, helping himself to a large sherry, enquired whether she had travelled a great deal. With another laugh Tilly replied, indeed she had, she was a walking Baedeker; and seating herself on the swing at once began to entertain them with reminiscences of travel. She had no need to do this, since she was not being paid, but again habit was strong. Amusing conversation was part of her working equipment, and a knowledgeable auditor would have been interested by the polish of her technique. Her most vivacious anecdotes were disciplined by two rules: never mention an hotel that was not first-class (*in case it gave wrong ideas about you*) and never be malicious about any one still alive (*in case it got round to them*). None of her present hearers, however, noticed this; Miss Cuff's appearance was so much more compelling than her words.

It was when she was still, when she ceased to patter on her high heels and sat, as now, relatively quiescent, that the contrast between her clothes and the creature inside them became most grotesque. For the thin sallow girl of Mr. Brocken's recollection had aged into a woman all skin and bone, and yellow as a plucked chicken. The green bangles slid up and down on arms like drumsticks, blotched from prominent wrist to pointed elbow with large brownish patches: the green beads emphasized rather than hid the salt-cellars at her throat and the tendons that jerked above: as for the face between the dangling earrings, it was so curiously made-up as to appear almost lipless. (*Rouge, but not lipstick.*) In shape it narrowed sharply to the chin, nose and mouth being extremely prominent, as though drawn forward from the rest of the skull, but colourless, or the colour of very old ivory, fleshless bone under tight-drawn skin, between brilliantly pink cheeks.

Through the independent minds of Mr. Brocken, young Humphrey, and Jacqueline Brown passed the same thought: how is it possible that any one, so recently as a month ago, has willingly taken her into their home?

They did Tilly Cuff an injustice. She was still extremely active. She could still perform the operative functions, make herself the arms and legs and mouthpiece, of an invalid. She could talk, to those who feared silence because death is silent. She had always earned her bread, and could do so still. But Humphrey and Miss Brown were too young to comprehend this, and Mr. Brocken too unimaginative: how, they all wondered, could anyone employ Tilly Cuff?

To which Simon added the grim rider: no one will ever employ her again.

He looked across at his sister-in-law. Isabel sat plump and innocent beside Miss Cuff like a pigeon by a battered macaw; her simple face wore an expression of bewilderment. For once Mr. Brocken sympathized with her. In the old days Tilly's chief characteristics had all been negative: she was unassuming, undemonstrative, unobtrusive; now it was as though she had turned herself inside out. The emotions of Jacqueline and Humphrey were naturally less complex. They were simply shocked, as youth is always shocked by any indiscretion in the old, and this had the effect of making them peculiarly formal in their manners: they sat up straight, sipped their sherry discreetly, as though to supply a missing quantum of decorum.

Miss Cuff's chatter ceased. It ceased upon a query. All realized this from the way her voice lifted, from her sparkling, inviting glance. The appalling thing was that no one knew what the question was. They had all been too much preoccupied to listen.

"Come on, chaps!" cried Miss Cuff. "What would *you* have done?"

Isabel opened her mouth and closed it again. Humphrey, Jacqueline and Mr. Brocken each gave the impression of waiting for the others to speak first. But no one spoke.

The situation was saved by Bogey. Limping out of the house — it was a day for two sticks, not one — suddenly he perceived the stranger. At once — oh, transport, oh delight! — his sticks were flung aside, forward he bounded, rending the air with acclamation. He hurled himself unerringly into Miss Cuff's lap, strove to lick her cheek: she clasped him to her bosom. For the first time the resolute brightness of that face cracked; frankly old, at last human, she turned to Mrs. Brocken and cried,

"Oh, Issy, Issy! Do you remember Puck?"

3

Half an hour later Isabel and Tilly were upstairs, and Jacqueline, Humphrey and Mr. Brocken in the stables.

Jacqueline had gone there first, to fetch in some washing; Humphrey followed; Mr. Brocken, hearing their voices from his new bedroom, went down to join them. This unusual act occasioned no surprise; they looked as though they had expected him.

"Well?" said Simon, fixing Humphrey with a gloomy eye. "Here's the result of your aunt's heroism and integrity and saintliness and all the rest of it. I hope you're pleased."

Neither Humphrey nor Jacqueline found any answer. Mr. Brocken noted their discomfiture with satisfaction, and stumped back upstairs.

4

Three hours later Isabel and Tilly had gone for a little walk, and Humphrey and Mr. Brocken were in the hall contemplating Tilly's luggage, which had arrived during her absence by van.

Its bulk was imposing: for the day and age she had a really enormous wardrobe. Numerous employers had made her presents of cast-off clothing. (Where there is a lady's maid, of course, pickings are almost nil, but of late the incomes of Tilly's employers had declined, and one rival was thus removed.) The material of these garments was usually excellent; snipped and sewn to her personal style, they lasted for years. She had twenty pairs of shoes, not all her size, but mostly wearable, and no less than fifteen bridge jackets. She had ten evening gowns, in every shade of purple, and six coats-and-skirts. She had four fur neck-pieces, and two muffs. She never sold anything, and never gave anything away. When entering on a new post she took with her only a suitcase, leaving the rest at a depository, and thus no employer hesitated to add to her store. She brought to Chipping Lodge, however, a full complement of three trunks, four hat-boxes, and one gunny sack (for the shoes).

They filled the hall. Mr. Brocken and Humphrey contemplated them resentfully.

"We had better," said Mr. Brocken at last, "start with the trunks."

Humphrey stooped. Upon a faded pictorial label — blue

sky and slanting tower—the words "Hotel Alix, Pisa" were faintly legible.

"It still leans," he said, taking a grip on the handle.

Mr. Brocken stooped to the other end; between them they humped the trunk upstairs and deposited it in Ruth's room. They then returned for the others. On their second downward journey they met Jacqueline coming up with two hat-boxes. She brought up the whole four, and Humphrey wrestled with the gunny sack alone.

"Well?" asked Mr. Brocken—this time with deceptive mildness. "How do you young people feel now?"

"Like hell," said Humphrey.

He said it rather loudly. There was a clatter of heels on the staircase, a patter of feet in the corridor, up ran Tilly Cuff, bracelets a-jingle as she clasped her hands in coquettish horror.

"Oh, naughty, *naughty!*" cried Miss Cuff. "Who's been swearing in *my* room?"

"I have," said Humphrey gloomily. "You'll find I swear a good deal."

Miss Cuff flashed him a roguish glance.

"I sometimes—tell it not in Gath—I *sometimes* use a little 'damn' myself. But we mustn't shock our elders—must we?"

The roguish glance—how well they were to know its mosquito-like flight!—flicked on, lit upon Simon, so that he shouldn't feel left out, so that he should know she was only joking. Jacqueline she ignored.

"I expect you'll want to unpack," said Jacqueline politely. "We'll leave you in peace."

PART TWO

Chapter 12

"We'll leave you in peace," said Jacqueline.

Can the trout leave in peace a pike thrown into a trout stream?—pigeons leave in peace a hawk loosed on their loft, or sheep a terrier unleashed in their pasture? Within the space of a week every one at Chipping Lodge, except Miss Cuff herself, had begun to look slightly hunted.

She had not, and this was the root of the trouble, enough to do.

She had not anything to do, for Isabel, resolutely upholding Tilly's status as honoured guest, refused to allow her any part in the housework. There was no one who needed nursing, except Bogey, whom she exercised so constantly that he developed blisters on all four paws. Tilly bathed them night and morning (Bogey shouting the house down) but even this double operation occupied no more than half an hour. The rest of her time was free. Free, but not idle; one of Tilly's strongest points being her ability to interest herself in other people's affairs. "Dull?" Tilly often exclaimed, at an interview, when a prospective employer began (as they often did) to lay unusual stress on a post's disadvantages—"But *I'm* never dull! So long as there's the *least* human interest, just one human being who needs my little mite of friendship and sympathy, I'm perfectly content. I take such an interest in people!" She did so at Chipping Lodge.

It was inevitable, to begin with, that her curiosity should be aroused by the Pooles. Their complete independence was a challenge, and in some obscure way an affront to her; she thought it very odd (and said so) that Isabel took no interest in them at all—especially when one remembered Mrs. Massey, so thoroughly conscientious about servants. "But I don't think the Pooles want to be taken an interest in," Isabel defended herself. "And they aren't exactly servants, they're caretakers; Simon engaged them, while I was away." "Mrs. Poole should at least wait at table," said Tilly angrily. "But she doesn't *want* to, dear," explained Isabel, "and Jacky doesn't mind a bit. Do you, Jacky?"

"Of course not," said Jacqueline; and added, a little dogmatically, "We're really very well organized, and the Pooles do all that can be expected of them; I am sure Miss Cuff knows how hard it is to get any help at all."

Miss Cuff's eye was unfriendly. "Do you imagine," it asked, "that *I* have waited at table?" But she did not pursue the subject. Pointedly addressing herself to Isabel, she observed that to get help was one thing, to keep it another, and in her experience quite impossible without just a touch of human kindness.

She could not leave the Pooles alone. Isabel and Simon, Humphrey and even Jacqueline, were far more prominent members of the household; but some instinct led Tilly, from the very beginning, to concentrate on the invisible couple in the kitchen. The Pooles were very difficult to get hold of, they had an extraordinary knack of self-effacement, which Jacqueline's masterly plan of operations greatly promoted: Mr. Brocken's embassy to the kitchen had been an occasion of note, and Mr. Brocken was an admittedly privileged person. Tilly had been specially asked by Isabel not to go into the kitchen unnecessarily. ("Because I could hardly say 'Not at all,' " explained Isabel to Jacqueline, "and there won't *be* any necessity, so it comes to the same thing . . .") But what is necessity? When Tilly unpacked her trunks she found an old pin-cushion, red velvet stuffed between two shells, so obvious a gift for a child that she felt an absolute necessity to bestow it upon Greta Poole.

"Here's a pretty thing!" cried Miss Cuff, popping her head round the kitchen door. "May I come in, Mrs. Poole? I've a pretty thing here for Greta!"

She intruded on a scene of great peace. For once the Pooles were giving their football coupons a rest, they were having a good read instead. Greta had a *Film Pictorial,* and her mother a *Film Favourites.* There was a bag of toffee on the table between them. They were having a lovely time.

"That's very kind, I'm sure," said Mrs. Poole.

The Pooles had excellent manners. Some one offered you a present; whether you wanted it or not, even before you had seen it, you said they were very kind. (Or some one saved your life in a blitz; the same phrase served.) But one wasn't over-enthusiastic, in either case; all codes of manners having their convention.

"Don't you want to know what it is?" cried Tilly, addressing herself to Greta. "Don't tell me you're *shy*—a big girl like you?"

Greta was in fact less shy than wary. But she smiled politely.

"It's—this!" exclaimed Tilly, producing the pincushion from behind her back.

The Pooles eyed it.

"There, now," said Mrs. Poole.

"What is it?" asked Greta.

"Why, it's a *pincushion*. See, it's made out of two shells!"

"Did you ever," observed Mrs. Poole courteously. "Greta, what do you say?"

"Thanks a million," said Greta.

Obedient to her mother's eye, she slipped from her seat, accepted the object from Miss Cuff's hand, and placed it on the dresser. Then she returned and sat down again, opposite *Film Pictorial*.

"All little girls like pincushions," pursued Miss Cuff. "When I was little, I had quite a collection of them." She paused; she was getting very slight encouragement. Greta, who had just discarded a collection of bomb fragments (some with dates on them), was perhaps to be pardoned for a lack of ebullience. But a child's values are arbitrary: the chestnut or conker is once more prized above shrapnel: some little girls no doubt like pincushions, and the special form of Miss Cuff's has frequently been admired by youth. The fact was that Greta did not like Miss Cuff. Yet the gift served its object, for at least Tilly was there in the kitchen, she could look about, see what the Pooles were up to. They were apparently up to nothing. Their surroundings were clean, tidy and unremarkable. The wireless was turned on, but so low that Olde Tyme Dance Music merely whispered over the air.

"Won't Mrs. Brocken let you have the wireless louder than that?" asked Tilly compassionately.

There was a short pause; the sort of pause that follows an innocent gaffe at a dinner table, a foolish remark made by some one who ought to know better, and who is at once presumed (out of politeness) to have seen their mistake.

"We don't ask," said Mrs. Poole.

It was a reply so full of dignity, such a complete declaration of independence condensed into three words, that for a moment Tilly was at a loss. Then she shrugged her shoulders, with a gay laugh.

"Dear me!" she cried. "There's no accounting for tastes, is there? But if *I* have the wireless on, I like to hear it without straining my ears."

"What *we* like," said Mrs. Poole patiently, "is peace and quiet. Thanks ever so for the pincushion."

The hint was unmistakable, and Tilly Cuff forced to

accept it. She withdrew with many gay good-nights, and a warning to Greta not to lose her beauty-sleep; but she withdrew.

2

Her friendship with Jacqueline Brown, as became a deeper, truer relationship, was founded not on material gifts (though she did once offer Jacky a pair of old kid gloves) but on advice.

This was a development as unexpected as unwelcome. Jacky, continuing to wait at table, had been fully prepared to do so under a fire of bright and humorous comment: she wasn't afraid of Miss Cuff's tongue, any more than she was afraid of a gnat bite, which is irritating rather than dangerous, and anticipated merely an exercise in self-control. But not a bit of it. The enmity she had surprised in Tilly's eye was simply a natural reaction, and no indication of what was to be the latter's considered course. When the time came Miss Cuff not only refrained from comment, but actually jumped up herself and pattered out to the kitchen on Jacqueline's heels — "I'll take the veg, dear; you take the meat" — and pattered back with the dishes, and out again with a forgotten soup cup. "Do sit down, Tilly," begged Isabel. "Tilly, I'm sure there's no *need* . . ." Tilly cast her a reproachful look, and said poor Jacky was on her feet all day.

How much worse was this than the pin-prick of a bad joke! Yet no one could tell — and least of all Jacqueline —

what was Tilly's motive. Perhaps it was genuine sympathy; perhaps a most brilliant stroke of malice; perhaps Tilly did not know herself. In any case, she took a particular interest in Miss Brown because they were both, as Tilly pointed out, in the same boat; and as the older hand she could give many useful hints.

"Is this your first post, dear?" asked Tilly. "I *thought* so; I thought so, from the way you let yourself be put upon. You should insist on at least one free period every day."

"But I'm not used to free periods," said Jacqueline lightly. "I've just come out of the ATS."

Tilly laughed incredulously.

"Running about in uniform, eh?"

"We wore uniform," agreed Jacqueline, "and sometimes we certainly had to run."

"If you ask me, you had a fine time," said Miss Cuff enviously. "There were ATS near my last place: they spent all their time looking in shop-windows."

"I suppose we did give that impression," said Jacqueline slowly. "People didn't see us, as a rule, except when we were off duty; and often we had nothing much to do, and didn't know any one, so we looked in the shops."

This was not a very promising start, but Miss Cuff persisted. Jacqueline found her peculiarly difficult to rebuff: her manner implied an alliance between them, even a secret understanding; for she talked very differently to Jacqueline according to whether Isabel (Jacqueline's employer) was or was not present. Before Isabel, Tilly exclaimed at Miss Brown's good fortune in finding so desirable a post; in private made it plain that her sympathies lay really with poor Jacky. Nothing could have been more disagreeable; by the mere fact of listening Jacqueline felt herself drawn into deceit, and yet could not avoid it. Evil communications corrupt not only good manners, but also good humour.

"I liked this place too," said Tilly once, "when I first came here. My word, I thought I'd fallen on my feet! But it's wonderful how people change, once they've got used to you."

Jacqueline said nothing. She was shelling peas, in the pantry; Tilly had come to keep her company. There was still half a basket to finish, but though Jacky shelled as fast as she could, haste made her clumsy; she had to run her thumb down the pods twice to be sure of emptying them, and now and then spilt a pea over the edge of the bowl. Miss Cuff watched intently.

"*I* used to do that too," she said abruptly. "I wasn't supposed to; I wasn't *supposed* to help in the kitchen; but it was wonderful what little jobs came my way."

"I rather like shelling peas," said Jacqueline.

"That's what *they* used to say—such a *nice* little job, let's all do it together!—and then we'd just get started when some one would come for Miss Ruth, and Miss Isabel was wanted to go calling, and I'd be left to finish alone . . ."

With her eyes on her hands, Jacqueline said softly,

"And you used to wash the dog."

"Yes, I did. How do you know that?"

"Mrs. Brocken remembered it. You used to wash Puck."

"And a messy business it was," said Miss Cuff. "Never any 'Oh-let's-all-do-it' about *that!* I'm very fond of dogs, I quite love Bogey, and I didn't dislike Puck; but he wasn't *my* dog, he was Issy's. I used to get soaked. But there you are: I dare say *you* wash Bogey, just as you shell peas, and I dare say you don't mind; all right, it's what you're paid for. But don't ever imagine you're thought good-natured for doing it. You're paid. And when Issy gets tired of you, or when she notices her nephew paying too much attention to you, out you'll go. Young men like to amuse themselves, and they may: but a companion mayn't. I'm just warning you, dear, because you and I are very much in the same boat; and so naturally I take an interest in you."

Jacqueline tipped a handful of empty shells over the full pods that remained and lifted the bowl from her knees.

"Thank you very much," she said politely.

"I haven't offended you, dear?"

"Not in the least. I'm sure you mean to be kind."

"Mind you — " Tilly laid her dry, bony hand on Jacqueline's arm — "if you *can* pull it off, I'd say take the risk. Has he — has he ever asked you to kiss him?"

Jacqueline shook her head, set the peas down on a shelf, and fled.

3

Humphrey Garrett, the confident young male, took the initiative.

"Miss Cuff," said Humphrey, "I wonder if you'd mind my telling you something?"

Miss Cuff opened her eyes in simulated alarm.

"My dear boy, how ominous that sounds! Have I trodden on your toes?"

"Not at all," said Humphrey. "It's just this: I don't reckon Aunt Isabel likes to be called Issy."

"But she was *always* called Issy, my dear! It's what every one called her!"

"I still don't reckon she likes it," said Humphrey.

Miss Cuff darted him a suspicious look.

"Has she been complaining?"

"No; of course not. The thing's simply obvious."

"Then it's obvious nonsense," retorted Miss Cuff huffily.

She ceased, nevertheless, from that moment, to use the disliked name. She called Isabel "Isabel," pointedly, accenting each syllable, with a bridling glance at Humphrey, if Humphrey was present. This lasted for some days; then with a sudden change of tactics she sought him out to confess that it *had* been naughty of her, she *had* done it to tease, but never, never, with the least intention of really hurting dear Isabel's feelings.

"She wasn't touchy as a girl," added Tilly, with a sigh. "I do hope she didn't consider it *presumption.*"

Humphrey muttered something about beer, and excused himself.

4

Upon Simon Miss Cuff exercised, or attempted to exercise, the spell of old, shared memories. When Simon did the *Times* crossword after dinner, on the terrace or in a corner of the drawing-room, Tilly came and sat beside him, ready to catch his eye.

"It's *your* being here," she told him, "that makes this house *really* like home to me. How well I remember you and Mark!"

"Do you?" muttered Mr. Brocken.

"You were here so often, you see. Always in and out. I used to admire you so much!"

"Did you?" said Mr. Brocken.

"Especially Mark," pursued Tilly, with an arch glance. "He was so dashing and handsome . . . I can see him now, in his white flannels, simply *dominating* the tennis-court. And I remember him when he'd beaten you, putting his arm round your shoulders — "

Mr. Brocken's pencil jabbed down a random string of letters. He said shortly,

"My sister-in-law is fond of piquet. Do you play it?"

"Of course." Tilly smiled ruefully. "I play *all* the two-handed card games. And of course I'll play whenever Isabel likes. Just as Mark used to play with her . . . Poor Isabel, how she must miss him!"

"Naturally," said Mr. Brocken.

"But not more than you do. I think," said Tilly earnestly, "there must be something very wonderful about deep, true, masculine affection; something no woman can ever really share. *I* saw it, between you and Mark, when perhaps nobody else did, because I was such a lonely little thing myself. Old Sobersides, Mark used to call you; and often he'd laugh at you; but always with so much affection — "

Mr. Brocken excused himself. He had had a long day, he said; would abandon the crossword and go to bed. Like Humphrey, like Jacqueline, he excused himself.

Luckily, however, there was one member of the household whose enthusiasm for Tilly's company greatly mitigated, and to a certain extent concealed, her unpopularity. The dog Bogey was her friend. He was more than her friend, he was her fan. Whenever they met, after the briefest separation, he put on a full-scale demonstration of delight; though he snapped at her once or twice (when she anointed his paws) it was without conviction. Miss Cuff addressed him in baby-talk, calling him her dear doggie, her nice pupsy, her old Bogey-wogey. He lay always at her feet, if not in her lap; and though this, since he was often muddy, was no loss to any one, his preference hurt Isabel's feelings. She tried to woo back his affection with scraps of corned beef. The faithless creature wolfed them down, and at once returned to Miss Cuff.

He even did what Miss Cuff told him. When she ordered him to go and sit by his real mistress, Bogey went, and sat at Isabel's feet, with an air of boredom and long-suffering. Tilly several times observed how wonderful it was that dogs always knew who truly loved them, for themselves, as personalities, not merely as pets. Tilly said she had always taken a great interest in dogs.

5

She had nothing to do. She was used to occupation, to a constant round of small duties, often disagreeable, but at least necessary. It had been necessary, in Birmingham, for instance, to wash and dress a semi-paralyzed old lady, and spoon food into her mouth; and necessary to go and change the library books, and then read from them after lunch; and then listen with patience to some long rambling tale of long-ago childhood; and at last to brush and braid a wisp of white hair for the night. By the faithful performance of such duties Tilly Cuff thoroughly earned her salary. Being valuable, and knowing it, she felt less need to push her claims to consideration. But at Chipping Lodge Tilly had nothing to do at all, except talk. She talked incessantly — to Isabel doing the rooms, to Jacqueline preparing vegetables, to Humphrey working in the garden; and the curious thing was that each of them had the impression that they had each been talked to continuously all day. Mr. Brocken had much the best of it, being absent at least eight hours; but as soon as he returned Tilly settled on him like a starving mosquito, leaving upon Simon the impression that she talked to no one else.

Even better than these tête-à-têtes, however, Tilly liked to join the conversation of others. At mid-morning, when Jacqueline carried out Humphrey a glass of beer, Miss Cuff was there too. In the afternoons, if they lay sun-bathing in the dell, Miss Cuff sat on its rim and chatted to them. Isabel could not consult Jacky about a meal without Tilly appearing round the doorway. She could scent a private conversation as a cat scents fish.

The motive for this behaviour was threefold. In the first place, as has been said, she had nothing to do; in the second she enjoyed exercising what was an undeniable gift; and in the third, she wished to be sure they were not plotting against her.

She had been plotted against, poor woman, so often. Ladies' maids always resented her; old servants were jealous. Relations were the worst, for it was a relation, in many cases, who had engaged and could dismiss her; the other relations criticized. It sometimes seemed to Tilly that no sooner was she settled in a new household than cousins, nieces, sisters-in-law arrived in swarms, with the sole object of casting doubt on the original relation's choice. What, asked Tilly bitterly, did they fear? That she would set her cap at some eligible male? Even in youth her charms were scarcely dangerous. That the old lady (all Tilly's charges were old, often senile) would leave her her money? In the course of thirty years she had received exactly three legacies, amounting in all to a hundred and fifty pounds and a seed-pearl brooch. The truth was that the relations never quite liked her. However anxious to be rid of burdensome duties—however ferociously weary of Great-aunt A.'s company—they nevertheless had consciences. They felt they might find Great-aunt someone nicer. They engaged Miss Cuff, but continued to look about.

Thus Tilly's path had lain through a sort of domestic mine-field. She had needed to tread warily, her detectors always working. Any conversation in which she did not take part was a potential danger. Did she ever listen at doors? She sometimes passed a door behind which something was being said.

Distressing as it is to relate, this unpleasant conduct was perfectly justified. Within a week of her arrival at Chipping Lodge, she was being plotted against again. Mr. Brocken, Jacqueline, young Humphrey, were all united in their desire to be rid of her.

Chapter 13

If Aunt Isabel is going to pay her off," stated Humphrey baldly, "the sooner she does it the better, because the woman, and I employ the term merely to spare Jacky embarrassment, is getting on all our nerves."

They were gathered in the bathroom, one of the few places Miss Cuff did not enter without warning. Mr. Brocken, washing his hands, had been joined by Humphrey, and Jacqueline came in to fill a water-can.

"There is such a thing," said Simon, "as jumping out of the frying-pan into the fire. I am just as eager as yourselves to be rid of Miss Cuff's company; but the idea of 'paying her off' is extremely repugnant. I should greatly prefer some other solution."

"Aunt Isabel," said Humphrey, after a moment's silence, "has a great respect for your judgment. After all, you're her brother-in-law. . . ."

"And you're her nephew, and she has a great affection for you," retorted Mr. Brocken. "So what?"

The colloquialism surprised even himself; but he was very much disturbed. Jacqueline (perhaps emboldened by the knowledge that she had no standing whatever) said frankly,

"*I* think Mrs. Brocken would be glad if you bullied her a little. Her generation doesn't mind being bullied by its menfolk. Can't you say that Miss Cuff arouses — arouses saddening memories, and that she must choose between you?"

"She arouses no memories whatever," objected Mr. Brocken. "She simply annoys me beyond endurance."

"Can't you say," suggested Humphrey, "that you once cherished a secret passion for her, and now the disillusion is too painful?"

"No, I could not," snapped Mr. Brocken. "What you both of you overlook — which, I must confess, surprises me, considering your recent attitudes — is that we have to deal not merely with a temporary nuisance, but with your aunt's whole future. You say 'pay the woman off' — as though it were a question of a mere fifty or a hundred pounds. Your aunt's idea of restitution is to make over her entire capital. Is she to be allowed to beggar herself for the sake of a peculiarly offensive incubus? I have done what I can: I have persuaded her temporarily to withhold from Miss Cuff the obligation behind this visit. All I can now hope is that a fuller knowledge of Miss Cuff's character will convince my sister-in-law that magnanimity is out of place."

"Do you mean Mrs. Brocken will get to hate her?" asked Jacqueline plainly.

It was what Simon did mean, though he hesitated to

put it into words: even he was still a little abashed before the embarrassing purity of Isabel's motives. But he hoped. Isabel as much as any of them had been shocked by Tilly's new personality: had actually confided (a week having passed) that she couldn't, really couldn't quite yet, make the confession she had planned. She would have to get to know Tilly first, all over again. "Because she's changed, hasn't she, Simon?" asked Isabel nervously. "I know she'll be angry with me, I expected it, and it's part of my punishment; but she's so different from the Tilly I remember, it would be like telling a stranger. . . ."

"I mean that my sister-in-law has agreed with me," said Mr. Brocken, "that until we know more of Miss Cuff's plans, until we know what sort of life would be most agreeable to her, nothing should be said of the future. The prospect of sudden wealth," said Simon sententiously, "often brings great distress of mind."

So the plot came to nothing. They could only, all of them, wait. Were they waiting to see hatred spring like an evil weed in Isabel's heart? Jacqueline at least hoped not. She hoped, though with an optimism that she recognized as faint, that in the gentle atmosphere of Chipping Lodge Tilly Cuff herself might become gentled, civilized from the barbarism of her servitude, a recipient worthy in magnanimity of so magnanimous a deed of restitution.

2

For the moment at least Isabel was in no danger. She could not love Tilly Cuff. She had meant to, she tried to, but somehow she couldn't. Indeed, it was a matter of grave self-reproach, and the most serious self-examination, that as the days passed, instead of loving Tilly more and more, she actually liked her less and less.

In some cases, however, neither love nor liking is more serviceable than pity. Alone at Chipping Lodge Isabel related Tilly's every word and deed, and even her appearance, to the circumstances of Tilly's past life; and as these gradually emerged — as Tilly, gaining confidence, grew less concerned to throw a rosy light over her career — Isabel was filled with pity.

"Mrs. Harrison?" said Tilly once, referring to her first employer. "She went to Switzerland to die, you know. Or didn't you know? I dare say not; I was rather young for the responsibility. But she died of T.B.; and that was in 1915; but fortunately I got a post as governess in Berne. They were short of English governesses just then."

"And — and what did you do next?" asked Isabel.

"I went to Paris. When the war was over, I went to Paris. *La ville lumière,*" said Tilly, with a peculiar bitterness. "I taught English, music and elocution to the three daughters of a professor of geology. We lived in the rue Vaugirard. Your mother would have been quite pleased, Isabel: we were *so* respectable. When the last of them married, I came home. . . ."

"I should have thought," observed Simon, "that an Englishwoman, with your qualifications, would have found more scope abroad."

Tilly looked at him sardonically.

"Odd as it may seem, I wanted to come home. I had been abroad nearly fifteen years. The best of my qualifications were French and German. So I came home — to find governesses were quite gone out. The families who could have afforded them sent their daughters to boarding-school instead. I suppose it made for quiet in the house. But there were always the sick and the elderly, and the people their families didn't want; so I made quite a niche for myself."

Such sad glimpses, together with many others, of Tilly's past life, left upon Isabel a deep and painful impression, and quite dreadfully strengthened her feelings of remorse; but saddest and most penetrating of all was a circumstance Tilly herself never mentioned, and which Isabel came to learn, indirectly, from Dora Tremayne.

3

Of course Isabel summoned so old a friend as Dora to greet so old a connection as Tilly. Miss Tremayne was invited to tea one Sunday, and came tramping up the hill from her ironmonger's decked in a hat of purple feathers and white kid gloves. When Humphrey, in the hall, frankly remarked on this unusual splendour, Dora with equal frankness explained that both hat and gloves dated from '29, and were kept for visiting the nobs. "Not that you folk are nobs any longer," added Dora, admiring her reflection in a mirror. "It's just the old atmosphere of the Ridge. . . . I used to live here and be a nob myself, you know, before I lost my money. Where's tea?"

"In the drawing-room," said Humphrey.

"Quite right," approved Miss Tremayne. "I'm glad to see Isabel recognizes my pretensions. If you're passing me the cake, if there is any cake, don't hesitate to pass it twice."

They entered the drawing-room in great good humour. The long beautiful room was looking at its best, with flowers gaying its dignity, and afternoon tea set out in the best china. A small flame burned under the silver kettle, there were three sorts of sandwiches, fish-paste, and cucumber, and tomato, and a large cake. It was a scene completely (in the current phrase) pre-war—except that both Isabel and Jacqueline wore a look of modest complacency, as though they had brought off a minor triumph, as indeed they had. Like Dora, they were dressed in their best—Isabel in flowered silk, Jacqueline in one of her less artistic creations, cream linen with a scarlet belt; but all three were outshone by Tilly Cuff.

Tilly wore jade-green: a short, tight sheath of jade-green taffeta, daringly relieved by jet necklace and ear-rings. Since jet is rarely made into bracelets, her arms were for once bare, the jangling which was so much a part of her personality being produced by a bunch of charms pinned to a black satin bag. This she held in one hand; in the other a cigarette in a black holder; and with Bogey at her heels pattered gaily in from the terrace crying, "Tea, tea, tea!"

"Good heavens!" said Miss Tremayne loudly. "It's Tilly Cuff!"

"Why, dear old Dora!" cried Tilly — and from the tone of her voice, no less than from Miss Tremayne's answering look, every one present knew that she had not been used to address Miss Tremayne quite so familiarly. "Dora, how ripping to see you! Our dear old Giraffe!"

"My good Tilly," said Miss Tremayne. Her voice, as they knew at Madame Esmé's, could be peculiarly expressive. "Isabel said you were to be here; and I was very glad, because I remember, as I was telling Simon, your mother."

There was a slight pause while Tilly looked about for an ash-tray; the trifling business occupied her for some moments. Then she turned back to Miss Tremayne with wistful eyes.

"But that's wonderful!" she said softly. "We must have a nice long talk . . . But not now, Dora dear; some time when we're just by ourselves."

Isabel, touched and helpful, suggested that they should both go and look at the garden; tea could wait.

"Nonsense," said Miss Tremayne brusquely. "I'm thirsty. And Tilly would only be disappointed. When I say I remember Mrs. Cuff, I simply remember her at Bournemouth, on the promenade — "

"Dear Bournemouth!" ejaculated Tilly. "That's where I used to live, Humphrey, when I was a little girl. The sea and the pines! And the heather! When I first came to Chipping Hill, and I know Isabel won't mind my saying this — I so pined for the pines — " she paused; the phrase was faintly comic — "I so pined for the *sea,* I didn't know *how* I could endure it. Was I very miserable, Isabel, dear?"

"You were always very quiet," said Isabel uncomfortably. "But we didn't know, we didn't guess, you were pining as much as that."

"You certainly gave no sign of it," observed Simon, who was sitting by the tea-table in an attitude of impatience.

Tilly smiled bravely.

"One learns, even a child learns — and of course I was little more — to hide one's grief. I'm so glad to know I didn't cast a shadow on Isabel, or Ruth. But how heroic children can be!"

Dora Tremayne did not refer to Mrs. Cuff again, and Tilly soon recovered her spirits; it was Isabel who felt the chief effect of this encounter. For how dreadful, as she said to Simon that evening, to realize that all the while Tilly had been with them, and apparently so contented (though quiet), she had secretly been pining for heather!

"Rubbish," said Mr. Brocken flatly. "Tilly was extremely lucky to find such a good home, and she must have known it. What Dora remembers is Tilly's mother pushing old George Cuff in a bath-chair."

But how should Isabel be comforted by this? To regret,

to the point of pining, a scene of so much unhappiness—a mother pushing, a father having to be pushed—revealed, surely, a heart of uncommon tenderness. "And we never knew!" mourned Isabel. "Mamma simply told us Tilly was an orphan, and that we were to be very kind to her, and really I think we tried—but we never knew about the bath-chair. Poor, poor Tilly!"

By this time Mr. Brocken thoroughly regretted his indiscretion; he also felt very much annoyed with Dora Tremayne. For Tilly he spared no sympathy whatever, and in this was unjust; her picture of youthful misery was not untrue but merely, so to speak, transposed.

She had been in fact extremely glad to get to Chipping Lodge; it was the period preceding, the period of her true childhood, that had called for endurance. Tilly's memory of her father was clear, and disagreeable: a cross old man, given over to self-pity, perpetually waited upon and never pleased. The years following his death were even worse. In the boarding-house opened by Mrs. Cuff, Tilly, from the age of ten, toiled up and down stairs with trays, waiting on three cross old men instead of one. Mrs. Cuff did the best she could, sent Tilly to school as regularly as possible, drove her to home-work in the gas-lit basement: but there was never a moment of leisure, never a pinch of unused energy, for fun or light-hearted affection. Long afterwards, in Paris, Tilly Cuff saw a drawing called "The Washerwomen"; in it a mother and childish daughter toiled up a flight of steps, each with her bundle; and Tilly looked at it, and began to cry.

Such were the memories, such the background, she brought with her, so long ago, to Chipping Lodge. Mrs. Massey came to Bournemouth to fetch her; wrote, with a face of dismay, half a dozen cheques before they left. Yet she was kind: "You shall come and be our little cousin," said she, and there was a moment in the train when Tilly, pressed close against a sealskin cape, felt a real impulse of gratitude and affection. It did not last. Her new cousins, Isabel and Ruth, were kind too—but how absently, how cavalierly! They were so pretty and secure, Tilly was so plain and waif-like; they so ignorant, and she so experienced. It would have taken a far larger nature than Tilly's to accept, unrancorously, the advantages of her position; and Tilly's nature, even then, and through the fault of heredity and circumstance, was mean.

4

Isabel was in no danger. The image of Tilly pining for pines was still fresh in her mind when an incident occurred that showed Tilly in a more favourable light still.

The element of contrast, so heightening to any moral illustration, was supplied, regrettably, by Mr. Brocken.

"Simon, dear," said Isabel, looking up from a card by her breakfast plate, "would you like to come with me to the hospital and give a pint of blood?"

"No," said Simon.

Isabel poured out Jacqueline's coffee. Humphrey was not yet down, and Tilly Cuff was having breakfast in bed.

For a few moments the big sunny room was quite silent, save for the clink of china and the rustle of Mr. Brocken's *Times*.

"I'll come," offered Jacqueline. "When is it?"

"Thank you, dear. On Tuesday afternoon, any time up till seven o'clock, so that people can get there after work." Isabel paused, and added, with what she believed to be great artfulness, "Don't you think Simon's blood is probably something very unusual?"

Jacqueline readily agreed that it was probably A.B.

"I'm just O," pursued Isabel. "It's dreadfully common, but *very* useful. It mixes with absolutely anything. What are you, dear?"

"I'm O too," said Jacqueline.

There was a brief silence.

"Simon . . ."

"Well?" grunted Mr. Brocken.

"It doesn't *hurt,* you know," said Isabel gently.

In some annoyance Mr. Brocken replied that he did not fear the pain.

"Then why won't you, dear? They're dreadfully short — "

"Because I need all the blood I've got," snapped Mr. Brocken.

Isabel's look immediately brightened.

"If *that*'s all, dear you make it up again at once — I believe in three hours, or else it's three days. I never even feel queer, though of course I always take the cup of tea, just in case. Do you feel queer, Jacky?"

"Not in the least," said Jacqueline. "I've done four."

"I've done ten," said Isabel, absently. "Simon, wouldn't you *like* to know which group you are?"

"No," said Simon.

Which, so far as he was concerned, ended the matter. As things turned out, however, it was Tilly Cuff, not Jacqueline, who accompanied Isabel to Chipping Hospital. Jacqueline had ironing to do, and promised to follow in an hour's time; but Tilly, as soon as she learnt of Isabel's object, volunteered both her company and her blood. She had taken no part in the conversation at the breakfast table, and Isabel, who felt that Tilly, unlike Simon, really did need all the blood she'd got, had no intention of pressing her into service: Tilly simply volunteered.

"Have you ever given any before?" asked Isabel anxiously.

"Oh, yes," said Tilly. "I'm B. I've my card somewhere upstairs."

Thus in due course they lay on adjacent couches, each squeezing obediently at a roll of lint; from each left arm — Isabel's so plump, Tilly's so meagre — the blood rhythmically pulsed. Neither spoke: but during these five or six minutes Isabel's mind was greatly eased. For she had in fact been uneasy: Simon's disapproval had shaken her: Tilly, in her new character, dismayed. Isabel was almost certain that Mark would not have liked the new Tilly at all. Was it really right, therefore, to give Tilly all Mark's money? So Isabel had pondered, and made herself wretched enough in the process; but now, watching the dark red fluid rise in Tilly's bottle, she felt a sudden clearing-away of doubt, a sudden conviction that Tilly, in spite of all her disagreeable ways, was *good.*

For wasn't it very good, to give up one's blood to some anonymous recipient? What else, except goodness, should make Tilly do it? Isabel never applied this reasoning to herself; she trotted off twice a year to the nearest hospital with no more than a vague sense of discharging some vague debt. Mrs. Massey's training had been thorough. "People who have a great deal, as we have, must always be particularly ready to help others. It's nothing to plume oneself on. Your papa doesn't plume himself on the Waifs and Strays." But Tilly, thought Isabel, lay under no such obligation. What debt did Tilly owe the world? Why should Tilly be a blood donor?

Tilly Cuff's motives were in fact mixed. In the first place, to give blood was the correct thing to do, it won approval: Tilly always kept on her bandage, and then her square of plaster, at least as long as was necessary, and on her thin arm, generally short-sleeved, these badges were very conspicuous. Other people besides Isabel wondered if she could really spare her pint, and admired her generosity. But even more than these words of praise Tilly loved the ten minutes after the tube was withdrawn, when she lay warm under a blanket (in some hospitals with a hot-water bottle) and a nurse asked her if she felt all right, and told her there was a cup of tea waiting. To Tilly Cuff, so little cherished, these moments of cherishing were peculiarly and perhaps pathetically delicious. For the sake of them she would have been glad to give blood once a week. Tilly wasn't in the least disinterested; but Isabel, though she might have been disappointed to know it, could have felt only compassion before the true motive.

Isabel did not know it. Glancing across at Tilly's small flat shape, so quiescent under the blanket, she thought, quite erroneously, *Tilly is good.*

"I'll just wait a day or two longer," thought Isabel comfortably, "just to satisfy Simon, and then I'll give her a lovely surprise."

It was a pity she waited. Much trouble would have been saved if she had sprung her surprise sooner. But Isabel, confident of her good intentions, anxious to placate her brother-in-law, allowed the days to pass; and Simon, bitter and most stubborn, trusted in time; and the situation (said Humphrey) rapidly deteriorated.

Chapter 14

There was only one major change in the domestic routine. Mr. Brocken, who never exposed himself to unnecessary discomfort, formed the habit of eating dinner at his Club and returning to Chipping Hill by the nine-o'clock instead of the five-twenty train. The evenings were light, the carriages at the later hour less crowded; he congratulated himself on an admirable notion. But over a summer week-end the Club was not altogether attractive: week-end sunshine in particular had a curious way of bringing out too strongly the smell of old books, old leather and old carpets which Mr. Brocken as a rule rather liked. On Saturdays, therefore, he returned as usual. This in turn produced a second habit, expensive but rewarding. Every week Mr. Brocken brought home two tickets for a Saturday matinée, and took his seat on the one-twenty down secure in the knowledge that Isabel and Tilly were even then emerging from the twelve-fifty up. It was the nicest thing, said Isabel gratefully, Simon had ever done; and Simon, attaching a preciser meaning to her adjective, was inclined to agree.

Thus he was sure of having the house to himself. Humphrey and Jacqueline, no less grateful than Isabel, never intruded on him; a tea-tray and an electric kettle were left in the dining-room, and he made himself tea when he wanted it. Mr. Brocken enjoyed these afternoons as much as he enjoyed anything; they rested and relaxed him. They also confirmed his opinion that the prime condition of rest and relaxation was the absence of any one else. Ten minutes of Greta, for example, once disturbed an entire afternoon.—Yet Mr. Brocken had been in a very good humour; it was in fact his unusual expression of benignity, as he strolled upon the terrace, that emboldened the child to come hovering up and ask him to do her a favour.

"Look," said Greta, "there's no one in but you, and Mum and me want to go out together."

There was a touching eagerness about her; Mr. Brocken was touched, also, by the way in which the Pooles gently but stubbornly persisted in regarding him as their patron. Still perfectly good-humoured, he replied that he saw no objection whatever to their both leaving the house at the same time.

"It's the beer," explained Greta. "It's because of the beer coming. It's Captain G.'s beer, and we said we'd take it in, but it hasn't come. I've got the money." And she held out a pound note, cajolingly.

"Do you mean you wish me to take it in for you?" asked Simon.

"Well, if you wouldn't *mind,*" said Greta. "You can hear the van from here, it makes ever such a row, and you can leave the crate just inside the door, don't bother with the empties, and there'll be three-and-ninepence change."

Her fingers, gently pushing the pound into Mr. Brocken's hand, left a curious impression of lightness, and brittleness, such as might be left by the claw of some small perching bird. Mr. Brocken allowed the note to remain. In a normal way he would have objected strongly to taking in Humphrey's beer — why couldn't the boy wait for it himself? — but Greta's brown eyes were exceedingly persuasive. With a real feat of imagination, he said benevolently,

"Are you going to buy a new dress?"

The child beamed.

"Guess again!"

"A new hat?"

"Warmer!" squealed Greta. "Go on!"

"A — a Tam o' Shanter?"

She shook her head. Her face grew solemn. She said impressively:

"*I'm going to get a perm.*"

There are few men in England to whom this term is unfamiliar; Simon Brocken was one of them.

"A perm?" he repeated blankly. "And what is that?"

"A permanent wave, silly!" (The child was plainly over-excited.) "You know, for my hair — like Mum has hers."

Mr. Brocken now understood well enough; but he by no means approved. That women had their hair waved he did vaguely realize: he had at once perceived, for example, that Mrs. Poole's coiffure was the product of some mechanical device; but for a child of fourteen — !

"Rubbish!" he said sharply. "You're too young."

"I'm not!"

"You are."

"I'm *not!*"

It was developing into a perfectly childish wrangle, such as Mr. Brocken dimly remembered from his own youth; the same memory warned him that Greta could keep on saying "I'm not" at least up to twenty, and possibly up to a hundred; he shut his mouth under the grim line of his moustache and turned away. Greta waited a moment, the response ready, and then ran after him.

"I can't go on looking like this all my life — now, can I?" she asked persuasively.

"You look all right. When you're tidy. How do you want to look?"

"Glamorous," said Greta.

She did not say it, however, with much confidence; her voice drooped. In the belief that he was making an impression, Mr. Brocken added that neatness and cleanliness rendered the appearance of all little girls equally attractive, and that nice manners were most important of all. But as Greta stood first on one leg and then on the other, he saw that his words were being wasted; he doubted whether she even heard them. Indeed, for some time after he had stopped speaking she continued thus to stand, on alternate legs, her large squirrel's eyes fixed on his face, until in an irritated tone he asked what she was waiting for.

"I'm not waiting for anything . . ."

"Then you had better run along. I have said I will take the beer in; what more do you want?"

"I dunno," admitted Greta sadly. "Thank you very much. You've just spoilt everything, that's all; and I wish I hadn't told you."

She trailed off, leaving Mr. Brocken with a wholly unmerited sense of guilt. What had he to feel guilty about? He looked at the pound note in his hand: was he not about to take in beer, a drink he personally disliked, to oblige a vain and silly child? Indirectly to oblige his nephew, gallivanted off with Miss Brown? His mind ranged further: were not Isabel and Tilly Cuff even then enjoying themselves at his expense? He was a man — good heavens! — universally benevolent. . . . Mr. Brocken looked at the note again: it was a very old one, creased and greasy, and across the back some one had written, in indelible pencil, "God send you back to me." Isabel would have found this touching; Mr. Brocken did not; he felt a strong impulse to crumple the note into a ball and toss it over the terrace. Yet it was still worth a pound, could buy as much as twenty new-minted shillings. No reasonable man would reject it, or consider it had been spoiled. . . .

Simon pushed the note into his pocket and dismissed the matter from his mind. Or rather attempted to do so; it remained a source of slight — and unmerited — annoyance for the rest of the afternoon. The beer came about an hour later, just as his kettle boiled.

2

Humphrey and Jacqueline, taking a cup of tea at Bob's, heard about the perm from Miss Tremayne. Dora often popped into Bob's about five: if the telephone rang at her deserted desk one of the girls ran out from a cubicle and answered it, and if a customer wanted to pay, Madame Esmé was summoned to receive the cash. For Miss Tremayne had no idea of being a bondslave, and Madame Esmé, recognizing her employee's unusual qualities, turned a blind eye to her idiosyncrasies. She had engaged Miss Tremayne in the first place purely for the sake of prestige, and been both pleased and surprised to find her reasonably efficient; Dora's real genius for handling a difficult customer, still more unlooked for, rapidly made her invaluable. She therefore popped out to Bob's (or up to her own flat, or round to the butcher's) unchecked, and unrebuked.

"Well, well!" cried Miss Tremayne cordially. "And where have you two been?"

"Up on the Common," said Jacqueline.

It was their usual Saturday walk: every Saturday Jacqueline and Humphrey, like dozens of other Chipping Hill couples, made their way up to the pleasant grassy stretches, the May-trees and birches, of Chipping Common. It was a simple outing; they looked at the trees and the pond — there was a small pond, with a few waterfowl — and looked at the people, and sometimes sat down on the grass, and sometimes took books with them; but the very familiarity of trees, pond and people, and the week-by-week regularity of the excursion, had a great charm for both young persons. They had been so flung about, for so many years, they could taste monotony as something sweet. This walk, however, had been less agreeable than usual; Jacqueline for some reason was rather silent; and they were both glad of the encounter with Miss Tremayne.

"In my young days," said Dora, "there used to be riding there. I went out myself, with Ruth and Isabel . . . and frankly I rode better than either of them, though perhaps with less grace. I must tell that to Madame: she loves these classy tit-bits about my past. By the way, I hope you're prepared for Greta's transformation: we've been working on her all afternoon."

Jacqueline stared in astonishment.

"That child!" she said (her expression for the moment rather like Mr. Brocken's). "Is Greta having her hair done?"

"My dear, she's being permed. She's under the drier at this moment, and I shouldn't be at all surprised if she's sick with excitement before she's combed out. However, her mother's there too, in the next cubicle — "

"You are throwing," said Humphrey, "an entirely new light on their habits. Is Mrs. Poole being permed as well?"

"But, my dear boy, she *is*. Haven't you noticed it?"

"We never see her," explained Jacqueline, "without a duster on her head."

"Then you've missed something," said Dora. "The Poole

coiffure is one of our triumphs. But undoubtedly a little elaborate for housework. Do you know — " Dora set her elbows on the table and regarded them with serious approval — "I think that's one thing you manage very well up at the Lodge; you do leave each other alone."

Humphrey and Jacqueline looked at one another.

"Miss Tremayne," said Jacqueline, "do you remember much — do you remember anything — about Tilly Cuff?"

Dora did not immediately answer. The moments passed: in the Beauty Parlour the telephone rang, one of the girls dashed out to answer, leaving her lady half-soused; a client waited for change while Madame Esmé dabbed lavender-water on Greta's pallid brow; still Dora sat meditative in Bob's. What she chiefly remembered about Tilly was the Bournemouth episode; generosity shut her mouth. For the rest, she knew certainly less than Isabel, and if she had seen more, or suspected more, of some characteristic slyness, had no proof of it. Discussing Tilly with Simon before Tilly's arrival, Dora had in fact stood up for her: it was the actual presence of Tilly that revived this forgotten mistrust. But what harm could the woman do, now, at Chipping Lodge?

"No," said Dora at last. "Tilly never made much impression. She was a quiet little thing. . . ."

"You don't remember," persisted Jacqueline, "a time when she seemed . . . broken-hearted?"

"Good gracious, no!" cried Dora. "Have I really been here half an hour? Humphrey, I'm leaving fivepence; Bob doesn't get tipped for tea."

3

It was important—Mr. Brocken and Humphrey and Jacqueline all felt this strongly—to get at the truth on a point which Isabel took for granted, and by so doing finally condemned herself. "Do you realize," Simon once demanded, "that we are absolutely in the dark as to Tilly's feeling for the fellow? She may not have liked Macgregor; she mightn't have wanted to marry him. She might have refused him."

"Of course she'd have married him," said Isabel mournfully. "She'd have married any one."

"You have a very low opinion of her."

"No, dear, I haven't. In Tilly's position marriage was the one hope. I don't say she'd have married the butcher—" Isabel paused doubtfully, and added—"not unless he had a *very* large business, when I believe they're called graziers, and not butchers at all; but she'd have married any one in the least suitable. And Mr. Macgregor was far more than that."

In his heart Mr. Brocken felt this was so; it was undeniable that even a butcher in a small way would have been a better fate than Tilly's actual one. At the same time—women were incalculable; and if it could be discovered that Tilly would have turned Macgregor down, the whole structure of Isabel's project would collapse. Her base act would remain base; but sterile, without consequences, calling for no feat of quixotry in expiation.

This hope, though faint, being the best he could find, Mr. Brocken cherished it; and at dinner that same Saturday was considerably heartened by a piece of evidence personally elicited from Tilly herself.

Tilly was describing the past glories of Chipping Lodge.

"What ripping dances we used to give!" exclaimed Tilly. "I've been to some very grand affairs since, but none more enjoyable. Do you remember sitting on the stairs, Simon, eating ices?"

Mr. Brocken grunted. At this point he was merely irritated; moreover the picture thus conjured up, of himself and Tilly practically sharing the same plate, was completely untrue; in fact he never remembered her sitting on the stairs at all, she was always in the dining-room, superintending the buffet.

"And on the first flight," continued Tilly vivaciously, "and on the second, up to 'Dignity and Impudence,' it was quite proper; but above 'Dignity and Impudence,' where the stairs turned, it was rather fast. What dear little innocents we were!"

"Where did you and Mamma sit, Aunt Isabel?" asked Humphrey. "Above or below?"

"Below," said Isabel simply. "We were hostesses."

"Of *course,*" corroborated Miss Cuff. "We were known as the Three Graces." (Simon regarded her with amazement. She might hope to delude Humphrey and Jacqueline, but how could she hope to delude either Isabel or himself?) "Don't you remember, Isabel, at that last dance before I went to Switzerland, we were standing under the chandeliers, waiting to receive our guests, when the band leader suddenly raised his glass to us? 'To the Three Graces!'"

"I dare say he did," said Isabel doubtfully. "I know Papa always gave him a glass of champagne before he started; and he was a very polite man. I—I remember the dance very well."

Acting on pure impulse, Mr. Brocken said,

"Mark and I brought a guest with us. A man called Macgregor."

He was watching Tilly closely. Her face became blank.

"Macgregor?" she repeated. "I don't remember him."

As soon as the meal was over Mr. Brocken baldly informed Isabel that he wanted a word with her, and went upstairs to wash his hands. Isabel had no hesitation in following; the bathroom was by this time the accepted spot for any private converse.

"Well?" said Mr. Brocken triumphantly. "That ought to relieve your mind. She doesn't even remember the chap."

Isabel, in the act of closing the door, turned on him a mild astonished gaze.

"My dear, of course she does!"

"But she told us she did not!" exploded Simon.

"Of course she'd *say* so," agreed Isabel patiently. "And that means she does."

Something in this calm certainty carried conviction. Mr. Brocken, violently drying his hands, reflected again that women were incalculable. Incalculable, irrational, incapable of straight dealing, and ungrateful to those who were doing their best for them.

"Dear Simon," said Isabel.

She opened the door — her hand had never left the knob — and went out.

4

Isabel was still determined. By this time she hardly liked Tilly at all, even though Tilly was good; which was manifestly unfair, since Isabel had been known to like even persons who were bad. Such, indeed, did not often come her way; but she had been really fond of her companion who received stolen property (a particularly nice, bright, clever girl) and of a particularly courteous gardener who sold the Priory vegetables for his own profit; and though this was of course before their delinquency was revealed, Isabel found that she weak-mindedly went on liking them even afterwards. But she didn't really like Tilly Cuff. The prospect of making confession to Tilly became increasingly painful. It had been difficult enough to confess to Simon; but even his hard words, Isabel suspected, would seem light, and even kindly, beside what Tilly might say to her. Isabel now heartily agreed with his advice to wait for the right moment of friendliness and good feeling: but the only time such moments ever occurred was in the theatre, at a matinée, when their common enjoyment of some thrilling love-song, or pathetic scene, united not only Isabel and Tilly, but the whole audience. Isabel could hardly plunge into confession then and there, and the intervals were too short. She postponed the evil hour partly out of cowardice, partly to placate Simon, and partly because her conscience was temporarily salved by the knowledge of her good intentions.

But she was still determined; and turning the matter over in her mind (for she naturally thought about it a good deal), and remembering how much Humphrey seemed to like Chipping Lodge, and glancing at her plan for joining forces with Dora Tremayne — turning all this over in her mind, Isabel decided that if her nephew wanted the house, he should have it. It would be instead, she explained carefully, of his five-thousand-pound legacy; and he could have it as soon as her affairs with Tilly were settled.

"Thank you very much," said Humphrey.

"Nonsense," said Mr. Brocken.

Isabel, who had made the suggestion in front of her brother-in-law to avoid telling him about it afterwards, felt very glad she had done so. She sat back comfortably and began to knit while they argued it out.

"Nonsense," repeated Simon. "What would you do with it? It's a white elephant."

"I should live in it, sir."

"Aren't you going back to New Zealand?"

"I reckon not," said Humphrey.

("How nice!" put in Isabel.)

"You should," said Mr. Brocken, who always liked to see his relations established as far off as possible. "There's no future for you in this country. What's to become of you?"

"A schoolmaster, sir."

"Then this house would be of no use to you whatever."

"Yes, it would," said Isabel, "if he taught at Broxbury. You take a bus from the station, Humphrey, and it's a twopenny ride."

"Broxbury College," said Simon, "is a school of some standing. What makes you think Humphrey would be acceptable there?"

"I have played Rugby football for the Army, sir." (Mr. Brocken scented irony; at the same time admitted the point.) "Broxbury is a Rugger school. I have also," proceeded Humphrey, "a degree in mathematics, and a decent war record."

"And Simon knows the headmaster," added Isabel.

"I do not," said Mr. Brocken.

"But, dear, you do." Isabel laid down her knitting and gazed affectionately back into the past. "We all knew him; he was that rather scrubby little Matthews boy who used to dance so badly. He once put his foot through the hem of my best white lace; so I'm sure he'd be glad to see you again."

Mr. Brocken looked at his sister-in-law for some moments, but fortunately without speaking, and left the room.

"He's just gone to get used to the idea," said Isabel comfortably.

For obvious reasons the matter was not to be discussed

openly, but Isabel told Jacky, and so, a day or two later, did Humphrey himself. The young people had been seeing rather less of each other; when Humphrey put his head into the pantry, as likely as not Tilly Cuff was there before him, and the collapse of the summer into wind and rain put sun-bathing out of the question. But Jacqueline still carried out a glass of beer when Humphrey gardened in the morning; sometimes stopped beside him to pick peas or beans, or to pull lettuces, while the rain pattered on the ground sheets with which they both in such weather habitually draped themselves. At the end of the vegetable plot a tumble-down grotto, covered with ivy, afforded some slight shelter; and here, refreshing himself, and with a proprietor-like air, Humphrey informed Jacqueline that the ground on which they stood was as good as his own.

"I'm glad," said Jacqueline seriously. "You wanted it, didn't you?"

"Yes," said Humphrey. "Uncle Simon thinks I'm crazy; but it's my idea of a nice house." He shrugged back the waterproof folds; the gesture, and his wet tousled head, turned him suddenly into a youngster Mr. Brocken would not have recognized. "I reckon all New Zealanders are sentimental about Home," he said thoughtfully, "and when we get here it's often a let-down, because it isn't what we expected. And then we come across a place like this, or a kind little country pub, or we're nursed in a big old house, and see a trench dug across the park, greatest depth two foot, three strands of wire, and that's where they were going to stop the Jerries; and back it all comes.

I don't know why I should feel it, I've lived in England half my life; I reckon I reverted to type in the war."

"But I feel it too," said Jacqueline. "I like this house too. That's inadequate. I mean, there's a lot of support in — in nice places."

They looked at each other seriously, as though they had discovered something new and important. Jacqueline was leaning in the grimy archway — constructed of small boulders, once so picturesque, now a weather-worn Victorian joke; but the rain-washed ivy leaves were glossy, and becoming to a fair head. She could lean comfortably, protected by her mackintosh cape; looked pretty and sturdy, another youngster such as Humphrey. It was inevitable that just then Tilly Cuff should join them.

"Caught!" exclaimed Tilly vivaciously. "Is *this* how Humphrey gardens? Not that I blame you, for it's pouring; but I simply had to give Bogey a breath of air."

She twinkled at them from under her umbrella — but with a special side-glance for Jacqueline, sympathetic, yet admonitory; dreadfully understanding. "*I* shan't tell!" murmured Miss Cuff. At such close quarters Humphrey naturally overheard, and Jacqueline was aware that he had done so; and to prevent his enquiring, with his usual precision, what Miss Cuff would not tell to whom, said quickly that if he had finished his beer she would take the glass back to the house. "I haven't," said Humphrey. "Then *I*'ll take it," offered Tilly. "We're going just *once* round the garden, and I'll pick it up on my way back. Come along, doggie!"

Bogey tugged her away past the bean rows. Humphrey emptied his glass and looked at Jacqueline enquiringly.

"You seem to be getting quite matey with the woman," he observed.

"I detest her," said Jacqueline.

"Well, what did she mean when she said she wouldn't tell?"

"Nothing. She simply said it to embarrass us."

"It didn't embarrass me."

"Possibly not," said Jacqueline; and felt in spite of herself a stirring of resentment. Naturally Humphrey wasn't embarrassed: no man, by the mere fact of his sex, was ever open to the particular disagreeableness of being taken for a husband hunter. She screwed the stopper back into the bottle, pulled her ground sheet over her head, and took the glass out of Humphrey's hand.

"Aren't you being a bit silly?" asked Humphrey.

"No, I don't think so," said Jacqueline; and plunged out into the rain.

Chapter 15

Mr. Brocken did not see Greta again for some days. This would have been perfectly normal, since he left the house early and returned late, but for the fact that the day after she had been permed was a Sunday. On Sunday mornings Mr. Brocken was quite accustomed to seeing her in the garden — in the distance, where she couldn't annoy him, playing about a winding path at the extreme limit of the ground. He strolled once or twice in that direction, before lunch and after; Greta was not to be seen. On the Thursday morning, however, as he emerged by the front door, she appeared round the tongue of shrubbery with a casual and disengaged air.

"Good morning," said Mr. Brocken. "I haven't seen you for some time."

"Well, I've been dodging you," said Greta frankly, "because you were so mean about my perm. This is it."

She stood gravely before him, and slowly turned her head from side to side. The result was not so bad as Mr. Brocken had feared. Greta's straw-coloured hair, parted low, now fell in one large wave over her right temple, and over the left showed a mere ripple, the ends being neatly rolled under all round.

"Well?" said Greta. "It's done now. What do you think of it?"

"You certainly look no worse," said Mr. Brocken handsomely. "In fact, if you push that piece out of your eye, it may even be an improvement."

"That's the whole thing," explained Greta patiently. "It's a Veronica Lake. I suppose *you*'ll say Veronica Lakes have gone out."

"I should say nothing of the kind," protested Mr. Brocken, in all honesty.

"Well, I know they've gone out. But Mum still thinks it's the best hair-do for my age, and Mum knows all about hair-dos. I'd look ever so silly upswept. Come on, say you like it!"

"Do you want me to say I do if I don't?"

Greta giggled.

"*I* think you do really, only it's against what you think's proper. Mum says — "

One can never resist the temptation to hear what others think about us.

"Go on," said Mr. Brocken.

"Well . . . you know how if you make a face, and the wind changes, you stay like it? Mum says the wind changed for you in the year dot."

Mr. Brocken was not displeased. He had not the least objection to being thought old-fashioned: the remark had the effect of restoring them to their old footing. They felt — and only a formal phrase serves — a certain good-will towards each other. Mr. Brocken perceived that for some obscure reason Greta rather liked him, and Greta, on equally nebulous grounds, perceived in Mr. Brocken a possible ally. It was perhaps this circumstance which accounted for Simon's unexpected attitude, some mornings later, in conversation with Humphrey Garrett.

Mr. Brocken, on his way out of the drive, found Humphrey at the gate stuffing newspapers into a plum-coloured sack. On the ground beside him lay two or three cartons and an enormous pile of cheap magazines.

"Where on earth do those come from?" asked Mr. Brocken at once.

"From the Pooles," said Humphrey. "They throw them away, and Jacky rescues them for salvage, and they're put out once a month."

Mr. Brocken poked at the heap with his umbrella. On nearly every cover appeared the likeness of a film-star, and on such inner pages as he exposed more portraits of film-stars, varied by scenes from films and diagrams showing how to reduce the hips.

"The Pooles *buy* these?" he said distastefully.

"Constantly, sir. At least four or five a week. The invention of movable type has been a great blessing to them."

"Trash," said Mr. Brocken.

"They like trash."

"They must indeed." The point of Simon's umbrella came to rest on a likeness of Greta Garbo, largely captioned, "Where Is She Now?" Mr. Brocken was perfectly incurious, but the name caught his eye: Greta, and Greta the child; the name was explained. Even upon the font, it seemed, film-stars shed their influence; it was like a new form of astrology. Trash! "And yet," said Mr. Brocken unexpectedly, "I don't know whether it has ever struck you, as it has me, that Greta and her mother, foolish as they are — that there is something attractive about them?"

Humphrey Garrett nodded.

"They don't feel the weight of the world."

"That's a strange observation," said Mr. Brocken. "I'm not sure I grasp what you mean by it."

"They know so little. You must admit that if one knew nothing whatever of economics or politics or foreign affairs, it would be a weight off one's mind."

"It would also reduce us to the level of animals."

"Who are so placid and self-contained," quoted Humphrey. "Certainly the Pooles don't lie awake at night worrying about their sins, or even about the sins of the Government. They disport themselves in all innocence, like Adam and Eve before they ate of the tree of knowledge. It makes them very restful company."

"I think perhaps you have said more than you intended," observed Mr. Brocken. "You employed the word 'innocence.' I agree that the Pooles appear to live entirely in their appetites and affections; but these, possibly by sheer hazard, are all innocent; and that is why they appeal."

He walked off down the hill, his umbrella cocked behind him like the last tail feather of an old bird. He was sagacious and well-informed; on him the weight of the world pressed heavily; and he was also, at the moment, troubled by a feeling that if young Garrett had said more than he intended, so had he himself. Innocent, indeed! The cinema, the dance hall, the cosmetic box — were these innocent tastes? Surely not: debauchery, rather. And what about the friendship between Mrs. Poole and Mr. Simmonds? The fellow's evidence, in the train, had carried conviction; but the relationship was certainly . . . indiscreet. "Innocent be damned!" thought Mr. Brocken — and what on earth had induced him to take such a line, he could not now imagine.

As a reaction from this weakness, he shortly afterwards found himself supporting Tilly Cuff, who wished to teach Greta to sew.

It was true that Greta sewed (and darned) abominably. The memory of Mr. Brocken's socks still rankled with him, and the child's own stockings, when she wore any, were deplorably cobbled. It was praiseworthy of Tilly to offer to take her in hand. The only difficulty was that Greta didn't want to learn, and her mother didn't wish Greta to do anything she didn't want.

As usual, they turned to Mr. Brocken. They caught him at the door as he returned in the evening, and drew him into the kitchen, and pressed a nice cup of tea into his reluctant hands.

"I don't say Greta's a wonder at her needle," stated

Mrs. Poole, with a great air of impartiality, "as few kiddies are; but what I do say is, if anyone's to teach her, then I'm the one."

Mr. Brocken forbore to point out that Greta appeared to receive singularly little maternal instruction on this point or any other; instead he observed tactfully that Mrs. Poole had a great deal to do, and that if Miss Cuff were an expert needlewoman, as he imagined her to be, it was a chance Greta should not miss.

"I'm sure I'd never stand in the kiddie's way," said Mrs. Poole uneasily. "It's just that she doesn't seem to take to the notion. But if *you* say so — "

"I consider it a thoroughly excellent plan," said Mr. Brocken — remembering his socks.

"Okay," said Mrs. Poole. "If you say so . . ."

So Greta was to spend an hour each morning with Tilly Cuff and the mending basket. Or such was the original plan; by the second morning Greta was sulking, on the third she simply disappeared, and on the fourth she most regrettably called Miss Cuff an old cow. To the general consternation Tilly answered the child with a reflection on her mother's character; and Mr. Brocken returned that night to an atmosphere like a thunder-storm.

"*I* didn't hear it," explained Isabel unhappily, "but Humphrey was in the garden — "

"She said Mrs. Poole neglected her maternal duties," said Humphrey. "I'm bowdlerizing. She asked if Greta knew who her father was — in fact, that's where I butted in."

"*I* was upstairs," corroborated Jacqueline. "I heard them on the terrace and ran down just as Humphrey came up from the beans. I said Tilly was wanted on the telephone — "

"*I* said I'd found a Colorado beetle," put in Humphrey. "She didn't know which to deal with first. But when she got to the telephone of course there was no one there, so she rang up the Ministry of Agriculture. We'd better find an earwig, in case they send a flying squad."

It was fortunately he who answered the phone when the Ministry, about an hour later, rang back. Humphrey described the Chipping Hill Colorado as being bright red, with black spots, and responsive to the cry of "Fly away home"; exchanged a few sentiments on the unreliability of women, and parted from the Ministry on friendly terms. It was an altogether ridiculous incident; important only as a warning, as a pointer to the direction in which Miss Cuff's malevolence was likely to turn.

For it was at this point, marked by this incident, that Tilly's characteristic quality first openly showed itself: a quality which no one ever named, as though in fear of attracting the evil eye: malevolence.

2

She wished ill.

She wished ill to every one at Chipping Lodge. She could not help it, they were too enviable. She envied Isabel's money, Jacqueline's attractive youth, Humphrey and Mr. Brocken their male advantages. Since she feared to attack any person openly, this malevolence vented itself upon such inanimate objects as they prized. Nothing was too large or too small for her mockery: the house was a great inconvenient barracks, the pepper-mill—Isabel's French pepper-mill, which she had cherished since before the war—a ridiculous fiddling contraption. The swing seat—she really couldn't help laughing at *that,* it looked such an absurd extravagance on the shabby old terrace; and to put cut flowers in the hall was too ludicrous for words. "We always had flowers in the hall," said Isabel defensively. "I like to see them when I come in." "My dear, don't tell me they welcome you with their pretty faces!" cried Tilly. Since this was exactly what Isabel fancied they did, she had no answer.

Tilly also found particularly foolish (and here was attacking the whole atmosphere of Chipping Lodge) Isabel's refusal to patronize the Black Market. "My dear, the butcher's known you for years!" exclaimed Tilly. "Don't tell me he can't slip you an extra cutlet!" "But I've never asked him to," said Isabel. "I—I don't ask him, Tilly." "Well, every one else does," said Tilly sharply. Since it is always embarrassing to appear more virtuous than one's neighbour, Isabel was silent again. "We get enough to eat," said Jacqueline, taking up her cudgels. "Only just," said Tilly angrily.—"And don't talk to me about Germany, because what *I* say is, Who won the war?"

"We won it," said Humphrey.

"Well, it doesn't seem like it," said Tilly, changing her

ground. "It certainly doesn't *seem* like it, living as we are. And Isabel won't take the least trouble — "

"If we hadn't won it," said Humphrey loudly, "I reckon I shouldn't be here. I should be either dead, or a labourer in Germany. Jacqueline's fate would be possibly more unpleasant. Aunt Isabel would starve. Uncle Simon would almost certainly get himself shot. So we, even living as we are, rightly prefer to have won. But of course I can't speak for you."

This rudeness was something else new at Chipping Lodge. Never before, in that small community, had discourtesy been heard. But Isabel, remembering all her nephew had endured, and how his shoulder still sometimes pained him, would not utter a rebuke; and Jacqueline, remembering a snow-bound Nissen, remarked angrily that it was always the civilians who complained; and Tilly retorted that the Army had notoriously wasted half its rations — and altogether the conversation at Chipping Lodge lost a great deal of its amenity.

All this, however, unfortunate as it was, was not yet serious. Tilly's real attack was launched against persons less able to defend themselves, simpler, and upon a more vital point. She attacked the Pooles.

It was not done lightly, without preparation. Impelled by a sense of duty, Tilly had no hesitation in slipping into the kitchen, while the Pooles were out at the shops, and sliding open a dresser drawer, and ruffling through their neatly arranged football coupons. Then she popped in one evening and caught them red-handed. "Football pools?" exclaimed Tilly. "Dear me, I've been to Monte Carlo myself, I've put my little five francs on the *rouge;* but *what* pleasure can you get, what possible interest can there be, in making noughts and crosses on a piece of paper without ever seeing a game?"

Like Isabel, the Pooles did not answer. Silence was their refuge; they simply waited, the ink drying on their pens, until Miss Cuff went away. But they must have been perturbed, must have felt as it were a need to throw out, from their cherished circle of isolation, some bridge into friendly territory; for the next day Mrs. Poole waylaid Humphrey Garrett (whose beer they regularly took in, except for the one occasion when they substituted Mr. Brocken) and requested him to post their coupons on his way down to Bob's. She could quite well have run out herself, or sent Greta; her real object was—in the Poole phraseology—to put in a word.

"We don't never spend more than we can afford," said Mrs. Poole earnestly. "Last year, on the year, we was ten bob up. Last week it was two pound. I dare say it'll go again, but what I mean is, we're prepared. If you see what I mean."

"Too right," agreed Humphrey. But his expression could not have been altogether approving, for Mrs. Poole added seriously,

"If we was lucky, we might win thousands; so it's a bit of excitement. Haven't you been dropping out of parachutes?"

"I usually managed," said Humphrey, "to retain contact. And to tell you the truth, I was always scared stiff."

Mrs. Poole gave him one of Greta's wide smiles.

"All you boys are the same," she said affectionately. "Always say you're scared, and then go and do it again. Well, I'm not scared, I know what I'm at; and we do like a bit of excitement, Greta and me."

3

Was it malevolence, or was it sense of duty, that set in train Tilly's subsequent course of action? Jacky, versed in the jargon of psychology, split her motive into conscious and subconscious; subconscious malice disguised, possibly even to Tilly herself, as eager benevolence. Isabel clung stubbornly to the theory that Tilly meant well. Mr. Brocken disbelieved it. But the question in essence remained posed; no one was ever really sure of the answer.

No one was ever sure whether Miss Cuff's violent emotion, one Saturday night, was genuine or not.

"I have *just,*" cried Tilly, bursting into the drawing-room, "seen the most *extraordinary person* at the back-door!"

All, naturally, looked up. Isabel, pouring coffee, suspended her hand. Jacqueline, pouring milk for Humphrey, over-filled his cup. As for Mr. Brocken, he felt a most disagreeable premonition.

"What sort of person?" asked Isabel anxiously. "A tramp?"

"My dear, no! A *woman*. A woman in the most *flashy* evening dress." (Simon felt his premonition confirmed.) "She's standing just outside the back-door, as though she were waiting for some one. I can see her from my window. I believe she's waiting to let in an *accomplice* . . ."

"Burglars," said Jacqueline, "don't go burgling in evening dress — at least not in this neighbourhood. It must be Mrs. Poole."

"And why should *she* be in evening dress? It certainly is not Mrs. Poole!"

Simon, by this time convinced that it was, observed that Mrs. Poole did, he had reason to believe, occasionally go to dances.

"And it's Saturday," corroborated Jacqueline. "There are dances on Saturdays at the Broxbury Palais."

"Of the highest respectability," added Humphrey. "Nothing stronger than ginger-ale."

Miss Cuff stared at them incredulously.

"But aren't you going to do anything? Aren't you even going to come and see? Isabel — "

"If Simon and Jacky say it's Mrs. Poole, I expect it is," said Isabel placidly.

"Then I shall ring up the police," declared Miss Cuff. "If no one will come with me to investigate this person, I shall ring up the police."

Remembering his own emotions at the first sight of Mrs. Poole in gala rig, Simon could not feel this to be altogether unreasonable; at the same time an instinct stronger than reason suggested that Tilly knew very well whom she had seen, had in fact recognized Mrs. Poole instantly, and was simply seizing the opportunity to make mischief. However, she obviously could not be allowed to ring up the police, there had been enough nonsense already over Humphrey's Colorado; unhappily but resolutely, Mr. Brocken set down his coffee cup and volunteered to accompany Tilly to the back-door. They arrived just in time to see a tomato-red gown, armed by a blue lounge suit, vanishing through the back gate, and Greta, by the shrubbery, waving good-bye.

"Who," shrilled Miss Cuff, her voice high-pitched and angry, "who, child, was that?"

Greta took a quick step backwards, towards Mr. Brocken. He received the definite impression that it was the pitch of Tilly's voice, much more than her actual words, that so frightened the child. For the child was frightened. Pressing close to Simon's sleeve, she said defensively—a leveret defending its doe—

"That's my Mum. What about it?"

"Your *mother?*" cried Tilly. "I don't believe you!"

"Well, it is," breathed Greta. "Gone dancing . . . What's wrong with that?"

She pushed hard against Simon's arm; he felt her thin body shake; and at the same moment was aware of Jacqueline standing behind them. She said cheerfully (but not too loudly: a welfare officer's pleasant voice),

"Greta, how nice your mother looks. I suppose she has the key?"

Greta nodded. Jacqueline had in fact seen no more of

Mrs. Poole than the tail of a bright skirt, but apparently the child did not realize it.

"Then that's all right," said Jacqueline. "In you go!"

Greta at once obeyed. She slipped through the back-door like a shadow, and closed it gently behind her. Mr. Brocken, who until that moment had said nothing whatever, observed that the coffee was probably cold. "Stone-cold," agreed Jacqueline. "And Miss Cuff's had none at all. I'll make fresh." Neither of them addressed or looked at Miss Cuff directly; her face was not pleasant. But Tilly had no intention of allowing an incident so promising of scandal to be so lightly passed over.

"How long has this been going on?" she demanded. "Or don't you know? Is no one except myself in the least concerned? Does—does that man come back into the house?"

"No, he does not," said Mr. Brocken.

"How do you know?" cried Tilly.

"From my knowledge of Mrs. Poole's character," snapped Simon. "Do you imagine that I should employ, in a position of trust, a person in whom I had not confidence? Are you implying that I have abused my sister-in-law's reliance upon my judgment? You had better control your tongue."

This was the first moment of open conflict between Tilly Cuff and any other person at the Lodge.

Curiously enough, Mr. Brocken had done something very rare with him: he had made a definite assertion unsupported by sufficient evidence. When he engaged Mrs.

Poole, it was on the verbal recommendation of a news-agent: she also looked neat and clean. Now her appearance at least was shown to be unreliable, the news-agent's good word, in retrospect, proved no more than a news-agent's good-nature, and Mr. Brocken himself by no means upheld the Poole-Simmonds alliance. Yet he had now no hesitation whatever in reaffirming his first favourable opinion. He was absolutely certain that Mrs. Poole would bring neither Mr. Simmonds, nor any other man, back into the house at night with the child Greta; and he was absolutely correct.

The moment passed; it was all over. Before Mr. Brocken's formidable eye, Tilly at once capitulated.

"Of *course,*" she said humbly, "of course, Simon, you know best . . . It was just such a shock, such a surprise, I'm afraid I made a *naughty* mistake." Her cheeks were still blotched with anger; she could control her voice more easily than her blood. She experimented with a chuckle. "I *did* put my foot into it, didn't I? But you mustn't be cross, because I'm very, very sorry."

"Thank you," said Simon stiffly.

He walked off. Behind his back Tilly made a funny face, to assure Jacqueline that the whole thing was only a joke. In the drawing-room (to which Simon did not return) she was very gay, laughing at her own silliness, and relating many amusing tales of mistaken identity. It was only towards the end of the evening that she dropped her flippant manner to sound a more serious note.

"Dear Isabel," said Tilly, "don't you think, don't you

really think that something should be done about Greta?"

Isabel, playing patience, scarcely heard and did not answer: she was nearly out. Jacqueline and Humphrey were reading. No one took any notice.

"Good night to you," said Tilly Cuff.

Her expression, as she left the room, was curious. If she was affronted, she did not show it; her look was rather demure. It was also anticipatory. Tilly's heels clacked up the stairs in a series of cheerful little taps; she was in a very pleasant humour.

Chapter 16

Tilly was gaining confidence. It did not come all at once: "A hard life?" Simon once exclaimed, in answer to some placatory remark of Isabel's. "Who hasn't had a hard life, since the last war? *I've* had a hard life. Why should Tilly Cuff be privileged to make herself a damned nuisance?" —and Tilly Cuff had wondered too.

She did not of course put the question in those words; but she wondered very much why Isabel had invited her to Chipping Lodge at all, and why, after she got there, no duties were expected of her, and why, above all, no period was suggested to her stay. It seemed inexplicable. When Isabel's letter arrived in Birmingham Tilly had read it with a certain malicious pleasure: so Isabel too (and at last) was feeling the servant shortage . . . she read it through again: there was no word about making herself useful; no doubt Isabel took the point for granted. But at least Isabel was not senile, and Tilly was ready for a change; there was an officious daughter-in-law whose eye she did not like, an ancient cook whose opinion of all companions was outspoken and impolite: moreover it was a rare pleasure to get in first with her notice. "Really, I must go back to my *people,*" said Tilly. "My cousin Mrs. Brocken, of Chipping Lodge—you don't know it?—it's one of those big old houses, quite historic, I believe, just outside London—my cousin really won't take 'no.' You do understand and forgive me, don't you?" The daughter-in-law forgave her readily; but was impressed all the same. Tilly left Birmingham with a flourish.

Thus she arrived at Chipping Hill prepared to cook. She would have made a great favour of it, but she would have cooked. Nothing of the sort was required. She found herself in Ruth's bedroom. She discovered that Simon had been turned out of it to accommodate her. "Buttering my paws," thought Tilly; and daily expected to hear that Mrs. Poole had left. But Mrs. Poole stayed. In Ruth's room, breakfast appeared on a tray. Little by little Tilly perceived that her position was for some reason not only secure, but privileged. When she had grasped the fact, the explanation that at once presented itself was that she had some hold over Isabel of which she, Tilly, was still ignorant.

How near the truth this was, and how far from it! Tilly's mind, poking and prying about the past, looked for an obligation on Isabel's side not moral, but legal. Could old Mrs. Massey, or Mr. Massey, have left her some substantial legacy, which Isabel had suppressed, and Simon only recently discovered? Was Isabel, in some strictly criminal sense, *guilty* of something? Was it in Tilly's power to send her absolutely to prison? Tilly fed upon the notion greedily, but without really believing in it; there was Simon to be reckoned with, the Brockens were the Masseys' solicitors: and though Tilly disliked Simon whole-heartedly, she acknowledged him to be both upright and perspicacious. He would never allow his sister-in-law to monkey with a will.

Cautiously, while her theory was still new, Tilly put it to a little test.

"I suppose no one," said Tilly, "would like to buy me a *lovely* house-coat?"

She said it at the tea-table, with a light, girlish laugh, looking up from the advertisement pages of a magazine.

"What's a house-coat?" asked Humphrey idly.

"My dear, you've seen your aunt in one again and again; they're worn instead of a dinner-dress. I've never had one," said Tilly wistfully. "It must be so nice to have something new." She sighed, and looked at the illustration again. "This one's brocade, peach or turquoise. Do look, Isabel; isn't it pretty?"

"How much is it?" asked Isabel.

"Fifteen *pounds.*" Tilly sighed again. "Well, it's no use wishing," she said bravely.

But it was. Both Jacqueline and Humphrey could detect, in Mrs. Brocken's pleased and cosy expression, the birth of a lovely surprise.

"Tilly," said Mrs. Brocken artfully, "will you give me eight coupons?"

This was where things nearly went wrong. Tilly had no coupons, because she had sold the whole book. "And why not?" enquired Tilly hardily. "Don't tell me you've never *bought* any!" Isabel had not, nor had Jacqueline; but there are circumstances in which virtue feels abashed; it is in general easier to be taken for a rogue than a prig. "We'll just have to see . . ." said Isabel vaguely. In the end, and despite strong opposition from Jacqueline, she sent off eight coupons of her own.

Tilly Cuff hung the garment in her wardrobe and thought about fur coats. (So a successful blackmailer, counting his first fifty pounds, begins to think in hundreds.) And she racked her brains. What was it she knew — as obviously she must — to Isabel's discredit? A long course of novelette reading suggested a secret marriage. If only Isabel had been married, in secret, before she was married to Mark! Wouldn't that make her a bigamist? Unentitled to Mark's money? But Tilly had never stolen forth, by night, to any shadowy chapel, there to overhear Isabel exchanging vows with some unknown male. She hadn't even chanced to pass a registrar's. . . . In cooler moments Tilly herself laughed the fantasy away as absurd. And in any case, why should Isabel, guilty of any crime from forgery up or down, so deliberately arouse the suspicions of its unwitting witness?

Tilly was baffled. A more agreeable nature might have seen a simple act of kindness; a more agreeable nature might have been right. But Tilly was at bottom a realist; consciously a ray of sunlight, in her heart she knew that no one really wanted her company. So she was baffled; her mind, continuing to poke and pry, could unearth nothing criminal in Isabel's past, and nothing more scandalous than one or two mild flirtations, certainly as apparent, at the time, to both Mark and Simon as to herself. It was a curious situation: feeling her way over thin ice, she found herself on solid ground; strong, while ignorant as to the source of her strength; and armed, however inexplicably, with a weapon of undoubted power.

Any one who believed that she had finished with the Pooles was mistaken.

Tilly allowed four or five days to elapse before returning to the attack. The unconsciousness of Isabel (her proposed cat's-paw) amused her. It amused her to say just a word to Mrs. Poole, and then, apparently, let the matter drop. She waited very happily; and in the meantime, out of sheer good-nature, said a word to Jacqueline Brown.

2

"Let me tell you this, dear," said Tilly, settling herself in the pantry for a chat, "if ever I make a mistake, I always own to it; and I think I may have been mistaken in my advice to you."

"Did you give me any advice?" asked Jacqueline, with deliberate obtuseness.

"Of course I did, dear, and of course you remember it," said Tilly, with a smile of understanding. "It was about you-know-who. But I'll tell you what I think *now*. Isabel's got very high principles. (And why shoudn't she have? She's led as easy a life as any woman alive.) And I believe that if Humphrey, for instance, got one of her companions into trouble, Isabel would take the girl's part. I don't think she'd make any objection to their marrying. And that's important, because it's Isabel who has the money, and *his* people are too far off to interfere."

Jacqueline, who had just finished preparing a salad, stood up. Her hands, untying her apron, trembled so noticeably that she let the strings hang, still knotted, behind her back. She said quickly:

"I must make a phone call. I must phone Celia. That's a woman who was in the ATS with me, I've had a letter saying she's in town — "

"I just mention it," said Tilly, "because naturally a girl's taking a risk. She's got to look ahead. But there are times when it pays. Because naturally, if a young man goes to his people and says he's going to marry a girl without a penny, a girl no one's heard of, well naturally they won't be pleased; and even if there's a very strong reason, they'll try and get him out of it. But Isabel's such a fool — "

"Miss Cuff," said Jacqueline, "damn you."

Was this any way to speak to her employer's guest? Certainly not. There was a difficult moment that night — the first difficult moment Isabel and Jacqueline had ever experienced — in Isabel's bedroom.

"Jacky, dear," said Isabel, "I can't quite believe it, but Tilly tells me — and really she seemed to mean it — Tilly tells me you *swore* at her."

"Yes, I did," said Jacqueline.

"But, my dear child — " Isabel's face was crumpled into

an expression of incredulous perplexity—"my dear child, *why?*"

Jacqueline bit her tongue.

"She annoyed me. That's all."

"But—but, Jacky, *dear,* that's no excuse for swearing at her. She annoys us all, sometimes . . ." Isabel sighed. "Tilly isn't as nice as she used to be. I hate to admit it myself, but it's the truth. And sometimes she says things she doesn't mean . . ."

"I won't swear at her again," said Jacqueline. "I promise." She took a quick step forward. Mrs. Brocken was seated at her dressing-table, brushing out her hair: it flared away from her head in a short curly halo, blond flecked with grey, lending to her simple face a look of peculiar youthfulness. Her lips, as she brushed, moved silently; she was counting up to a hundred. "Mrs. Brocken," said Jacqueline, "not every one is generous, like you. Or even scrupulous. I don't think Miss Cuff is . . ."

In the mirror, Isabel's eyes were troubled. She said gently,

"Tilly's had a very hard life; so we must make allowances. She can't hurt us, you know."

"But she can!" cried Jacqueline. "She says things . . ."

"You must just take no notice of them. As I do. I must say—*seventy-nine, eighty*—I was very glad when she stopped calling me Issy; I always hated it even as a child. And she can't blackmail me," said Isabel, with rather surprising matter-of-factness, "because I'm going to give her everything anyway. I'm just waiting for Simon to get used to the idea—and I should like Tilly to get a little nicer; but in the meantime, Jacky dear—*eighty-seven, eighty-eight*—don't pay too much attention, and always remember what I said, that Tilly's had a *very* hard life."

"I never forget it," said Jacqueline.

3

This was true. Tilly's wry little anecdotes of past employers had begun to weigh most burdensomely upon Jacqueline's spirits. Hitherto (as she told Humphrey) she had not looked very far ahead; and this chiefly (as she did not tell him) because of a certain possibility, in the immediate foreground, before which, as before a dazzling ray of light, she averted her eyes. To love and be loved, to marry and be happy—how simple and how tremendous a future! But if she were not loved? "Young men," said Tilly Cuff, "like to amuse themselves . . ." No young woman should have been better armoured against such thrusts than Jacqueline: she knew Tilly's past history, could even realize that Tilly was employing upon herself exactly the same tactics that Isabel had once employed upon Tilly. But the words stuck nevertheless, like burrs. In spite of every resolution to the contrary she began to be less frank, even a little priggish and defensive in her conversation with her friend.

Thus she set out to paint the Priory ruins alone. It was a fine afternoon, an afternoon for a picnic, but to fill a thermos just for herself was too much trouble; Jacqueline carried only her old paint box, and a sketching pad, and a bottle of water. The loosestrife was still in full bloom, and so happily disposed as to conceal the trickier bits of perspective; Jacqueline without difficulty outlined the shell of the bay-window in front, and the stump of chimney behind, and prepared to blob colour in between. She dipped her brush into the water; into the red, into the blue; and there for a moment let the brush lie, in a purple puddle, while she listened.

She was listening, she admitted it to herself, for Humphrey's step, in case he should have followed her. But how should he follow? Even if he looked for her, and did not find her, at the Lodge, was it likely he would remember a half-joking scheme to paint the Priory? The emotion Jacqueline felt was illogical: it was her own action that had put her thus in suspense, yet she was angry with Humphrey because he was not with her, and because she could not settle to her work for wondering whether he would come. How different this was from the first weeks at Chipping Lodge!—when she could go about her business unimpatient, tranquil in the knowledge that because they were under the same roof, with all time before them, no encounter had to be schemed for! What wealth it had been! They were still, certainly, under the same roof; but Miss Cuff was there with them, a perpetual third, and in Jacqueline's mind a seed of mistrustfulness was taking root. Had she been a little too quick to see that dazzling future, and to open her mind to it? A little too ready in response to what was perhaps no more than the casual attentions of a young man at a loose end? All young people have a great idea of their dignity, and rightly: men and women are often more generous, more disinterested—better human beings—in their twenties, than they will ever be again; and the world has a way of knocking them from their high ground. Jacqueline felt her dignity in danger, though in this case unjustifiably; and when Humphrey did come, she was angry still.

Seeing him, from the tail of her eye, cross the broken ground between the pavement and the broken house, she began to paint very busily; and had laid a second streak of purple (with too much blue in it) against a streak that was too red, before he reached her side.

"More pink, my girl," said Humphrey at once. "Why didn't you tell me you were coming?"

Jacqueline painted away.

"I didn't know what your plans were. . . ."

"Had you asked me," said Humphrey, with something of his Simon-baiting manner, "I should have returned a civil answer. But if art flourishes best in solitude, I'll go away."

"You know there's no question of art," said Jacqueline sharply. "I'm doing this to please Mrs. Brocken. It's going to be terrible, but I dare say she'll like it, and at least I shall have done my best."

Humphrey looked at her. She was sitting on the butt of a wall, her sketching pad on her knee, paint box and water bottle balanced beside her; whenever she took a brushful of paint the box wobbled, her fingers were rapidly becoming purple, and so was the water in the bottle. In all this — combined with her serious looks, the way she held her brush at arm's length and closed one eye — there was something so amateurish, yet so whole-hearted, as to be engaging — as Humphrey would have found had they both been better-humoured. As it was, her earnestness struck him as affected. He said disagreeably,

"Shall I tell you something, my darling? You're beginning to behave exactly like a companion."

"Am I?" said Jacqueline, mixing brick-red for the chimney.

"Yes, you are. Just now, when I called you 'my darling,' you bridled away. For heaven's sake!"

"But I am a companion," pointed out Jacqueline. "Will you tell Mrs. Brocken I'll be back to get tea?"

"I shan't see her," said Humphrey. "I'm going up to town."

He had spoken, and Jacqueline at once guessed it, on the spur of the moment. Humphrey did not go to London often; his fidelity to the mild pleasures of Chipping Lodge (which at first caused Isabel to ask him whether he was short of money) had come to be so taken for granted that this sudden departure was almost momentous.

"Shall you be back to dinner?" asked Jacqueline.

"I don't know," said Humphrey. "Does it matter?"

"Only because it's herrings, and it's a pity to have yours cooked if you won't be there to eat them."

"Then I shan't," said Humphrey. . . .

Isabel liked Jacqueline's picture very much; she said it wasn't modern. With an air of connoisseurship she pointed out the particularly clever way in which the colours of the flowers all ran into each other — a result only to be achieved, as she knew from sad experience, by painting unnaturally fast. Tilly Cuff also admired the daub, and advised Jacqueline that though the art of water-colour, as a professional asset, had rather gone out, it was not for that reason to be neglected. "For most employers give you a little something at Christmas," explained Tilly. "It used to be a handbag, before they went up so, now it's generally bath-salts — but in any case you have to make a return: and there's nothing more acceptable than a nice little painting of the house or the grounds, and it won't cost you a penny. Take my tip."

It was the last Jacqueline received for some time. Tilly's attention was thenceforward centred on the Pooles.

4

"My dear Isabel," said Tilly, "I know I'm no one here — " the phrase seemed to give her pleasure, for she repeated it — "I know I'm no one here, but I have my opinions and beliefs; and I can't see you neglecting a most obvious duty without speaking of it."

"Oh, dear," said Isabel involuntarily. "Let me give you some more coffee. . . ."

Tilly was down to breakfast. A suspicion had crossed

her mind that the tray sent up to her room was sent to keep her out of the way; so now she came down.

"I'm talking," continued Tilly, "about that child Greta. She's very intelligent. She ought to be sent to school."

"But she's been to school," protested Isabel. "She was fourteen this year."

"Don't you believe in raising the school leaving-age? Next year, of course, she'd have been made to stay till she was fifteen. But I'm not talking about that. She ought to be sent to a boarding-school."

"Good gracious me," said Isabel, in genuine and as yet cheerful surprise. "Greta's a bright little thing, I'm sure she is — except that she's so good and quiet I never see her — but I don't think she's at all *bookish.* Why boarding-school?"

"To get her away from her mother," said Tilly Cuff. She paused, aware that she had now not only Isabel's attention, but that of the whole breakfast table. "That woman's a bad influence. Do you know how the child spends her evenings?"

"Doing football pools," said Humphrey. "The other week they won two pounds."

"Exactly. That's bad enough. Teaching the child to gamble. But what is far worse is for Greta to see her mother painted and bedizened, every other night, to go dancing with a man she's picked up in the street."

If she shocked her hearers, it was far more by the virulence of her tone than by this coloured account of Mrs. Poole's recreations. She was like a person naïvely recounting dreams before an audience of Freudians. Even to Isabel's innocent mind the word "repressed" uncontrollably presented itself. Jacqueline said hurriedly,

"Not every night; only Wednesdays and Saturdays. And I think it's usually with Mr. Simmonds."

"A married man!" cried Tilly.

Isabel was quite interested. She knew Mr. Simmonds well, by sight: he was an estate agent; but she had never known he had a wife.

"Well, he has," said Tilly. "I've made it my business to find out. She lives with her people at Torquay. *Why* she left him I don't know — "

"You will," muttered Humphrey.

" — but it can't be for any creditable reason. If this affair with Mrs. Poole goes on, I'm not sure it won't be my duty to write to her."

"If you do," said Mr. Brocken, emerging unexpectedly from behind his paper, "you will undoubtedly lay yourself open to misconstruction, and possibly to heavy penalties." His grim eye placed her, not without relish, in the dock. Tilly, as always before any threat of bullying, at once retreated.

"I don't suppose I shall, of course. But doesn't it all show, really, that Mrs. Poole is quite unfit to have charge of the child? It's Greta I'm thinking of; and that's why I want Isabel to do the generous thing, and send her to boarding-school. It wouldn't cost so very much . . ."

This change of ground, this implicit accusation of meanness, was particularly cunning. Isabel could never bear to be ungenerous. She said doubtfully,

"If you really think so . . . and if Mrs. Poole thinks so . . ."

"She won't," said Tilly swiftly. "I just dropped a word — very tactfully, of course — and she wouldn't even discuss it. You must override her. You must send the child away."

So this was it, the point Tilly was aiming at. This was the objective she had set herself: the victory that was to crown her assault. The challenge was explicit in her voice, in her eyes, in the movement with which she snapped open her cigarette case. Before any one spoke she had lit a cigarette, and risen to her feet; no one attempted to detain her.

"Now Bogey's going walkie-walkies," smiled Miss Cuff. "Where's my Bogey-wogey?"

The Sealyham exploded from beneath her chair. Mr. Brocken, who had risen at the same moment, received the full impact of his solid body; but it was not Bogey upon whom he directed, as he left the room, his unspoken maledictions.

Chapter 17

To return to Isabel. Her demeanour at this time was a source of general wonder: she went about gentle, good-tempered, tranquil, the one person at the Lodge whose serenity Tilly could not ruffle. Mr. Brocken, having always considered his sister-in-law a fool, wondered least: Humphrey and Jacqueline both wondered and admired; none of them guessed that this serenity, this pleasantness, were the result of conscious effort.

Isabel was greatly perturbed. She had come (in Chipping Hospital) to the conclusion that Tilly Cuff was good: therefore — in the old phrase — deserving: yet what one might call the *results* of Tilly Cuff were all bad.

Sadly Isabel acknowledged it: sadly reviewed the disintegration, since Tilly's arrival, of all the pleasantness of Chipping Lodge. She thought of Simon: the successful domestication of her brother-in-law had been a great triumph to her; she had taken pride in seeing him settle at the Lodge as one takes pride in seeing some difficult, pedigreed cat settle on one's hearth; had felt he really liked staying with her. Now she felt he stayed only because his house had no roof. The happiness of Humphrey and Jacqueline, equally delightful, was something else Tilly had spoiled; Humphrey was more and more often in London, Jacqueline had grown prim and touchy, and the former's ironic references to the duties and habits of companions showed all too clearly where the trouble lay. As for the Pooles — poor Mrs. Poole, whom Tilly called a bad influence, and poor Greta, so fond of her mother — as for the Pooles, Isabel could only suffer, on their behalf, all they would suffer themselves should Tilly really give her mind to their welfare.

And this, it seemed, was what Tilly meant to do. "Wherever I go," said Tilly humbly, "I always try to do just one good deed: to leave behind just *one* person a little better off than I found them." Pinned down (by Mr. Brocken) to cases, Tilly described an old lady whom she had introduced to the methods of M. Coué, another old lady reconciled with her stepchildren, and a butler weaned from Philosophic Doubt. ("All no doubt better off as they were," said Mr. Brocken sourly.) But at the Lodge Tilly had found something really worth doing: if she could save a child, and such a child as Greta, from an influence so deleterious as Mrs. Poole's, then indeed would her stay have borne satisfying fruit.

"To me," said Tilly, "a child is something sacred. I suppose no one else here feels that." (Isabel winced.) "Your mother — " she addressed herself to Humphrey — "your mother would understand."

"Did you know there were four of us?" asked Humphrey.

"Oh?" said Tilly—a little taken aback.

"I've two sisters and a young brother. Aunt Isabel always forgets the rest of us, because she's never seen them. But I've an idea—speaking from my mother's point of view—that four children seem less sacred than one."

"If Ruth were here now," cried Tilly—with one of her little darts into gaiety—"she'd say you were a *bad,* ungrateful boy!"

It was with this same gaiety, prettily veiling the same earnestness, that Tilly dropped her tactful words to the Pooles. She dropped the first, it may be remembered, almost immediately after she got her house-coat. "Greta, tell me the capital of Egypt!" cried Tilly, popping into the kitchen with an atlas in her hand. "You don't know? I *thought* not—and that's why I'm going to give you this nice old atlas I've just found among my books. My dear child, you ought to be still at school!"

"Greta's bin to school," said Mrs. Poole.

"Quite so," retorted Tilly, "and if the Education Act were in force, she wouldn't have left. Well, we must see what can be done about it. . . ."

That was all; she scampered out, leaving the Pooles an out-of-date atlas and a rankling dread. Her second word was even briefer: she needed only to put her head round the door—"Oh, Mrs. Poole, such a wonderful plan for Greta! Mrs. Brocken's going to send her to boarding-school. You'll hear all about it in a day or two!" It was noticeable about this time that Greta appeared less often in the garden; she kept strictly within the Poole quarters, or walked down with Mrs. Poole to the shops in Station Road, always her mother's shadow. Even the Pooles, it seemed, were feeling the weight of the world at last: and if their apprehension was narrowed to a childish dread, it was about as much as they were capable of.

In the midst of all these distresses, however, Isabel possessed one great and unguessed-at source of strength. The truth was that she regarded Tilly as a punishment. Her thoughts on this point as on all others were incurably woolly; but she felt that if some one was taking the trouble to punish her, then some one would forgive her in the end. She was very sorry that Simon and Humphrey and Jacqueline and the Pooles had to bear her punishment with her, and so was taking particular pains to be agreeable and good-tempered herself. Her apparent serenity was in essence sheer good manners. She was good-mannered with her household. At the same time it could not be denied that she had a great gift for living in the moment, and could go with Tilly to a matinée, and enjoy the performance, and enjoy, afterwards, tea at a Corner House, in a sort of vacuum. She enjoyed *The Dancing Years* so much that she asked Simon to get tickets for it again. When the situation finally resolved itself, no one grudged her these care-free interludes; but at the time they surprised.

"The fact is," said Mr. Brocken once, in answer to a comment of Humphrey's, "that your aunt's mind is incapable of dealing with more than one sensation at a time. While pleasantly bemused by some simple entertainment, she is conscious of Tilly Cuff merely as a sharer, and therefore a heightener, of her enjoyment. I've no doubt," said Simon grimly, "that they both shed tears at precisely the same moment." (This was correct; any sad bit in a play, any well-tried piece of tear-jerking, was sure of an immediate and simultaneous response from both.) "Your aunt," continued Simon, "has just achieved a remarkable intellectual feat: she put together an ill-judged phrase in a sermon, and her own shabby treatment of Tilly Cuff; she then took action—an action which has already produced the most unfortunate consequences—but one which logically followed. We cannot expect any further mental activity for some time."

Humphrey, sitting on the edge of the bath (of course they were in the bathroom), said thoughtfully,

"Then you reckon we're in for an indefinite spell of Tilly, before Aunt Isabel comes to the point?"

"Not exactly," said Mr. Brocken, drying his hands. "Isabel is remembering her promise to me, to wait for some favourable moment. By which I mean, and I trust Isabel does too, a moment when Tilly shows herself capable of decent feeling. She has not," said Simon coolly, "done so yet."

"If that's what we're waiting for," said Humphrey, "my gum, we're going to wait."

Mr. Brocken nodded. He was not young, he was not impatient. He believed that the longer Tilly Cuff stayed at the Lodge, and the better Isabel got to know her, the readier Isabel would be to come round to his own viewpoint. For the money Isabel proposed to give away was in fact Mark's money; however unwillingly, Simon acknowledged, in Mark's widow, an affection for Mark that equalled his own. (Or very nearly; there were old memories of boyhood, old brotherly intimacies, that no woman could ever share.) Isabel would not give away Mark's money to any unworthy object. And with every day, thought Simon, Tilly Cuff was so proving herself. Give her rope, thought Simon. . . .

"So we wait," said Humphrey. "My gum, it's like being in a test-tube. We're all here in a test-tube, awaiting the result of an experiment. It's like—it's like Racine."

Mr. Brocken started.

"What do *you* know about Racine?" he enquired suspiciously.

"We did him in the Upper Fifth. With Doggers."

"With whom?"

"His name was Cairns. He taught us French. And he used to explain—" Humphrey frowned, evidently rummaging the débris of an expensive education—"that the reason they were all kings, and so on, was so that their moral problems wouldn't be obscured by economics."

"I gather that was dictated to you," said Simon.

"Yes, it was. But the thing is, Aunt Isabel is in rather the same situation. She's perfectly independent, she hasn't any children—"

"She has her duty to her kin."

"Quite, sir; but who are her kin? My mother, who's perfectly well off in New Zealand, and yourself, who—

who must be pretty comfortable, and me. I've no real claim on her. I should like to have this house, but in a way that would be an advantage to her, because of course Aunt Isabel could live with us as long as she liked. She's a perfectly free agent; and that, in these days, must be very rare."

Mr. Brocken replaced his towel and moved towards the door.

"Your aunt," he said, "does not, perhaps unfortunately, fit into the picture. The chief personages of Racine were left free in order to exercise their intelligence. Your aunt has no intelligence at all."

"Yet you expect her to rumble Tilly," said Humphrey Garrett.

Mr. Brocken paused.

"Your aunt is, after all, a gentlewoman," he said. "Let her get to know the creature" — and went out to find the subject of their conversation, Tilly Cuff herself, hovering sponge in hand outside the door.

"You greedy, *greedy* man!" cried Tilly. "I suppose I can go in *now?*"

"Certainly," replied Mr. Brocken.

2

In the end the period of waiting turned out to have been shorter than either Humphrey or Mr. Brocken anticipated. Tilly Cuff had been at the Lodge just under two months, though to every one except Tilly it seemed much longer; she had arrived towards the end of July, it was now the end of September; and there were only two weeks yet to run before the second and final show-down. During this next fortnight, however, Tilly's power for mischief reached its height.

"Simon," said Isabel, waylaying Mr. Brocken one evening in the hall, "Simon, dear, I want to ask your advice."

Mr. Brocken hung up his hat in silence. Though he was away from the Lodge from morning till night, and though he saw as little as possible of Tilly Cuff, he was aware of her influence, upon his sister-in-law, and the Pooles and the whole household, as a sort of infection. Distress of mind is catching; Simon took every precaution he could, came home later than ever (the grandfather clock was then striking ten) and successfully resisted every attempt of Isabel's to corner him alone. He said brusquely,

"I'm very tired, I've had a long day, I'm going to turn in."

"Do, dear. I'll come upstairs with you," said Isabel.

If it wasn't the Pooles, thought Mr. Brocken angrily, it was Isabel; was there no peace in the world?

"I'm going straight to bed," said he.

"I'll bring you a night-cap," said Isabel, "while you take your boots off."

At least this was better than cups of tea: old Mr. Massey, and then Mark Brocken, had each in turn left a fine conservative cellar, and Isabel had been trained in a sound school; she brought Simon a large pre-war whiskey.

"Because I know you must be worn-out, dear," she said

sympathetically. "And though I don't want to bother you, I must. Water or soda?"

"Water," said Simon.

Isabel added exactly the right amount. She could always remember anything Mark had told her. Simon looked at her almost approvingly.

"Simon," said Isabel, "Tilly won't stop talking to me about Greta."

"A topic one would imagine soon exhausted," said Mr. Brocken.

"She wants me," Isabel reminded him, "to send Greta to boarding-school. She's set her heart on it. And she keeps putting it to me as a duty, until I'm really not sure it isn't. I wish you'd tell me what I ought to do."

"Nothing," said Mr. Brocken unhesitatingly.

"But Tilly says — "

"Your protégée Tilly Cuff," pronounced Mr. Brocken, "is a pernicious mischief-maker. You may take it from me that she has no more real interest in the child than the man in the moon."

Isabel looked shocked.

"Oh, but I'm sure she has, dear. Don't you remember how she tried to teach Greta to sew?"

"And I remember what came of it," said Simon.

"That was just unfortunate." To Mr. Brocken's surprise Isabel laughed appreciatively; he did not guess that her mind had suddenly switched to Humphrey — bad Humphrey! — and his Colorado beetle; as usual, she had been unable to resist a crumb of amusement. "In fact," said Isabel, "it's one of Tilly's best points — "

"One of them?" interrupted Mr. Brocken. "Has she any others?"

"Of course, dear; we all have." Isabel paused. "For instance, she's very good to Bogey . . . What I was going to say was that I'm *sure* she takes a real interest in Greta. And when she puts it to me as a duty — "

"Have you consulted Greta's mother?"

"No. But Tilly has," said Isabel. "She *will* go into the kitchen, and I can't stop her. And I'm afraid Mrs. Poole didn't like the idea at all. And the trouble is, Simon, and this is what I really want to consult you about, that while I dare say it would be a very good thing for Greta to go to boarding-school, I feel it would be almost cruel to part her from Mrs. Poole."

"It would be worse than cruel," said Simon. "It would be wrong."

He spoke without reflecting, rather as he had once spoken to Humphrey Garrett. But this time reflection supported his judgment. He had no great opinion of the Pooles. He considered them incurably frivolous. They had not the slightest sense of conscientiousness. When they finished with some trashy magazine, they simply threw it away; Jacqueline Brown, for salvage, salvaged their leavings. Upon the same magazines they squandered their wages, upon equally trashy films, and upon cosmetics. They were inveterate gamblers. The one good thing in them was their mutual affection. But for that, one could write the Pooles off as worthless. Destroy that, and you destroyed the root of any other good to come. . . .

"I don't think much of them," said Mr. Brocken, "but they're fond of each other."

Isabel looked at him gratefully.

"That's just what *I* think, dear. And if Greta goes to boarding-school, it's bound to separate them — I don't mean just in term-time, but in all their ways. . . . Need I do anything about it?"

"No," said Simon. "Just put the whole thing out of your mind."

He was an abstemious man. The whiskey had undoubtedly heartened him, made him feel less tired; but no more than that. He believed the advice he had just given his sister-in-law to be perfectly sound, and certainly possible for her to accept. But he reckoned without two factors: the simplicity of the Pooles, and the subtlety of Tilly Cuff.

3

The simple Pooles were afraid. They were afraid of Tilly Cuff, and they were terribly afraid of the Education Act.

This admirable measure put the school-leaving age up to fifteen; it was to come into force the following year, and Greta had only just dodged it. (The phrase was her mother's, and succinctly defined the Poole point of view.) What they now feared was that Miss Cuff could in some way invoke the Act to send Greta to boarding-school.

"Nonsense," said Dora Tremayne.

It was the following afternoon; the Pooles were seated each under a drying machine, the curtain between their cubicles drawn aside to facilitate conversation; and Dora Tremayne had as usual popped in for news of the Lodge. As a rule this amounted to no more than the bare statement that all were okay; but the Pooles were rapidly being forced from their self-sufficiency. Their fears, overflowing into speech, overflowed upon Miss Tremayne.

"Nonsense," repeated Dora roundly. "The Act won't touch Greta — more's the pity. If you were both of you a bit better educated, you might at least understand the laws of your own land."

Mrs. Poole, looking unconvinced, observed that they neither of them wanted anything to do with the Law at all, it was better to keep clear of it.

"My good woman — " Dora never hesitated to employ this outmoded form of address — "the law's to protect you. It's nothing to be afraid of."

"Well, Greta isn't afraid of policemen," said Mrs. Poole, rather proudly. "I was, when I was a kiddie; but Greta's not. She asks them the way and everything."

"I ask 'em the time," corroborated Greta, with a giggle. "*If you wants to know the time, ask a p'liceman!*"

She sang the phrase, rather tunefully, her small voice echoing inside the drier; her mother joined in a reprise.

For a moment their volatile spirits soared. Miss Tremayne looked at the pair with exasperation; at the same time it occurred to her that perhaps such small bursts of melody quite often punctuated their conversation; they ended in very neat unison.

"Doesn't Mum sing nice?" asked Greta fondly.

"Very nicely indeed," said Dora. "I am glad to see I have reassured her."

Mrs. Poole was silent. She was not reassured in the least. The ways of authority were ineluctably mysterious to her; moreover a wartime experience of wardens and billeting officers and evacuation ladies had led her to accept the presence of authority under almost any disguise. A lady not unlike Miss Cuff would have sent Greta to Land's End, if Greta hadn't hid in the attic: why couldn't Miss Cuff send Greta to boarding-school? Hadn't she *said* she would? "Oh, Mrs. Poole, we've just made *such* a plan for Greta! Mrs. Brocken is going to send her to boarding-school!" But the Pooles knew well enough it wasn't Mrs. Brocken who menaced them, it was Miss Cuff, and the Education Act. Mrs. Poole had had a feeling that if any one could stand up to Tilly Cuff it was Dora Tremayne; now Miss Tremayne too said Greta needed more education. "But she's *bin* educated!" thought Mrs. Poole, in genuine bewilderment. "*I* never kept her back! I did her sums for her and everything!"

So she was silent. Miss Tremayne, on the point of returning to her desk, saw reflected in the mirror an expression of such complete and hopeless bewilderment that she halted. But what was there to say? How could one introduce, to such minds as the Pooles' (and in half a minute, in a hairdresser's cubicle), the notion that education might be not only useful, but pleasurable? And even more?

Miss Tremayne, seeking rapidly for some concrete example, remembered how once, on the way to an extremely painful interview with her solicitors, her eye had been caught by the name "Elizabeth Collins" over a shop front. It at once set up a most amusing train of reflection—Elizabeth Bennet in fact married to Mr. Collins, and the subsequent revolution at Hunsford: the rest of the journey passed quite pleasantly. That she had thus been spared a most lowering quarter of an hour, and arrived at her interview in excellent fighting trim, was a result, in the long-term sense, of education. But she could not convey all this to the Pooles: the most elaborate exposition (for which she had not time) would be boiled down, by them, to the simple fact that she could read. And Greta could read already: there was a *Film Pictorial* in her lap at that moment. . . .

"You must be nearly dry," said Dora. "I'll send one of the girls."

As soon as she was gone, Greta said softly,

"We can always do a bunk . . ."

Mrs. Poole nodded.

"If it comes to it. But it does seem hard, when we're settled so nice. I've liked that house."

"So've I." Greta lifted her voice again in a shrill little pipe. "'*Ours is a nice 'ouse, ours is,*'" sang Greta persuasively; but her mother did not join in. They waited for the girl in silence.

The Pooles were not reassured in the least. It had been easy enough for Simon to reassure Isabel; easy, and a great relief, to Isabel, to accept his flat statement that she need not send Greta to school. But the Pooles knew nothing of this decision taken, as among Olympian gods, on higher levels. Mr. Brocken himself couldn't have reassured them, for the simple reason that he couldn't have understood what it was they feared. He had no idea of the panics, the formless dreads, that drifted like fog shapes — swelling at a breath to enormous proportions — through their unfurnished minds. (Set Mr. Brocken down in the mind of Mrs. Poole, and he wouldn't have known where he was: that monstrous bulk, looming up like some Easter Island image — was *that* the Education Act?) The Pooles felt trouble coming upon them as swallows feel the approach of winter; but less fortunate than swallows, did not know where Cairo was.

Chapter 18

The Poole instinct was sound. Confronted by Isabel's personal brand of mild obstinacy, Tilly hit on a new and most fruitful approach.

Isabel had spoken to Tilly Cuff quite plainly, and with Simon's moral backing quite plainly told her that she, Isabel, was not going to send Greta to boarding-school; but perhaps unfortunately based her refusal on the attitude of Mrs. Poole. "If her mother doesn't want the child sent away," said Isabel, "then I think it's wrong to interfere." "Is that your only reason?" asked Tilly. "Yes, it is," said Isabel. "I am *not,* Tilly, thinking about the money." "You mean, if her mother wanted Greta to go to school, you'd pay?" "Yes, I should," said Isabel — anxious only to have the matter finally settled. It was no doubt with all this in mind, and seeing the opportunity to do good to the Pooles in spite of themselves, that Tilly made her next point.

"Where," asked Tilly, "is the child's father?"

This question, launched upon the Sunday lunch table, produced at first no more than a slight ripple.

"He's dead, dear," replied Isabel at once. "Mrs. Poole's a widow. Isn't she, Simon?"

"Certainly," agreed Mr. Brocken.

"You never know," said Tilly.

How did Mr. Brocken know? Because Mrs. Poole had said so. Examining the point at greater leisure, he admitted a possibility that Mrs. Poole had not been speaking the truth; but it was after all her own business. Widowhood, Mr. Brocken knew, was considered in some circles a particularly desirable state: his own Mrs. Evans was a widow — or said she was; it was almost a convention.

Simon dismissed the matter from his mind; but Tilly Cuff did not. It might have been thought (had any one thought about it) that she was setting herself a task altogether impossible: she had no right to cross-examine Mrs. Poole, no standing in the matter whatsoever; if in answer to the flat question, "Mrs. Poole, is your husband in fact dead?" Mrs. Poole returned the flat answer, "Yes, he is," there, surely, all investigation must end. But the Pooles were very simple, and already in a high state of tension owing to their fears of the Education Act. Tilly Cuff's method of approach was simplicity itself, and one which Mr. Brocken, as a solicitor, should have foreseen.

Mr. Brocken was not in fact present; but Jacqueline was, for Tilly had seen all the importance of securing a witness. Thus she had to watch for her moment; it was now more rarely than ever that Mrs. Poole came into contact with any other member of the household. On

Monday mornings, however, such laundry as was not washed at home had to be sorted and listed; Mrs. Poole, bearing the Poole bed linen and the kitchen roller-towel, met Jacqueline in the back passage and there called over each item for Jacqueline to write down. It was no great task, but more easily performed by two persons than by one, and Mrs. Poole, in the first halcyon period, had volunteered to co-operate.

"Six sheets," called Mrs. Poole, "and six pillow-slips. Six towels — "

The door from the hall opened. Tilly Cuff pattered through. She carried no forgotten table-cloth or bed linen; she had come with a definite, and quite different purpose.

"Mrs. Poole," said Tilly brightly, "I've just seen your husband!"

Mrs. Poole dropped back on her heels among the used sheets: white as the towel in her hand. "*Keep your wits, woman!*" thought Jacqueline suddenly, fiercely; but she could not give the warning aloud, and in that moment Mrs. Poole was lost. She spoke one word, and it betrayed her.

"*Where?*"

Tilly laughed, a high bark of triumphant mirth.

"My *dear* Mrs. Poole," she cried. "That was only my *joke!* I *have* just seen a man called Poole, only I think it was Pole, I heard him give his name at the Post Office. Asking for letters, you know. But it does *show,* doesn't it, how easily these tarradiddles are found out? Where *is* your husband, may I ask?"

Mrs. Poole moistened her lips. Too late, she said quietly, "I haven't got no husband. He's dead."

Tilly raised her eyebrows. She had taken to pencilling them, rather boldly; they made two black semicircles above her bright black eyes. She looked at Jacqueline.

"I'm afraid Miss Brown and I can't *quite* believe *that,*" she said. "Can we, Jacky? Of *course* your husband is alive; and I'm sure we're all very glad to know that little Greta has a father."

The door closed behind her; she knew, said Jacqueline afterwards, grimly, when to get out. Mrs. Poole did not move. Still crouched among the linen, the towel still in her hand, she seemed to collapse into herself like a hamstrung puppet. Jacqueline, moving her pencil at random over the page, said what she could.

"It doesn't matter, Mrs. Poole. I'm sure it doesn't matter. Oughtn't there to be a best table-cloth?"

Mrs. Poole raised a white, suddenly lined face. She said, "I left him. I left him for Greta's sake, because he was a brute. Can she — can she set him on to us again?"

"No," said Jacqueline. "Have you three tea towels?" — for she could think of nothing else to say.

2

Tilly, on the other hand, said a great deal. She was so glad to find a real means of doing good. She was certain she could find Mr. Poole — he couldn't be very old, he must have been in the Forces — and equally certain of his co-operation. "Mothers are always so *possessive!*" cried Tilly—"at any rate in *that* class; but a *man* will take longer views. Men always do. And if Isabel will pay Greta's fees—"

"But I won't," said Isabel. "At least, I haven't said I will—"

"But if her *father* asked you to?"

Isabel looked across the breakfast table at Simon.

"The question," said Mr. Brocken, "is purely academic." He regarded Tilly with open dislike. "Miss Cuff talks of finding Greta's father. May I ask what business it is of hers?"

Tilly met his eye.

"It's my business as a *Christian,*" she said gently. "I believe in the sanctity of family life. In my little way, I'm trying to *help.* After all, it's not a *very* common name."

The following day Simon paid another visit to his house in Kensington. So far as he could see nothing whatever had been done to it. Tarpaulins still sagged across the roof, still patched half a side. The only new feature was a notice tacked to the door-post: "Premises unsafe, danger, keep out."

Mr. Brocken surveyed it gloomily, and went on to Red Lion Place. Could he possibly sleep there? Put up some sort of cot, wash and shave at the hand basin? The idea appealed to him so strongly that he actually, during the lunch hour, enquired the price of a camp-bed at the Civil Service Stores. The sum was not exorbitant, but did not include bedding; the linen department was full of women.

Simon abandoned the whole project and returned that night as usual, but much later than usual, to Chipping Hill.

He was not late enough. At the end of the drive, waiting for him, stood the child Greta.

3

She had evidently been there some time; her face was pinched, and the Veronica Lake wave drooped limply over her forehead.

"Why aren't you in bed?" asked Mr. Brocken at once.

Greta pushed a skinny paw, cold as a fish, into his hand.

"Will you come into the kitchen?" she asked softly. "There's a nice cup of tea for you. Will you come straight in by the back?"

She was tugging at him as she spoke, like a puppy—but not from any puppyish exuberance. Not cold alone pinched her face, but also distress. Mr. Brocken looked at her uneasily, and without further question allowed himself to be hurried past the front-door, round the tongue of shrubbery, down the passage to the kitchen. To his surprise, for he had assumed Greta to be a messenger from Mrs. Poole, it was empty.

"Where's your mother?" asked Mr. Brocken.

Greta dropped his hand and stared at him defiantly.

"She's gone dancing with Mr. Simmonds. She didn't want to, but I made her. I thought it might take her mind off. It's me that wants to talk to you, because you've been ever so nice to us, and Mum said we'd bothered you enough."

"You have been no bother to me whatever," said Mr. Brocken. "You may say whatever you wish. Only let me say something first: if you are worried about Miss Cuff's interference in your affairs, remember that it is quite unjustified. You are not forced to take her advice, and no one can make you."

"It's not about school," said Greta. "They could send me, but I'd run away. It — it's the other thing she's going to do."

Greta paused. Her squirrel's eyes, fixed on Mr. Brocken, were no longer defiant, but so terrified that he pusillanimously averted his own. To look at the child just then was like looking at a small trapped animal.

"She's going to find my dad," breathed Greta.

"Nonsense," said Mr. Brocken automatically.

"It isn't nonsense to Mum and me," said Greta. "It's disastrous."

The unusual word came oddly from her lips, and at the same time impressively; Greta must have sought long before she found it; it did not belong to the Pooles' slipshod and stereotyped vocabulary. Mr. Brocken corrected himself.

"When I say 'nonsense,' " he explained, "I mean that it is nonsensical of Miss Cuff to take up such a position. How can she find your father?"

"I don't know," admitted Greta, turning away as the kettle began to sing. "But *she* does. She said so. There's societies and things, and something called Army Record, and Ex-Prisoners of War — she said if a man's been in the Forces you can just track him down. And everyone *was* in the Forces; and my dad was the right age."

Mr. Brocken reflected. All of this was true; he himself, attempting to find such a needle in a haystack, would follow precisely the same lines: from Army Record to S.S.A.F.A. There was a thousand to one chance, he supposed, of Tilly Cuff (presenting herself no doubt as some welfare-worker) being successful. Greta meanwhile had turned the gas up under the kettle, was warming the teapot, turning it carefully between her hands; even in the midst of her distress remembering the promised cup of tea. A good child, thought Mr. Brocken suddenly: a good daughter for a man to be fond of . . . He said gently,

"My dear, is it after all such a trouble to you to think of finding your father?"

"Yes," said Greta.

The kettle boiled; she measured tea into the pot, and filled it, and fetched two cups from the dresser.

"I can hardly believe — " began Mr. Brocken.

"You didn't know him," said Greta.

"Then tell me what he was like."

The child shivered.

"He used to shout at us," she said softly. "He used to come in at night, and throw things about, and shout at us for hours and hours. And sometimes he socked my mum. She never let him lay a finger on me, she used to put me in the cupboard; but I heard."

Mr. Brocken was deeply shocked. He knew that wives and children were sometimes ill-treated; he knew, because he read of such cases in the papers. It was a purely intellectual knowledge, on a par with his knowledge of the death-rate from tuberculosis. This was the first time it had ever approached him personally; and in the person of a child. He did not know what to say.

"So we ran away," continued Greta. "One morning, while he was still sleeping it off, Mum packed all our things, and we slipped out, and took a train to here. We'd have gone to — to Australia, but for the fare; and Mum was here in service once. And she got a job straight away as washer-up at Bob's; and he let her bring home the bits, and we had a room over the newspaper shop. Milk and sugar?"

"Milk, please," said Mr. Brocken.

"Okay. But Mum was on her feet all day long, and o' course she didn't see much of me; and then you turned up, and so we came here, and — and we've been happy ever since."

Mr. Brocken had never yet seen Greta cry; she was crying now, hopelessly and unbecomingly. Her Veronica Lake hair-do was all awry, pushed back behind both ears; nothing softened the tragic mask of her face.

"My dear child — " began Mr. Brocken helplessly.

From the depths of her misery, Greta spared him compassion.

"It's lousy for you, isn't it? It's not your funeral. But I got to talk to some one. . . . What I want to know is, why can't she leave us alone? What have we done to her?"

"Miss Cuff," said Simon, with an effort, "believes she is thinking of your welfare. She believes school would be good for you. And as your mother can't agree — "

"But Mum's done everything for me!" cried Greta passionately. "She got me orange-juice and cod-liver and everything; she did all the clinic told her. Why should my dad have a say-so?"

"Because in the eyes of the law," said Simon, "his is the legal right."

"Does that mean because Mum married him?"

"Exactly. That makes him your legal guardian."

"So if she hadn't married him we'd be okay?"

"My dear child," said Mr. Brocken, "if your mother hadn't married your father, you wouldn't be here."

Greta gave him a long, gentle look.

"It's because I was on the way she did it. So I wouldn't be a little basket. She'd do anything for me, Mum would. If we'd only known!"

There was a considerable silence. Simon drank his tea: it was there before him, so he drank it. Greta drank hers; she had stopped crying, but every now and then a sob rose in her throat. Sometimes she choked it back, sometimes it defeated her, and the short tragic sound escaped. So they were sitting, one on either side of the clean kitchen table, when the door opened upon Mrs. Poole.

She was arrayed in more than usual splendour. To the bodice of her tomato-coloured gown was pinned a great bunch of artificial orchids: more orchids bloomed among the mazes of her ruddy curls. The diamonds with which Woolworth has outdone Golconda gleamed in her ears. But her face was Greta's face, small and pinched.

"It's no good," said Mrs. Poole. "I couldn't bear it. I told him I was feeling faint, and he brought me home straight away."

"He know what's up?" asked Greta anxiously.

Mrs. Poole hesitated.

"I had to tell him, love. I couldn't keep it back. But I made it sound joking-like. He won't worry." She glanced at Mr. Brocken indifferently. "So you got him here after all, did you?"

"He doesn't mind," said Greta swiftly. "He's not angry with us."

"That's kind," said Mrs. Poole, without irony. She pushed the fur from her shoulders and sat down next to Greta's place. "Well, this is it," she said wearily. "I might have known it was too good to last. We dodged the bombs all right, but this is it."

Greta slipped an arm round her mother's naked shoulder.

"Cheer up, Mum . . ."

"How can I cheer up, when it's all beginning again? *She* won't let it rest, that I do know. She'll write letters to the high-ups . . ."

"Mum," said Greta urgently, "when you married Dad, are you sure it was legal?"

"So far as I know. He put 'bachelor.' And I had no ties."

Mr. Brocken coughed.

"Has it struck you," he asked, "that your husband may be dead? If he were in the Forces, as is extremely probable, it is possible he has been killed. To know this as a certainty would surely be a great relief to you. Moreover, you may be entitled to a pension."

Mrs. Poole shrugged.

"We don't want his pension. We just don't want anything to do with him. . . ."

Greta placed a tea-cup by her mother's hand, and for a moment Mrs. Poole's face relaxed.

"That's just what I wanted," she said. "There's nothing like a nice cup of tea, is there? P'raps Mr. Brocken will have another?"

But Simon had pushed back his chair and begun to pace up and down the kitchen.

"If your husband should reappear," he said, "he undoubtedly has authority over Greta. I may say I consider the possibility remote. On the other hand, if you will allow me to make enquiries myself, we may establish the fact of his death. You say you don't want a pension, and indeed it might be difficult to substantiate your claim. But wouldn't it be any comfort to you to know that he died a brave death on the battle-field? Wouldn't you like to have that memory for Greta? And when you think of Greta's future, as I'm sure you do, might it not be a help and a guide to think what his wishes would have been for her? Leave this business of school out of it," said Mr. Brocken, "but consider, I beg of you to consider, whether Greta is to go through life with none but bitter memories of her father."

Some minutes passed. The two Pooles, seated close together on the farther side of the table, had followed his words with deep attention; but their faces were stubborn. At last Mrs. Poole spoke.

"My own mother," she said slowly, "Greta's grandma, came to a very sad end."

"Well?" said Mr. Brocken.

"Yes," said Mrs. Poole. "She was seventy. And she went out in the black-out, to see a neighbour that had just been brought to bed. A very cold night it was, snowing and freezing. And coming back she thought she'd take a short cut across the allotments. She got in, see, and she couldn't get out. There was some booby had had his potatoes stole, he'd fastened up the other gate with a bit of barbed wire, and what with that and the black-out, she couldn't get out. When they found her in the morning her apron was all torn on it. So it was death from exposure, and every one was very sorry. She still had the bit of washing she'd brought back, in a parcel under her arm." Mrs. Poole wiped her eyes. "Well, she was seventy; you might say she'd had her life; but she was a gay old thing just the same. . . . Why I tell you this is because when you say, 'Maybe he died on the battle-field,' it just cuts no ice. I think *she* died just as brave."

"Undoubtedly," said Mr. Brocken. "Performing a charitable act . . . yes, undoubtedly."

"It wasn't charity to her," said Mrs. Poole sharply. "It was something she did every day of her life. Well, she didn't think much of my husband; and she was right. 'Clear out,' she said, 'and keep Greta away from him, and mind you look after her.' Because she'd looked after me the best she could. And I did. Now you say, he died so brave, what would *he* have wanted for Greta? I'll tell you: he'd have said, 'Put her in the box factory at fourteen, and she'll bring her money home to me.' And I say, my mother died just as brave as he did, why shouldn't I do what *she* told me? I've never left Greta, not for so much as a day. And as for her future, we've got it all planned; she's going as apprentice to Madame Esmé."

"I'm going to be a Beautician," murmured Greta.

"They get good money," said Mrs. Poole, "and it's nice work. And that's another reason we don't want to leave here, because Madame Esmé's some one we know, and there's that Miss Tremayne there too. I can see you mean well," said Mrs. Poole, "but you just don't understand. If Jim's dead, I'd be glad to know it; but I just won't take any risk."

Again silence fell. Greta, indeed, from nervous excitement and the late hour, was almost asleep. Her head drooped against her mother's shoulder; Mrs. Poole gently pulled up her fur to make a nest of warmth.

"I'll just give her a minute or two," she said softly, "and then we'll go to bed. You've been ever so kind, and I'm sorry Greta troubled you; because what can you do?"

Chapter 19

What could Mr. Brocken do? If anything?

He considered the problem carefully: first that same night, before he slept, when his thoughts remained merely unhappy and confused, and again in the morning, at his office, where his brain began to work more satisfactorily. The results of this second cogitation were indeed highly rewarding: Mr. Brocken, who at Chipping Lodge had been unhappy because he did not see what he could do, in Red Lion Place absolutely welcomed the conclusion that he could do nothing, because he had also reached the conclusion — in those sane, familiar, unemotional surroundings — that nothing needed to be done. Let Tilly Cuff exhaust herself on a wild goose chase: the man Poole was quite possibly dead, or if living had quite possibly changed his name — though this was a more difficult matter than it used to be. In any case, it was long odds against Tilly laying hands on the fellow; she had, Mr. Brocken reminded himself, no standing. . . . Nor had she the money to pay Greta's school fees herself, and Mr. Brocken was pretty certain that on this point Isabel would not waver. Isabel could be extremely stubborn, and though it was a quality he usually deplored in her, and never more than during the last months, he now admitted its usefulness. With her brother-in-law's advice to back her own instinct, Isabel would not budge; and so the whole thing would blow over, and there was nothing for any one to do.

Thus reasoned Mr. Brocken, who in the kitchen, under the beseeching eyes of Greta, had shown himself so genuinely sympathetic. But the truth was that to sympathize came unnaturally to him: he rather disapproved of sympathy, as exhausting to the sympathizer and enervating to the recipient; the reaction which now set in was so strong, indeed, that Simon's annoyance with Miss Cuff very soon began to embrace the Pooles as well. They should have had more sense. With only a modicum of sense, thought Simon resentfully, they would simply have sent Tilly Cuff about her business. (He could not enter the mind of Mrs. Poole, where now the Easter Island images loomed ever more menacing.) Undoubtedly they should have had more sense; since unfortunately they had not, the only course for a rational man was to avoid their company.

During the days that followed Simon came home even later than usual, and if Greta was at the gate, or lurking about the shrubbery, showed so formidable a face that she feared to address him. He showed the same face to his sister-in-law; he re-entrenched himself in detachment. An embittered ostrich, he buried his head in the sand, and thus procured for himself (what no one else at this period enjoyed) a brief holiday from mental distress. Had Isabel behaved so, Simon would have been first to point out her foolishness; but then Simon had a brain to be benefited by such a holiday, whereas Isabel, in his opinion, had not. So he buried his head in the sand — but not for long; only for these few days, only until the Pooles gave notice, when Isabel herself mildly and innocently pulled it out again.

Humphrey, who had a turn for humorous caricature, about this time made a little prophetic drawing of his aunt as Alice in Wonderland, clasping an ostrich instead of a flamingo on the royal croquet ground: the bird's expression of dignified repugnance, as it twisted up its head into Alice's face, was extraordinarily like Mr. Brocken's. Isabel laughed till she cried, and gave Humphrey a scolding. He did not show the sketch to Jacqueline. An unfortunate by-product of the whole affair had been an open quarrel between Humphrey and Jacqueline Brown.

2

Though no longer on good terms with each other, they had not before quarrelled openly: their relationship was chequered. The deliciousness, the exquisite hush and tranquillity, of their first days at the Lodge, was irretrievable; but now and again, when Jacqueline pulled herself together, they could be friendly and easy for an hour or an afternoon. It was Jacqueline's fault they were estranged — and yet not her fault altogether: she had made a great effort to forget Miss Cuff's opportunist advice, and believed that she had succeeded. There were some lessons Jacky was in no danger of learning, and how to make an advantageous surrender of her virtue was one of them — nor had she ever attributed to Humphrey the selfish weakness necessary, on the male side, to such transactions: on this point Tilly had done no more damage than is done to a fruit by rubbing the bloom off. What Jacqueline was in danger of learning was not venality, but self-pity. "I was born," she once told Humphrey, "to be the hanger-on of a great house" — and could then, hardly three months before, say it unresentfully, simply admitting what was perhaps a weakness in her character, but knowing Humphrey thought no worse of her for it, and perfectly aware that a passive disposition had its compensations. Tilly's conversation showed her the reverse side of dependence, and in particular its terrible condition of insecurity.

"The trouble with me," said Jacqueline, "is that I'm not educated."

"You're very nice as you are," said Humphrey lazily.

They were sitting perched side by side on the terrace balustrade; Mrs. Brocken, much impressed by Jacky's water-colour, had driven her out to draw from the antique. (All artists, said Isabel knowledgeably, drew from the antique; and in the absence of plaster casts the two statues would do just as well, or even better, because they weren't dusty. As a girl Isabel had drawn from plaster casts herself, and frequently been confused between dust and shadow.) Jacqueline obediently took out her sketchbook, and finding Humphrey on the terrace already, and remembering uneasily her own behaviour at the Priory, let him sit beside her and laugh at her in the old way. They neither of them meant to quarrel; but Humphrey laughed once too often, and when he remarked that she'd better stick to companioning, for she'd never make an artist, Jacky snapped shut her book.

"I'll never make anything," said she. "The trouble with me is that I'm not educated."

"You're very nice as you are," said Humphrey.

"Thank you," said Jacqueline. "How patronizing."

"Darling, don't be an ass," said Humphrey.

"I'm not an ass. I'm simply stating a fact—just as I'm stating a fact when I say I'm not educated, in the sense that I'm not equipped to enter any decent profession. I went to school till I was seventeen, but I didn't even learn how to work."

"You'd better tell that to Tilly Cuff," said Humphrey. "It might make her lay off Greta."

Jacqueline raised her eyebrows.

"I suppose you think Greta's very nice as she is too?"

"Yes, I do."

"I don't agree."

"Then you're wrong. I like Greta very much."

"You know nothing about her."

"I know she doesn't make a nuisance of herself, and I know she's fond of her mother. A quiet and affectionate female, of whatever age, cannot be improved."

Jacqueline laughed. Her laugh as a rule was pretty, frank without being hoydenish; now, because she was forcing it, it curiously echoed Tilly Cuff's.

"But this is extraordinary!" she exclaimed. "This isn't

Victorian, this is—this is Japanese! Do you really mean that because Greta has an affectionate disposition, she shouldn't be given a chance to find out whether she has brains as well?"

"I mean," said Humphrey stubbornly, "that I don't think Greta has any more brains than a rabbit. And if she had, I'd still reckon her disposition was more important. She's wrapped up in her mother—"

"Exactly. Which isn't always healthy, you know."

"Oh, bull's-eyes," said Humphrey rudely. "A child loves her mother, a mother loves her child, so you look up a piece in a text-book and take them away from each other. I never in all my life heard such pernicious balderdash."

They sat in angry silence; they had each of them gone farther, and in opposite directions, than they originally intended, and were now too angry to find a way back.

"Need we discuss it?" said Jacqueline coldly.

"No, by gum, we needn't," said Humphrey; and swung himself over the balustrade on to the lawn below.

3

When Isabel told him that the Pooles had given notice, Simon, stout in his newly recovered detachment, replied that it was just as well.

"But I don't think it is, dear," said Isabel unhappily. "They've been so good and contented—and it does seem hard that they should be driven from their home."

"This isn't their home."

"They've lived here six years, Simon. I know Tilly says I take no interest in them, and I didn't, in the sense of interfering; but you can always *feel* a happy kitchen, because if the kitchen isn't happy the house isn't either." Isabel paused. "Of course, I didn't *take* their notice."

"A pity," said Simon.

"I just told Mrs. Poole she could go *without* notice if ever she felt she had to."

"I fail," said Simon, "to see the distinction."

"I dare say, dear. But Mrs. Poole did, and it eased her mind. And I promised her I wouldn't send Greta to boarding-school." Isabel paused again. "And I told her — I told her that quite soon Tilly would have other things to think about. . . ."

It was plain that Isabel (a more practised sympathizer than her brother-in-law) had done something. No doubt the Poole mind was eased considerably. Mr. Brocken's was not.

"And what did you mean by that?" he demanded suspiciously.

"About Tilly, dear? I mean when I tell her about the money," said Isabel simply. "You asked me to wait, Simon, and I've waited; but I think it's been long enough. Tilly isn't," said Isabel moderately, "very nice. I've tried to close my eyes to it, but I can't. I did hope she'd get nicer, so that telling her wouldn't be quite so dreadful; but now if she gets any worse I'm afraid I mayn't be able to tell her at all."

The corollary was so unexpected that Mr. Brocken spent some moments examining it. "Do you expect," Humphrey had asked, "Aunt Isabel to rumble the woman?" Isabel had apparently done so. "Not very nice" was, on her lips, a phrase of strong condemnation. But what followed? Admitting that Tilly might deteriorate still further, Isabel proposed not to delay, but to hurry on her insane sacrifice, before its object became too blatantly unworthy. . . .

"Tilly *needs* something to think about," explained Isabel. "That's her whole trouble."

From this moment Mr. Brocken lived in a state of irritated apprehension. The knowledge that Isabel might at any moment give away forty thousand pounds haunted him even at his office, and put him in the unnatural state of being uneasy all the time he was away from Chipping Lodge. This was serious; for it will be readily realized that by this time Mr. Brocken's office in Red Lion Place had become far more than his place of business. It was his refuge as well. As a rabbit into its burrow, as an infantryman into a slit-trench, so Mr. Brocken plunged each morning into its dingy portal. Whatever problems the day might bring — whatever messes his clients had been getting themselves into — the solution of these problems, the extricating of those clients, was certain to prove far less harassing than the problems left behind at Chipping Lodge. Now all this was changed; and with the peace of his days destroyed, and his nights ruined by calculations, Mr. Brocken's existence became so altogether burdensome that when this last preliminary period ended, he felt almost relieved.

He, like his sister-in-law, had been waiting for the moment: he, with much the same sensations as when he had waited for the moment when a V-I cut out its engine, she, with pleasanter expectancy, for a moment of friendliness and good feeling that would make all smooth. But the moment, when it arrived, arrived precipitately, and as the result of a most painful scene.

It was a wet Sunday afternoon. Jacqueline had just carried the tea-tray into the drawing-room; the rattle of china woke Isabel from her nap on the sofa, and at the same instant (a common domestic phenomenon) Mr. Brocken, on his bed, also awoke, and Humphrey awoke on his, and the two men came downstairs together. They were all a little somnolent; it was a Sunday afternoon like any other, lazy because of the rain, but rather comfortable. Mrs. Brocken looked at Humphrey and wondered whether he would play piquet with her; Simon cast a preliminary glance over the *Observer* crossword; Jacqueline meditated letter-writing. She held the caddy in her hand, ready to make tea as soon as the kettle boiled, and since it was the electric kettle, in the dining-room, had left the drawing-room door open to catch the first rattle of its lid. Through this open door the dog Bogey, smelling like a grampus, now strolled.

He had not long finished a fish dinner; his friends shunned him. "Poor fellow!" exclaimed Mrs. Brocken — but fending him off. "Down, Bogey!" cried Jacqueline.

Full of frustrated affection, Bogey insinuated himself under Simon's chair and rubbed his odorous muzzle up and down against Simon's calves.

"Why you keep the animal!" ejaculated Simon, kicking violently backwards. "He ought to have been dead years ago! He ought to be shot!"

None of them noticed Tilly Cuff, who had appeared in the doorway just in time to hear Simon's words. Their effect on her was terrifying.

4

She had passed the afternoon alone, and perhaps her thoughts had been bitter. Perhaps even the new house-coat in her wardrobe, even her belief in her secret power, and her plans for using it, could not always drive away apprehensions for the future. Perhaps she had looked in the glass and seen there a face so inexorably sealed for ill-fortune that no other fortune seemed possible. Entering the drawing-room, she heard Simon's words, and saw the dog cringe forth from under his chair; she ran forward and dropped on her knees and gathered Bogey into her arms and began to wail. Wailing, crooning, she rocked back and forth with the animal clasped to her bosom, railing against their common fate.

"We're not handsome, are we, my darling?" wailed Tilly. "We're simply old and worn-out and faithful — so we ought to be shot! We can't help it, can we, we can't help growing old! We can't help eating what's thrown to us, and then being abused for it! But we ought to be shot all the same, because we're old and worn-out and we don't die . . ."

No one tried to stop her. They were all too much horrified, too much embarrassed, to speak. Mr. Brocken could have pointed out that Bogey at any rate had led a consistently pampered life; but it was not, as even he realized, a moment for the voice of reason. Tears streamed down Tilly's face; Bogey licked them away. Three persons at least silently accused him of playing his part for all it was worth, but of Miss Cuff's genuine agony there could be no doubt. For once she had forgotten herself, the springs of bitterness were unsealed and could not be stopped again: with raddled cheeks and distorted mouth, grotesque and tragic, she abandoned herself to despair; and it was the final touch of grotesque tragedy that the partner of her sorrows was a Sealyham smelling of fish.

Isabel rose. She made no move towards Tilly, but walked straight to the door. She said,

"Tilly, will you come upstairs, please? I have something to say to you."

5

With horror, with pity, the other three watched a succession of emotions alter Tilly's face. She was first of all, immediately, terrified. She realized what she had done: she had made a scene; she knew what happened to companions who made scenes. And she had given away her age.

Worse, she had given away her fears. She had dropped the mask of youth and brightness which had (perhaps? who knew?) deluded Humphrey and Jacqueline into thinking of her as a contemporary. So she must reassume it. With little dabs of hand and handkerchief she dried her cheeks, smoothed back her hair, coaxed the curls above her ears: terror gave place to secretiveness as she ran over in her mind what she had done, what she had said: in a moment her line was taken, she sat back on her heels and faced them all with a jaunty smile.

"Dear me!" said Miss Cuff gaily. "Am I in for a wigging?"

"No, no," said Simon. "No; of course not." And he added obscurely, "I must beg your pardon."

"For being so *brutal* to poor Bogey? I should jolly well think you ought!" cried Miss Cuff. "I can't *bear* to hear such things! And Jacky and Humphrey just stood by — "

"We knew he didn't mean it," said Humphrey uncomfortably.

"But did Bogey know? *That*'s the point." Miss Cuff jumped youthfully to her feet. "And now what does Isabel want me for? Why am I summoned upstairs like a naughty girl?"

"You needn't go," said Mr. Brocken. "If I were you I shouldn't. It can be nothing of importance."

But Tilly looked at him shrewdly; looked at Humphrey and Jacqueline. Their faces told her two things: that they knew what Mrs. Brocken was going to say, and that it was worth hearing.

"Oh, well," said Tilly. "We mustn't hurt poor Isabel's feelings. So long, chaps."

She pattered out; they heard her high heels tapping up the stairs.

An hour later Jacqueline, passing through the hall, saw the door of Tilly's room open on the landing above. Mrs. Brocken came out alone; she had evidently been crying. When she saw Jacqueline she asked her to take Tilly a cup of tea, and some very thin bread and butter; and then went on to her own room.

6

Tilly did not come down to supper. Soup, and more thin bread and butter, were left outside her door. But Isabel courageously appeared, her eyes swollen and her face thickly powdered, and took her usual place at the head of the table.

"Well?" said Simon. "Have you done it?"

Isabel nodded. She looked so exhausted that it seemed unkind to question her; but the general curiosity was naturally intense.

"Was it awful?" asked Jacqueline anxiously.

Isabel nodded again. Humphrey got up, walked round the table, kissed her, and walked back.

"I'm sure we all sympathize with you," said Mr. Brocken, in a nonetheless business-like tone. "The point is, how did she take it?"

"Dreadfully." Isabel wiped her eyes. "We've all been

wrong about Tilly. At least, I always did say she'd have accepted Mr. Macgregor; but I never guessed she was passionately in love with him."

"Humph," said Simon.

"Was that what she told you?" asked Humphrey.

"Yes, dear. As soon as I'd told *her* about—about the letter, it all come out. She fell in love with him at first sight. She never gave a sign of it because she was afraid—this is what's so pathetic—she was afraid of putting herself forward. I never realized till now that we'd been so cruel to her."

"Nonsense," said Mr. Brocken robustly. "No one was cruel to her."

Isabel sighed.

"I'm sure we didn't think we were. We thought she was treated just like one of ourselves. But she wasn't, you know: she only had one new evening dress all the time she was with us, and that only cost four pounds."

"Has she just reminded you of it?" asked Jacqueline.

"Yes, dear. I'd quite forgotten; but it was a blue taffeta. So you can see how she felt; and she didn't even imagine Mr. Macgregor would think of her, she was so used to being overlooked. But she loved him all the while, and that's why she never married." Isabel looked round the table; the lack of responsive sympathy was becoming marked. "I was surprised too," she admitted ingenuously. "Somehow I never thought Tilly would have another chance. But she had; she had three. One was a doctor, and one was a parson, and one had an hotel at Lucerne. Tilly

said Isabel, unconsciously obeying this law. "It will make it seem more businesslike. Would you like to go up after supper, dear?"

"No, I should not," said Mr. Brocken. "And if Tilly has been crying all evening, she will hardly be fit to receive me."

Isabel hesitated.

"Perhaps you're right, dear. She — she doesn't look very nice; and she did say she was going to cry herself to sleep. But you'll tell her to-morrow?"

"If you insist," said Mr. Brocken. "I will tell her when I return from town."

His sister-in-law gave him one of her unexpectedly shrewd looks.

"I am not going to change my mind, Simon. One day won't make any difference."

"I was in no hopes that it might," said Mr. Brocken, with measured bitterness. "You won't come to your senses in twenty-four hours. You'll never come to your senses. I merely wish to avoid losing a morning's work."

He left the table and went up to his room.

7

During the remainder of the evening Humphrey played six games of piquet with his aunt and cheated himself to let her win; unnecessarily, as it turned out, since Isabel held very good cards and played with all her usual determination. It was remarkable how quickly her spirits could rise; the kindness of her nephew, and a couple of repiques, rapidly restored her to cheerfulness. Outside the rain fell heavily; a westerly wind drove it against the windows, and Jacqueline, who sat watching the game in silence, felt the sound getting on her nerves; but it didn't, apparently, get on the nerves of Isabel. The dark sky darkened the room, usually, at that hour, still light and cheerful. Presently Jacqueline could bear it no longer, and got up to switch on the lights.

"That's better," said Isabel approvingly. "I'm sure I don't know why we should sit here in the gloom."

"Because we feel gloomy," said her nephew.

"*I* don't," said Isabel stoutly. "I feel tired, and I think I'll go to bed; but I don't feel gloomy in the least. And to-morrow I shall go and see Dora Tremayne. I shall *enjoy* living with Dora," said Isabel. "When you get to my age, if you haven't your husband, there's nothing so nice as being with some one who was young when you were young, and lived in the same place, and knew all the same people. I look *forward* to living with Dora — "

"Aunt Isabel," said Humphrey, "have you spoken to her yet, or is it to be a lovely surprise?"

Mrs. Brocken looked at him triumphantly.

"My dear boy, Dora suggested it herself. After Tilly came, when Simon got so disagreeable, Dora *suggested* it. Because we were both young together — "

"All right," said Humphrey. "You win. You're protected. What's going to happen to this house?"

Isabel, on her way to the door, paused.

"It's yours, of course, dear—if Tilly doesn't mind. I'd much rather it stayed in the family, because I've had a great deal of bother keeping hold of it, as poor Simon knows only too well. But perhaps we should ask Tilly first."

"Then I shall fight for it," said Humphrey, "tooth and nail."

Isabel kissed him fondly and trotted out. Humphrey turned back and saw Jacqueline, still silent, by the card table. At something in her face—an aloofness, a disapproving chill—his own cheerful expression altered.

"And what's the matter with you?" he asked brusquely.

"I am not," said Jacqueline, "convinced."

"Convinced of what, for heaven's sake?"

"That all—" she was imitating (how curiously! as though his turn of speech had become hers) his own mixture of slang and preciseness—"is hunky-dory."

Humphrey turned back to the door.

"Then you're simply being psychic," he said, over his shoulder. "Aunt Isabel will be all right with Dora, Tilly will gallivant off to some Hydro, and I shall become the hermit of Chipping Lodge. It's a damn good arrangement all round."

"It's too good," said Jacqueline. "Too perfect. Like a fable or a fairy story. It can't happen. That's all."

Chapter 20

At least Mr. Brocken had not next morning, in Red Lion Place, to worry about what might be happening behind his back at Chipping Hill. It had happened. He knew the worst. It was bad enough; the notion of making over his brother's money to Tilly Cuff was still extremely repugnant to him; but he was determined to save Isabel not one hundred a year, but at least two, out of it; she would pay practically no income tax, and by joining forces with Dora Tremayne could expect a certain modest comfort: the house, made over to Humphrey, was something else saved from the wreck. Because all this was as good as settled, even on that Monday morning, when Isabel made him promise to come back to dinner, and with an interview of the most disagreeable in prospect, as Mr. Brocken turned into Red Lion Place his spirits lightened.

What kindness and piquet did for Isabel, bricks and mortar did for him. The solidity of the old buildings (they had been bombed, but not bombed out) matched something solid in his own character; if they were undecorative, so was he; and none the worse, thought Simon, for that. In the tiled entrance hall a charwoman was gathering together her swabs and brushes; and she wasn't decorative either, but her puckered old face—one eye slightly distorted—was familiar, and therefore agreeable. Simon never spoke to Mrs. Grum, and Mrs. Grum never thought of speaking to Mr. Brocken; but each was a fixture in the other's world, and therefore valuable.

Believing himself to be free of Chipping Hill for at least nine hours, Simon observed with extreme irritation, as he passed through the outer office, the large, the monumental figure of Mr. Simmonds seated in a client's chair.

His clerk was apologetic. The gentleman had arrived half an hour earlier, and was prepared to wait all morning on the chance of five minutes with Mr. Brocken. His business was personal with Mr. Brocken. Should that morning prove inconvenient, Mr. Simmonds would call again. In short, Simon received the definite impression that Mr. Simmonds was an inevitable evil.

He looked at the diary on his desk. He had no appointment for half an hour. He nodded, though reluctantly, and the estate agent was shown in.

"Good morning," said Simon distastefully. "Sit down. You want to see me?"

Mr. Simmonds sat. He did not sit, in any sense of the word, lightly; he lowered himself into the chair, as though testing its strength, and placed his hat carefully beneath. He made himself secure. He then spoke.

"I take this kindly," said Mr. Simmonds. "You're a busy man; so am I. And let me say at once, I haven't come to consult you as a solicitor. I have a solicitor. I have come, if you will spare me no more than five minutes, to speak to you man to man."

"Quite," said Mr. Brocken. "Five minutes."

The estate agent breathed deeply, but did not immediately continue. Mr. Brocken glanced at the clock and waited.

"You are already aware," said Mr. Simmonds, "of my domestic situation."

"Torquay," said Mr. Brocken. "Torquay, Christmas, fortnight in August, week at the Great Western." (It had been, after all, a conversation with intent.)

"I thank you," said Mr. Simmonds. "You've got it pat. A position, as you may say, highly satisfactory to all parties. Including my friendship with Mrs. Poole. Now we're coming to it."

"From what you told me, and I refer to this friendship, it can come to nothing."

"That's right. No expectations on either side. Which is why," explained Mr. Simmonds frankly, "it's lasted. Over six years, not a moment's anxiety. But at the same time — "

"You are employing," pointed out Mr. Brocken, "a frequently disastrous phrase. At the same time —?"

"I've had a doubt," said the estate agent. "I've had just one doubt, no more than a very faint doubt, at the back of my mind."

Simon waited.

"I shouldn't have cared," said Mr. Simmonds, "to see Mr. P. turn up."

"Is not Mrs. Poole," asked Simon, "a widow?"

The estate agent shook his head.

"No," he stated. "*I* tumbled to that straight away. And for why? Because a widow," explained Mr. Simmonds, evidently out of a wide experience, "will talk about her late husband. He may have been a bad lot, she may be better off without him, but still, now and then, she'll drop a word. Mrs. P., never. At first—well, I wondered. It didn't detract from my respect for her. I respect Mrs. P. highly. It just crossed my mind, as you might say, that there had never been a Mr. P. in question. But something she said about the kid put me right. Greta was born in wedlock," said Mr. Simmonds.

From either side of the big desk the two men looked at each other seriously. It was still, after all, after the publication of a hundred books on sex relations, after a hundred defences of the unmarried mother, a point worthy of respect.

"She's nuts about that kid," went on Mr. Simmonds. "Well, I'm all for it. They bring out, as you may say, the best in each other. And putting two and two together, I arrived at a conclusion. The late Mr. P. wasn't dead, or not to her knowledge; she'd just left him. It was no business of mine. All *I* cared was that he shouldn't turn up, and maybe get a wrong impression of our friendship, and maybe make trouble. It was just," said Mr. Simmonds, "at the back of my mind. Even after I'd seen him— "

Mr. Brocken jumped. He actually moved so violently and incautiously that he knocked over a pen rack.

"Even after you *what*— ?"

"Even after I saw him," repeated Mr. Simmonds, with remarkable stolidity, "I didn't worry much; but what, I ask, about this Miss Cuff?"

It took Simon some little time — the five-minute limit tacitly ignored — to make himself master of the facts; the estate agent could not be hurried. But at length the facts were established. Mute upon the subject of her husband, Mrs. Poole nevertheless, and inevitably, dropped now and again, in the course of six years' conversation, certain allusions to her past life. Like all Londoners, she was fond of talking about her own particular neighbourhood; and Mr. Simmonds early reached the conclusion that before she came to Chipping Hill she had lived in Paddington. He did not think much about it; his own contacts with the place were limited to the one week in each year when he stayed at the Great Western Hotel, and the double journey from Paddington en route for Torquay. On these occasions the thought of Mr. Poole did casually present itself; particularly after the war ended, as khaki in the streets gave place to demob suits; men were coming back, Londoners in particular returning like homing pigeons — a Battersea man to Battersea, a Pimlico man to Pimlico; it seemed at least possible that Mr. Poole had returned to Paddington. Mr. Simmonds had certainly no idea of looking for him; but both ear and eye were so to speak warned, alerted; as one's own name leaps from a page of print, so the name "Poole" over a stationer's, for example, jumped to the eye of Mr. Simmonds. It was however too large and thriving an establishment to interest him. He did not visualize Mr. Poole as a thriving man; and in this was perfectly correct, for Mr. Poole, whom he had actually seen face to face four times in one week the previous October, held a collecting box at one curb for a barrel-organ at the other.

"I must have seen him," repeated Mr. Simmonds earnestly, "nearly half-a-dozen times, and closer than I am to you. They had a pitch just off Praed Street, in a road bang opposite the hotel, that we went down to get to the Park. He pushed his box right under your nose. 'You'll get into trouble,' I thought, 'you'll have the police after you.' I as you might say noticed him. I noticed his face, and it came to me, 'You're like some one.' And then it came to me who. I crossed the road — it so happened the ladies weren't with me — and asked his partner, 'What's that chap's name?' 'What's that to you?' he asked. 'Five bob to *you*,' I said: and he told me, Jim Poole."

Mr. Simmonds took out a large handkerchief and passed it round the inside of his collar. The narrative, into which he had thrown considerable expression, had exhausted him.

"And the man resembled — ?" said Mr. Brocken.

"Greta. I know. It's rum. That kid, you're going to say, is the spit and image of her mother. So she is. But she's like her dad too. I've looked at her since," said Mr. Simmonds, "and now I can see it every time. It's the eyes. Greta's got brown eyes, you may have noticed, and so has he. Mrs. P.'s are blue."

Up from the depths of Simon's memory floated a tag

of biological information: a brown-eyed child postulates at least one brown-eyed parent: Mendel: well-established.

"Yes," said Mr. Brocken heavily. "It seems possible . . . Did this man observe your interest in him?"

Mr. Simmonds shook his head.

"Not a chance. There was a bit of traffic, and his mate never stopped turning the handle. It was all over before you could say knife."

"Yes," said Mr. Brocken again. "Quite so. Did you mention the incident to Mrs. Poole?"

"I did not. I saw no use in worrying her with it. *She* never left Chipping Hill; and those chaps mostly stick to their own beat. Why look for trouble?"

"You were probably right," agreed Mr. Brocken. "But what is the point you now wish to raise?"

"The point is this," said Mr. Simmonds. "The chap's alive. If this Miss Cuff goes looking for him, he's there for her to find. It's out of reason she'll walk slap into him, as I did; but if she goes searching about, what I mean is, he's *there*. And if she does find him, there'll be trouble. There'll be trouble straight off for Mrs. P., and if Miss Cuff should put ideas into his head, there may even be trouble for me. I'm a man," concluded Mr. Simmonds simply, "who wants no trouble of any kind."

"The universal human wish," thought Simon. "The pathetic human hope . . ." Aloud, he said severely,

"There are annoying possibilities in every irregular situation. What I do not understand is why you should have come to me."

The estate agent looked at him in surprise.

"Miss Cuff," he stated, "is your cousin."

"She is nothing of the kind," said Simon. "Miss Cuff is a distant connection, a very distant connection, of my sister-in-law's. We are not related in any way."

"Then Mrs. P. got it wrong," said Mr. Simmonds. "Not that it matters. Mrs. P. tells me you're the boss. All I want you to do is just stop Miss Cuff making a nuisance of herself. Just stop her. That's all. I thank you," said Mr. Simmonds, "for allowing me so much of your valuable time."

2

That evening when he left the office Mr. Brocken took a taxi to Paddington and had himself set down at the Great Western Hotel. Thence he crossed Praed Street to the turning opposite, the turning which would lead to the Park, and walked its full length. No barrel-organ played; the only music sounds came, through open windows, from wireless sets. He retraced his steps, and worked down Praed Street as far as the Edgware Road. Thence he took a bus back and nosed towards Bayswater. There was a barrel-organ, grinding out some forgotten tune, in Craven Hill.

Mr. Brocken slackened his pace. Through the sparse traffic he could examine from a distance the figure with the collecting box. Of medium height, but with a curious disproportion in the build: rather heavy shoulders, a thickness through the trunk, and short, shambling legs. There was a passer-by, not far ahead, a woman: Mr. Brocken saw the box thrust out in a gesture not altogether ingratiating. He felt in his pocket for a sixpence, then dropped it back; he wanted to look at the fellow.

"Quite," said Mr. Brocken, as the box thrust at his own elbow. "One moment . . ."

He looked, and at once saw—not Greta, but Greta's caricature. Should he have been so quick to see, had not Mr. Simmonds prepared him? Mr. Brocken did not know: he knew only that this was Greta's father. Under a low forehead, from which the straw-coloured hair grew in a thick stubble, the eyes, in all save expression, were Greta's: very dark brown, set wide apart, a little tilted at the outer corners; squirrel's eyes, but informed with a furtive viciousness all too human. The lower part of the face was heavy, and totally unlike: but the eyes were unmistakable.

"Here," said Mr. Brocken, pushing a sixpence into the box.

Mr. Poole saluted. Upon his breast a triple row of medal ribbons, framed and glazed with cellophane, caught the light. Simon glanced across at the organ: there was a legend chalked across its back in large letters. DUNKIRK TO ROME, it ran. EX-R.A., EX-P.O.W's. Mr. Brocken discounted the lot, but thought it probable that Mr. Poole had seen, if not service, at least the inside of a barracks. And possibly of a glass-house . . . He nodded and walked on; behind him the organ continued to play, "Smoke Gets in Your Eyes."

3

Altogether forgetting his promise to Isabel, Mr. Brocken dined at the Club. There was lobster on the menu, but he did not enjoy his dinner. The image of Mr. Poole cut his appetite. He was not an imaginative man; he could not subtract fourteen years, glimpse the Jimmy Poole, blond, compact and swaggering, cock of a local barnyard, whose lustrous brown eyes had played havoc with a dozen ready hearts. He could not, in short, imagine why the deuce Mrs. Poole had married him. ("So I wouldn't be a little basket," murmured Greta.) But before that — ? Mr. Brocken gave it up; accepted one more proof that women were in general imbecile, and complained to his waiter about the salad dressing.

The waiter was very sorry: they could not get the proper oil.

Although most women were imbecile — Mr. Brocken's mind took a leap forward — Mrs. Poole had at least seen her error. She had removed Greta from an intolerable domestic situation. Greta, uninstructed, little better than a pagan, showed nevertheless affection and intelligence. She was in fact rather a nice child. She was — gentle. Mr. Brocken found himself almost violently opposed to the notion of handing her back into the authority of her father. ("Put her into the box factory," whispered Mrs. Poole.) Or worse. "Yes," thought Mr. Brocken obscurely, "or worse. And what am I to do about it? What business is it of mine? Why should I be dragged into this?" And suddenly the answer came to him: it was no business of his, but of Isabel's.

Chapter 21

Mr. Brocken, returning to Chipping Lodge, was extremely anxious to see Isabel before he saw Tilly. To do so might be difficult: in the train he remembered his promise to be home to dinner, and hoped the meal had not been long postponed for him; but if they hadn't waited for him then, certainly they were waiting for him now. As he turned in at the gate Simon half-expected to see both Tilly and Isabel on the door-step; in which case he was determined to take his sister-in-law by the elbow and without a word propel her before him into the house and up the stairs. ("No doubt to the bathroom," thought Mr. Brocken angrily.) Though he rather hoped, by entering quietly and looking about for Jacqueline, to secure Isabel's attention without resorting to melodrama, it was a measure of his concern that he was prepared, at a pinch, to be melodramatic.

There was no one on the step. There was no one, when he entered it, in the hall. Indeed the whole house was peculiarly still. It was also, after the near-daylight without, very dark. Mr. Brocken was aware of, and approved, his sister-in-law's conscientiousness in the matter of electricity;

but it surprised him that no lights showed even in the drawing-room. For a moment he stood hesitant in the big shadowy room: hesitant and disconcerted, for a trick of memory had suddenly unshrouded the chandeliers and set twenty couples revolving to the strains of "Destiny Valse." Irrelevant, nostalgic scene! "Or is that where all this started?" thought Mr. Brocken. He made a considerable effort (peering as it were among the circling couples) to remember what Macgregor had looked like: no handsome figure rewarded him. However fascinating—however much like Lewis Waller—the fellow had left absolutely no impression. "I dare say *he* wouldn't remember *me,*" thought Simon grimly. "I dare say he's forgotten the lot of us—Isabel and Tilly included"; and shaking himself free of such imaginings walked to the French window.

It was slightly ajar. Outside on the terrace stood Jacqueline Brown, unfamiliar in a long coat. She was leaning against the balustrade, with her back to him; his voice made her start.

"Where," asked Simon, "has everybody got to? Where is Mrs. Brocken?"

"Gone to bed," said Jacqueline flatly. "So has Miss Cuff. And Humphrey couldn't stand it, so he went down to Bob's . . ."

"Humphrey, indeed!" thought Mr. Brocken. What had young Humphrey to stand? And why, for that matter, should Miss Brown be mooning about with such tragedy airs?

"Why didn't you come back to dinner?" asked Jacqueline.

"I was delayed," said Mr. Brocken. "If you made any special preparations, I apologize. Now I should be obliged if you would go up and ask my sister-in-law if she will see me. It is unlikely that she will yet be asleep."

While he washed his hands he heard Jacqueline tap at Mrs. Brocken's door, and go in, and after a slight interval come out again. How that interval had been employed was immediately clear; when Simon entered Mrs. Brocken was in bed, but sitting up, her hair in order, her upper half neatly arrayed in a pink bed jacket. The result was in one sense unfortunate: the pink silk (collared in frilly white muslin) threw into painful relief the puckered old face above. For once Isabel looked more than her age; her cheeks were colourless, her eyes rimmed with red; even her small plump hands, bare but for her wedding-ring, fidgeted over the coverlet like the hands of an old woman.

"Sit down, dear," she said. "I'm so glad you've come, because I want to speak to you — "

"Isabel," said Mr. Brocken, "I have seen Greta's father."

Isabel's eyes widened. Whatever she had been going to say was forgotten. She stared, speechless, with such a foolish look, that Simon in his impatience with her repeated the words almost roughly.

"I tell you I've seen Greta's father. Are you listening?"

Isabel moistened her lips.

"Then — Tilly's found him?"

"No," snapped Mr. Brocken. "When I say I have seen him, that is all I mean."

With that he did sit down, heavily, in a low embroidery-covered chair. It had belonged, had he known it, to Mrs. Massey; and Isabel had always meant to take it to the Priory, and then, when the Priory was bombed, been very glad she hadn't. Isabel moistened her lips again.

"Tell me about it, Simon. What is he like?"

"He holds a box for a barrel-organ, in the street. His appearance corroborates all that Mrs. Poole has told me of him, which is all bad. He looks a brute. I should have the gravest fears for any child unfortunate enough to be placed in his hands. Wait," said Mr. Brocken. "Let me finish. I discovered him, in a sense, by hazard. Hazard has operated once, and may operate again. Even should it not, Tilly Cuff has great funds of persistence, the man has apparently served in the Army, and there are channels through which he might be traced. I do not for one moment suppose him to be disinterested. Offered a large enough bribe he would agree to anything Tilly proposed; certainly to so apparently respectable a measure as sending his daughter to school. At the same time, he probably has some idea of a child's value. The point is this: any money you give to Tilly Cuff will be employed to separate Greta from her mother. As for Mrs. Poole, if her husband returns to her, the result can only be miserable. In short," said Mr. Brocken, "give Tilly money, and you precipitate, for both mother and child, disaster."

"But I've given it her," said Isabel.

2

For some moments they stared at each other dumbly. Isabel was crying. Then Mr. Brocken stood up, and began to pace up and down the room.

"When?" he threw over his shoulder.

"This afternoon. It's been a dreadful day, Simon." Isabel struggled with a sob; but she was making a great effort to control herself. "Tilly's been worse; she cried all morning, she wouldn't let me speak, she just wanted me there to listen while she talked and talked, going over every time she'd seen Mr. Macgregor, and how dreadfully she'd loved him, and how her heart was broken. I couldn't blame her, but it was dreadful."

Mr. Brocken believed it. Given such an opportunity, he thought bitterly, Tilly could be trusted to exploit it to the full. He was sorry for his sister-in-law; but much sorrier for the Pooles.

"Go on," he said curtly. "What then?"

"She cried herself out. She slept most of the afternoon. I sat beside her," said Isabel, "and really it was pitiful, Simon, to see how she tossed and turned and — and kept saying his name. So — so when she woke up, I told her. I *gave* her the money, then."

"When she was, I presume, comforted."

Isabel hesitated.

"I *think* she was, Simon. At any rate, she was much quieter."

"Eight hundred a year would quieten most people."

"I explained everything," went on Isabel. "I told her how I was going to live with Dora, so she wouldn't have to worry about me, and I *did* say I'd like to give the house to Humphrey, if Tilly didn't want it. I explained everything. But—" Isabel paused again—"she didn't believe me."

At the farther end of the room Simon swung round.

"You mean she didn't think you were serious?"

Isabel considered; and said simply,

"I think she thought *I* was; but she didn't think you'd let me. She asked several times, Simon, had I spoken to you about it; and I said I had. And I told her you were coming home to dinner, specially, to explain to her about it. But then you didn't come. . . ."

"Then there's your loop-hole," said Mr. Brocken. "You've got to give the woman something, that's plain. But not the lot. Allow her a hundred a year, and she'll be grateful. And from a hundred a year she'll waste precious little on the Pooles. Leave it to me," said Mr. Brocken, with a quick, bitter smile, "and I'll deal with her. . . ."

Isabel, sitting up in bed, her eyes fixed on her mother's chair, was silent. Mr. Brocken looked at her in sudden mistrust. Her simple, silly face was deeply troubled; it was also stubborn.

"No," said Isabel.

"Then you're a fool," said Mr. Brocken.

"I know you've always thought me one," said Isabel

gently. "And even Mark didn't think I was very clever. But I can only do what I think right."

"And have you thought of the Pooles?" demanded Mr. Brocken harshly. "Have you thought of the effect your virtue will have upon them?"

Isabel sighed.

"Yes, dear, I have. I've thought and thought. Greta's father being alive, and—and not nice, makes it much worse. But it's all so mixed up, I can't see my way clearly: so I must hold on to the one thing that *is* clear, and right. Come here."

There was in her voice an unexpected, a purely feminine authority. So her mother might have said "Come here," or Simon's mother: gently, authoritatively, with no notion of being disobeyed. Simon approached the big old-fashioned bed, and Isabel took his hand between her own.

"We both loved Mark very much," she said. "You think he'd disapprove of what I'm doing. I know he'd have said I was right. He didn't think I was clever, but he—he trusted me in matters of conduct. And he wouldn't like us not to be friends. Don't be too angry with me, Simon."

"It's Mark's money," said Mr. Brocken.

"Yes, dear; and that's why I have taken such pains to allow for your point of view. That's why I didn't tell Tilly at once, before all this harm was done. You shouldn't be too angry, Simon."

Mr. Brocken was silent. There was a certain truth in this—though how obscured! How it was all, in Isabel's phrase, mixed up! He said grudgingly,

"What do you want me to do?"

"Tell Tilly it's true about the money."

"I will tell her. In the morning."

"Now," said Isabel. "I've sent Jacky to wake her up."

There was no time for further argument. The door opened, and there was Tilly Cuff.

3

She was wearing her new house-coat. Like Isabel's jacket, it was unkind to the ravaged face above. Yet Tilly had not neglected her appearance; all that rouge and powder could do for her had been done. Her eyes were very red.

"Come in, Tilly," said Isabel. "Simon was kept late at his office. That's why he couldn't be here to dinner. Now he wants to tell you what I've told you, that you're to have all my money."

Tilly laughed.

"I wasn't asleep," she said. "I wasn't in bed, or I wouldn't have bothered to come. I've had enough of this farce. I'm not taken in by fine words. Is it likely that you'd strip yourself, when you needn't? Simon's here to see that you don't. Simon's going to offer me a hundred pounds," said Tilly loudly, "to forgive you and clear out. Well, I don't think it's enough."

"Tilly," said Mrs. Brocken, "Tilly, listen to me. I—I did you a great wrong. When we were both girls together, and I had every advantage, I did you a great wrong. But

I'm going to make amends. All I can do is to give you my money. And I will: I'll give you every penny, except a hundred a year, and I'm keeping that because I don't want to be a burden on either Simon, or Dora Tremayne. They say any one can find work now," said Isabel humbly. "I can look after children, and I can cook, and Dora will have me to live with her. I'm going to be perfectly all right, Tilly; and you shall have my money, and never be a companion again."

Tilly turned her head. She looked not at Isabel, but at Simon. He nodded bleakly.

"She can do it," said he.

"She can give me all her money?"

"Yes," said Mr. Brocken.

"And you won't stop her?"

"It is not," said Mr. Brocken, "within my power."

Tilly took an uncertain step forward.

"And Isabel really means to do it?"

"Yes," said Mr. Brocken loudly. "And let me say here and now, for it should be said, that I consider her behaviour quixotic to the point of insanity. If I had the power to stop her, I would. Does that reassure you? I don't consider you worthy of such generosity. You are odious to me. You're a detestable woman. It was an unlucky day for all of us when Mrs. Massey brought you into this house. I don't for one moment—"

"Simon!" cried Isabel. "Stop!"

"Let me finish," shouted Mr. Brocken. "For it's time some one spoke the truth—I don't for one moment believe that you were ever in love with Macgregor, or that your heart was broken, or any of the rest of it. I believe you are simply taking advantage of my sister-in-law's simplicity. You'll beggar her and laugh at her. But she can do what she likes with her own property, and I can't stop it. Now will you have the decency to admit that my sister-in-law is speaking the truth?"

For perhaps half a minute Tilly stood looking from one to the other of them: from Simon's mask of fury to Isabel's tear-stained face. Then she ran forward, and dropped on her knees by the bed, and so crouched clutched at Isabel's hands.

"Oh, Issy, Issy!" she cried. "My darling, but I don't want it! I don't want your money! If you give it me, I want to share it with you! All I want is that we should never be parted again!"

Isabel reined back. It was a purely involuntary movement; the next instant she had leaned above Tilly, stroking her hair.

"My dear," she said, "that's nonsense. You must take it all. You must go about, and travel, and buy yourself things . . . Think, Tilly, of all you'll be able to do. . . ."

Miss Cuff raised her ravaged face.

"I don't want to do things," she said. "I don't want to travel. I just want to be with some one."

Her voice shook with an unmistakable, a heart-rending sincerity. Isabel, stroking tenderly and steadily, as one strokes the head of an anguished child, said soothingly,

"So you will, dear. You'll make friends. You've never been able to make friends, you've been too worried and —

and nervous. But you'll make friends now. You'll stay in nice hotels — "

"With you," said Tilly. "With you! Don't turn me away, Issy! I can't make friends by myself, I've forgotten how. You say you're going to live with Dora, but Dora's no relation, and I am. We'll live here together — "

"The house too?" threw in Mr. Brocken bitterly. "The house too, Isabel?"

Isabel shook her head.

"No, dear. The house is for Humphrey. I'm giving it to Humphrey, Tilly, because I shan't have anything to leave him, and he's fond of it. I hope you don't mind."

"I shan't mind anything, if we're together. We can both live in an hotel." Tilly's voice was steadying: as though the word "hotel" brought everything into focus, made all real and solid to her, she dwelt on it eagerly; her face brightened. "I'd much rather live in an hotel," said Tilly. "We'll find a nice hotel — won't we, Issy? — or if we want to travel we'll travel — but we'll stay together all our lives, and never be lonely. *That's* what I want, that's what I've always wanted — "

"What you forget," said Humphrey Garrett, "is that I also am a relation; and I very much hope that Aunt Isabel will live here with me."

4

He had opened the door, and held it for some moments ajar, so quietly that no one had noticed him. Mr. Brocken was forcibly reminded of a moment on the terrace, when from under the covered seat a foot emerged. But he now surveyed the young man without animosity, as a possible ally.

"I gather," said Humphrey, "that all is over bar the shouting. Dear Aunt Isabel, I'm very fond of you."

Mrs. Brocken beamed at him. She had now, in a most extraordinary manner, plumped out again; the pink in her cheeks matched her bed jacket. But Tilly, still on her knees, still clutching at Isabel's hands, turned in anger.

"You!" she said. "*You!* What do *you* know about growing old? What will you want with Isabel, when you're married and have a family here? We'll give you the house and welcome; but Issy and I won't live here." She raked him with her eyes, and turned back to bury her face in Mrs. Brocken's lap. "Tell him you'd rather be with me, Issy! I'm owed it, aren't I, after all I've suffered? Tell them you'd rather live with your cousin!"

Isabel looked at Humphrey over the bowed head, motioning him away. When he did not move, she said softly,

"Will you both go away, please? Tilly and I have a great deal to talk about. . . ."

They obeyed. With reluctance, with misgiving, Humphrey and Mr. Brocken left the room. They went out and left Isabel and Tilly Cuff alone.

PART THREE

Chapter 22

Incredible as had seemed, to Simon and Humphrey and Jacqueline, Mrs. Brocken's original design, this issue was at first harder still to accept. Any one of them would have given up any amount of money rather than share it for life with Tilly Cuff. They would have worked, and earned money, and given it to Tilly, rather than endure her society. By comparison with such a lot, a room over an ironmonger's appeared even to Mr. Brocken an abode of bliss. It was Mr. Brocken, however, who from the first believed that Isabel would in fact sacrifice herself; long inured to the general cussedness of things, he could not be surprised to find the attainment of a greatly desired object — in this case the preserving to the Brockens of Mark Brocken's money — accompanied by some unexpected disadvantage. In his ointment there was ever a fly, in his pound of sweet ever an ounce of sour; the sympathy he was forced to feel for his sister-in-law was simply this fly, this pinch of aloes. He did not exaggerate it. When Jacqueline and Humphrey, with the optimistic indignation of youth, cried that such a sacrifice could not be permitted, Mr. Brocken sensibly pointed out that Isabel was her own mistress.

A great part of this argument took place at once, on the landing, at the head of the stairs; for Jacqueline met the two men as they emerged from Mrs. Brocken's room, and Humphrey immediately acquainted her with the situation. "But we mustn't allow it!" cried Jacqueline at once. "It would kill her!" "Of course I shan't allow it," said Humphrey. Mr. Brocken pointed out that, so far as they knew, Tilly's company had killed no one yet; and added that his sister-in-law had remarkable reserves of vitality. "All *you* care about is the money," said Jacqueline brusquely. "At least Humphrey doesn't. At least Humphrey's disinterested. And Humphrey won't let her." "I certainly shall not," said Humphrey.

Mr. Brocken, listening to their energetic young voices, was reminded of the afternoon — how long ago it seemed! — when he had spied them lying side by side, sun-bathing, in the dell. He had experienced then an odd poetic illusion; glanced backwards at a nymph and shepherd of Arcady; noted that Jacqueline had pretty feet. Now there was nothing Arcadian about them, each was fully clad and a little dishevelled; but they produced the same impression of vigorous and ready youth. As the shepherd would have sprung up, stone in sling, against a wolf, as the nymph would have flown to succour her kids, so Humphrey and Jacqueline now leapt to the defence of Mrs. Brocken. No doubt the wolves pulled down a shepherd or two, no doubt the nymph sometimes mourned her goatlings; Mr. Brocken considered neither young person a match for Isabel's conscience, and Tilly Cuff.

He yawned. Their outraged glances accused him of hard-heartedness. Mr. Brocken, being naturally sleepy, yawned again.

"Good night," he said. "I don't expect you to take the reasonable view. But I warn you that my sister-in-law can be very stubborn. I've known her all my life. I have not, as you may know, a high opinion of her intelligence; but on a matter of conscience I believe her to be quite immovable."

2

So, in the course of the next few days, the young people found her.

"Aunt Isabel," said Humphrey flatly, "you can't."

"Dear Mrs. Brocken," echoed Jacqueline, "you can't . . ."

This was at breakfast next morning. Jacqueline had taken Tilly a tray in bed, so that they could have Mrs. Brocken to themselves. Isabel looked at them affectionately.

"But of course I can," she said placidly. "*You* couldn't. But Tilly won't worry me nearly as much as she would you. We can talk over old times together, and I'll teach her piquet, and after all, we'll be company for each other. We'll find some nice hotel — "

"You know you hate hotels," said Humphrey.

"No, I don't. My hotel at Bath was very nice. There was a waiter — "

"She'll be rude to the waiters," said Jacqueline.

"I can always smooth them down afterwards. I get on with waiters," said Isabel complacently. "They tell me about their families. The one at Bath — "

"I expect she cheats at bridge," said Humphrey.

"I shan't let her, dear. If she cheats I won't play with her, and if *I* won't play with her," said Isabel shrewdly, "Tilly might find it quite difficult to make up a four. Simon, aren't I right?"

Mr. Brocken, just then appearing, replied that any glutton for punishment who played bridge with Isabel could probably stomach Tilly also. Isabel looked pleased.

"That's just what I meant, dear. Tilly needs someone to — to make way for her a little." Isabel reflected a moment, and added thoughtfully, "Jacqueline and Humphrey don't understand; but in my young day, and Simon will remember it, people put *up* with their relations. Some of ours weren't very nice, but they all came and stayed with us, and Ruth and I even had to go and stay with them. It's only lately that people feel they have a right to choose their company. Oh, dear," said Isabel, "I *had* looked forward to living with Dora . . . But there it is."

"But it *is*n't!" cried Jacqueline. "You haven't *got* to endure Miss Cuff — "

"Yes, I have, dear. It's no good giving people things they don't want. And Tilly honestly doesn't want the money. It's exactly as I said last night; when you get to our age, there's nothing like living with people who were young when you were — "

"Shall you find," interrupted Humphrey — and his voice had a strong family resemblance to Mr. Brocken's — "shall you find so many pleasant memories in common? Aren't Tilly's memories all rather . . . resentful? Won't they all lead back to Macgregor?"

"Yes, of course," agreed Isabel, apparently without apprehension. "Of course Tilly will talk about Mr. Macgregor a great deal. But I shan't mind talking about him myself, because he *was* fascinating." (Something of Mr. Brocken flickered in Humphrey's eye.) "In a way," pursued Isabel, "Tilly wouldn't be *without* Mr. Macgregor; because all women like to have a man to talk about; and she'll know how truly I can sympathize. If Tilly talked about Mr. Macgregor to just any one — well, they mightn't quite believe her; but I do, because I read his letter. And of course *I* shall talk to Tilly about Mark. You'll find," said Isabel, "that we shan't do at all badly."

To Jacqueline's surprise, Dora Tremayne, whom she visited at the shop later that morning, took much the same view.

"My dear, Tilly's *family,*" said Dora, after listening with deep interest to Jacqueline's tale. "I dare say they'll get on very well: Isabel's very good-tempered, and Tilly won't seem nearly so tiresome to her as she would to you. Tilly takes devotions, you know; I expect she'll take a devotion to Isabel, and though that may be very tiresome too, at least Isabel will be able to keep her in order."

"I can think," said Jacqueline, "of no worse punishment, for the worst crime, than to live all my life with Tilly Cuff."

Over Miss Tremayne's long face passed a look of great gentleness: gone before Jacqueline had noticed it.

"But it won't be all Isabel's life," said she. "Isabel has lived her life, or all the best of it." ("As I have," thought Dora Tremayne. "As I have!") "You could say the same of Tilly, though Tilly hadn't such good luck. They'll do very well together, and when Tilly upsets people, Isabel will calm them; and if Isabel is sick, Tilly will nurse her — and of course Isabel will nurse Tilly. I shouldn't be surprised if they grew to be a very devoted pair."

3

At this point both Humphrey and Jacqueline, though shocked by the fatalism of their elders, were still full of fight. Isabel had spoken truly: they believed — and believed still, after five years of service life, for so eternally hope springs in the youthful human breast — that one could choose one's company; and that this was moreover a right, like *habeas corpus* or free speech, only voluntarily to be abdicated. They considered Isabel criminally weak, but did not for that reason cease to try and protect her from herself. What they did not realize was that the whole situation had been altered, and by influences which neither they nor any one else could control. They did not allow, for example, for the effect upon Tilly Cuff of the knowledge that she would never again be out of work. They knew her only as mean and malicious, and saw the unfortunate Mrs. Brocken perpetually shadowed by meanness and malice. They did not realize that the pleasure of giving affection had been the pleasure above all others that poor Tilly had lacked. Whether or not she had truly loved Mr. Macgregor was something no one ever knew; but it was soon, and astoundingly, apparent that she was going to love Mrs. Brocken.

While Jacqueline hurried down to Madame Esmé's to tackle Dora, Humphrey stayed behind at the Lodge to tackle Tilly Cuff. Confident and resolute, he took up his position in the drawing-room and waited for Tilly to appear. It was raining again; the dampness without, and the gloom within, seemed somehow appropriate to his unpleasant task. He did not flinch from it: he intended to speak to Tilly very sternly, with masculine authority, even if it meant reducing her to fresh tears; his exact words he left to the inspiration of the moment.

Upon Humphrey, confident, resolute and sombre, Tilly Cuff burst like a ray of sunshine.

He had not seen her since the previous afternoon. She was wearing her pink house-coat (she loved it, because Isabel had given it to her). Its length hid her bony shins; in it she was less grotesque. Nor was her make-up quite so startling as usual, a little natural colour in her cheeks warmed the rouge, and her nose, still swollen under the powder, seemed less protuberant for its pinkness. Had Humphrey seen her then for the first time, he would have found no harder name for her than an old trout.

"Miss Cuff — " began Humphrey sternly.

"Dear boy," cried Tilly, pattering towards him and seizing his hands. "You know — of course you know — of Isabel's *wonderful* plan?"

"I'm not sure that I do," said Humphrey. (At least he wasn't going to take it for granted.) "I've heard some vague talk of her going off with you to some hotel, and what I have heard, I don't approve of."

Tilly dropped his hands to clasp her own.

"My dear, you *wouldn't,*" said Tilly. "And I know it's just because you're so fond of her, and that's why I can't be cross with you, or expect you to share *all* my happiness. *You* want Isabel to stay here and run this great house for you — and Simon is just as bad, all *he* thinks of is his own comfort. But hasn't Isabel any rights of her own?"

Humphrey, considerably taken aback, replied that such was precisely his own attitude.

"Then there you are!" cried Tilly. "That's just what I feel too! When Isabel said, 'Tilly, let's get right away and find some nice hotel,' I was so *glad,* because I felt at last she was standing up for herself. This house," said Tilly earnestly, "has been too much. *You* wouldn't realize it, of course; but I did, the moment I got here: poor Isabel, I thought, a houseful of people — two men — and only those shiftless Pooles! I was really terribly distressed, though I hope I didn't show it; and I thought then, the only thing for Isabel is to get right away. But of course I couldn't say anything; I had to wait for Issy to make the first move. (And I may tell you," threw in Tilly, possibly from sheer force of habit, "that there's a most desirable post simply *waiting* for me. Most charming people, in Somerset; five indoor staff. But I wouldn't take it, I just held off and held off, thinking that if Isabel really needed me, of course she had first claim.) But I didn't say anything; oh, no. I never said a word. I thought, there's Humphrey and there's Simon, Issy has so *many* friends; and much as I love her, who am I to put myself forward? And then," continued Tilly swiftly (for rhetorical questions are dangerous), "this most wonderful thing happens. The person Isabel wants is *me*. When she told me, I could have cried. I believe I did cry. And Issy cried too, you'll think we were a couple of silly old women, and so it was all settled."

Humphrey was dumbfounded. For the first time in his life he was faced by the human phenomenon of self-delusion. Watching Tilly Cuff, listening to Tilly Cuff, he did not know what to believe. She sounded utterly sincere. (She was utterly sincere.) Yet everything she had said was false. He said stubbornly,

"We'd better go back to the beginning. If this house really were too much for my aunt, which frankly I don't believe—"

"*Just* my point," interrupted Tilly. "Men always imagine a house runs itself. I'm not blaming you, dear boy, not for one moment."

"If Aunt Isabel really wants a change," began Humphrey again, and omitting the intervening steps, "of course I'm all for her having one — "

"I knew you weren't really selfish," said Tilly warmly. "First we're going to the Lakes."

"I am perfectly prepared to take her there myself," said Humphrey.

Tilly smiled at him with great understanding.

"Dear boy, I know it must be difficult for you to realize! But Issy and I have been making plans ever since breakfast, and that's half the joy of them — that we shall be just together by ourselves, so perfectly *free*. If the Lakes don't come up to our expectations (fancy, we've neither of us ever seen them!) off we shall go again, foot-loose as gipsies, just vagabonding about as the spirit moves us. — Then for the winter we *think* of Falmouth, but it may just as well be Torquay, or even Penzance — but the *great* point is that with me as courier (and with no one else to consider) Isabel won't have a moment's worry. Isabel *oughtn't* to be worried," said Tilly rather severely. "She's too sweet and simple; and it's just because I'm such a tough little thing by comparison that *I*'m the right person to look after her." Tilly paused; ceased looking severe in order to look modest, and then looked understanding again. "Dear Humphrey," she said affectionately, "I can well imagine your anxiety, I know all you were going to say to me, and it does you great credit; but I assure you, I assure you from the bottom of my heart, you need have no fears."

Modest, sunny, affectionate, away she ran; and when Jacqueline came back from Madame Esmé's and reported what Miss Tremayne had said about Tilly's taking devotions, Humphrey was forced to admit there was something in it. What they could neither of them credit, however, was that Isabel would find Tilly's devotion any more tolerable than her malice. "You should have heard the woman," said Humphrey gloomily. "She was . . . well, nauseating." "You should have heard Dora," said Jacqueline. "She was absolutely *callous* . . ."

The two young people — they had instinctively drawn together again, in alliance against their elders — exchanged anxious looks. They weren't allied against Mrs. Brocken — or did not wish to be; they still hoped to save her, if only she would make the least motion towards saving herself. They felt like firemen holding a safety net, crying, "Jump, jump!" to some one who persisted in pottering about in a fire.

"Aunt Isabel could live here as long as she liked," said Humphrey. "We could all live here on twopence. She should tell Tilly it's the money or nothing."

"Dora," said Jacqueline doubtfully, "thinks she'll be able to keep Tilly in order . . ."

"No one could keep Tilly in order," said Humphrey. "Short of wringing her neck."

4

A day or two later, however, they witnessed a scene which rather supported Dora's view. Mrs. Brocken, rising from the lunch table, said briskly,

"Tilly, how long will it take you to go through all your boxes?"

"My dear, I needn't go through them at all," said Tilly. "At least half can go straight back into store."

"Then I don't see why you keep them," said Isabel. "In fact, I don't think you ought to keep clothes you don't wear. I'll have them for my Quakers."

Miss Cuff hesitated. It was an interesting and important moment. For the first time (both Humphrey and Jacqueline realized) Isabel was dealing with Tilly unhampered by a sense of obligation; her cheerful confidence was rather impressive. Isabel for her part was quite unconscious that the moment had any importance at all. She wasn't applying any little test, as Tilly had once done. She simply thought no one ought to keep clothes they were never going to wear.

"It isn't rubbish, you know," said Tilly.

"The Quakers *will* be pleased," said Isabel. "Thank you very much, dear."

"And I certainly shan't give away half. There are some things I've never even had on. There's a cloth cape—"

"Tilly," said Isabel.

"Well?"

"Don't be such a jackdaw," said Isabel. "We're going upstairs this minute, and I'm going through your boxes with you, and we'll give the Quakers a lovely surprise."

With these firm yet kindly words Mrs. Brocken left the dining-room. After only a moment's hesitation Tilly Cuff followed. They could be heard arguing all the way upstairs, but arguing as it were intimately. The incident, if it foreshadowed the future, foreshadowed a future in which they would argue with each other a great deal, but intimately, and perhaps, in due course, rather cosily: a future in which Dora Tremayne's judgment, callous but experienced, might be vindicated after all.

5

Jacqueline in particular was struck by the success and extent of Mrs. Brocken's depredations. It may be remembered that when Tilly arrived at Chipping Lodge she brought with her three trunks, four hat-boxes, one gunny sack, and a suitcase in the hand. The loot collected in the hall to await Carter Paterson filled one trunk—the largest, dome-lidded and obese—the gunny sack, and four paper parcels. It had been, said Mrs. Brocken subsequently, an extraordinary experience; besides wearing apparel Tilly had collected such things as old foot muffs, old work boxes, an old eiderdown, and quantities of unfinished crochet work. At the bottom of one trunk was folded a faded green motoring veil, curiously gathered round a flat button, which Isabel actually recognized as having belonged to Mrs. Massey. "Did you send that away too?" asked Jacqueline. "Of course," said Isabel. "I can't think what they'll do with it, but they're very clever . . ."

This was slightly disingenuous. Isabel had so lightly discarded the relic because Tilly possessed another: a strip of camphor-smelling sealskin, once the collar of a cape, which also had belonged to Mrs. Massey. "Your mother wore it when she came to fetch me," said Tilly, sitting back on her heels among the open boxes. "When she came to fetch me from Bournemouth. I remember leaning my cheek against it, in the train . . ." This Isabel did not repeat to Jacqueline, in case Jacky should point out that Tilly simply hoarded anything she could lay hands on — which was true, but in this case irrelevant. Isabel was quite sure that Tilly kept that strip of fur out of pure gratitude. They had both cried a little — cosily.

It was curious to watch the rapidity with which Isabel and Tilly merged all their interests. Hearing them discuss guest houses, one would have imagined them cronies from childhood. Yet no two women could have been less alike: they presented the two sides of the female character, the two sides of female experience: all they had in common was certain memories. They had been young together. ("Before 1914," Simon would have added.) It seemed as though the mere fact of contemporaneousness could soften all differences of temper, and unite the unlike.

Jacqueline and Humphrey, before this phenomenon, were offended. Youth is always a little offended to find itself not preferred: it cannot help feeling that when it admits the old to its society, it confers a benefit. Jacqueline and Humphrey were genuinely fond of Mrs. Brocken, the Lodge had been more agreeable to them because she was its mistress, and they had shown their affection openly. (As the young often do not; Jacqueline, with her own mother, was far less attentive.) To see Tilly preferred, therefore — to see Tilly Cuff, by gum! — preferred to themselves, offended them deeply. They abandoned all attempt at rescue, and listened with aloof and cynical expressions while Isabel and Tilly discussed hotels.

Simon advised them to go straight back to Bath. He had a great notion of seeing them fixed somewhere, somewhere a good way off; and since Isabel had given him less trouble while at Bath than at any other period, naturally stressed that city's amenities. And on Bath, in the end, Isabel and Tilly settled. They were not, when it came to the point, quite the vagabonds they fancied themselves. Isabel knew the hotel at Bath was nice, the manageress was almost a friend, and with luck they might get the same elderly chambermaid, so reliable about hot-water bottles. Isabel wrote at once, and was able to report with triumph that they could be squeezed in, as a personal favour to herself, at the end of the month. The prospect of seeing her favourite waiter again, and contemplating again her favourite view, and sitting again in her favourite chair, afforded her a great deal of pleasure; her affections, as had been said, were very easily engaged.

The reasonable solution of a dilemma is often accompanied by a sense of anticlimax.

Mr. Brocken, still literally without a roof to his head, proposed to stay on at Chipping Lodge till he should be furnished with one; and this reminded Isabel (among one or two other odds and ends to be cleared up) of the Pooles.

6

Amid the varied emotions of the last few days, the affairs of the Pooles had been completely overlooked. Nothing could have been more agreeable to them; to be overlooked was what they asked; scenting, hopefully, the new preoccupations of their employers, they lay very low, did not again give notice, but waited. As Jacqueline later observed, it was remarkable how the Pooles, isolated within their own territory, always knew in broad outline what went on in the rest of the house. The Pooles knew in fact only that something was up, but drew hope from any change in the existing circumstances. They were not surprised, but hopeful, when Mrs. Brocken suddenly visited their kitchen, and at one stroke altered the whole situation.

Before this, of course, Isabel had spoken to Tilly. She found it perfectly easy to do so, though she had a little difficulty in securing Tilly's attention, for Tilly happened to be deep in the "Situations Vacant" columns of the *Telegraph,* which she now read every day, right through, from beginning to end. It was a great luxury to Tilly Cuff to read advertisements without having to answer them.

"Tilly," said Isabel, "I know you want me to send Greta to boarding-school, but I'm not going to."

Tilly, without looking up, agreed that it would be a great expense.

"I'm not thinking of the expense," said Isabel. "I just don't believe the child would benefit by it, and moreover her mother will need her help, because of course Simon can't cook. Tilly, are you listening to me?"

"Of course, dear; you're quite right. Do listen to this one: 'Elderly lady, not bedridden' — that's what they *all* say — 'but some occasional nursing' — "

"Then I think," persisted Isabel, "you ought to drop your idea of looking for Greta's father, because it's upsetting them."

"My dear, if they don't want to be helped, I'm sure I don't want to help them. Why should I?" asked Tilly Cuff — and how reasonably! Why indeed should she interfere with the Pooles, and make their lives a misery, except for the reason that her own life was miserable? When one has no consequence whatever, there is much consequence in being feared. When one is starved of all emotion, stir up any, even hatred, of which one is the centre! But now Tilly had no need of such stimulants. The prospect of life in an hotel at Bath, in the company of Mrs. Brocken, would not have exhilarated every one; but it exhilarated Tilly Cuff. She would never more be lonely, and never destitute, and she had the wit to realize that her escape from these two real and enormous evils had been very narrow. And moreover, Tilly loved hotels. She was used to them. She liked the diversity of the company, and the interminable gossip. She had the makings in her of a happy (if objectionable) old woman; and why on earth should she bother about the Pooles?

"It's their own business," added Tilly Cuff—with no sense of anticlimax whatever.

Isabel for her part simply informed Mrs. Poole that she and Miss Cuff were leaving for Bath at the end of the month. "Is she going for good?" asked Mrs. Poole. "For good," replied Isabel. "You will never see her again." Mrs. Poole drew a long breath. "Then Greta won't have to go to school?" "No," said Isabel; and after a moment's reflection (for she was very anxious that Simon should have some one to cook his breakfast) added frankly that Miss Cuff would make no more trouble of any sort. Again Mrs. Poole sighed, the long sigh of the convalescent relieved—yet not quite trusting in the relief—from pain. She looked round, as though for Greta; but Greta was not there, and Mrs. Brocken next took the opportunity to explain that Mr. Brocken, for the time being at least, would remain at Chipping Lodge and want his breakfast.

"Just him?" asked Mrs. Poole.

The question brought forcibly to Isabel's mind another odd, or end.

Chapter 23

The idea that her nephew now owned Chipping Lodge — or would own it so soon as Simon had completed the necessary formalities — pleased Isabel very much; and she confidently expected that he would live in it, starting off, oddly enough, with Simon as his guest. That such a house as the Lodge was hardly suitable to a junior master at Broxbury troubled her not at all; to Isabel it was simply the proper place for Humphrey to live, and when he rose to be Head, as she had no doubt of his doing, it would be very appropriate indeed. What did trouble Mrs. Brocken was the position of Jacqueline Brown. Jacky, who might possibly be left at the Lodge with Simon, could hardly, to Isabel's mind, be left there with Simon and Humphrey; especially as the former would one day get his roof put on. To take her to Bath was out of the question; Simon had warned his sister-in-law very seriously that with Tilly Cuff to support as well as herself, her income no longer permitted extravagance; and this warning Isabel took to heart. She had not asked the manageress for her old room in the hotel; she and Tilly were going two flights further up. For a day or two Isabel hesitated; and then, as she watched Jacqueline begin to read the advertisement columns of the *Telegraph* (like Tilly, but without Tilly's enjoyment), decided to take action. Isabel was wonderfully active at this period. The unburdening of her conscience had released such a fine flow of energy that she was positively looking for action to take.

"Humphrey, dear," said Isabel, "now that you and Jacky have stopped quarrelling — "

"I was not aware," said Humphrey, "that we had ever quarrelled."

Isabel (full of energy and optimism) could not help regarding him impatiently.

"That's nonsense, dear, and you know it. You've bickered and avoided each other for the last month at least. And the reason was that Jacqueline was out of sorts, and the reason for that was of course Tilly. Not that Tilly meant to do any harm," added Mrs. Brocken hastily, "I've no doubt she just meant to give Jacky good advice; only perhaps Tilly's advice is a little realistic." She paused, momentarily distracted by pride in her use of this modern and (she hoped) psychological term. She wondered if Humphrey understood it. "What I mean," elaborated Isabel, "is that poor Tilly was always so afraid of putting herself forward, she thought Jacky should be too: and I dare say she gave Jacky hints. But what I really mean," finished Isabel, suddenly pouncing from this thicket of verbiage, "is, do you mean to marry her?"

With commendable readiness and his usual precision, Humphrey replied:

"Not exactly."

Isabel's look of impatience returned.

"I asked you a serious question, dear; please don't start imitating your uncle. Do you want to marry Jacky?"

"I am giving you a serious answer. At the moment I rather dislike Jacky, because up to the last few days she's been behaving like an idiot. At the same time I must undoubtedly be attached to her, because it doesn't seem possible that I should marry any one else. Whether Jacqueline would accept me — "

"I don't think you need worry about that," said Isabel.

"Possibly not," admitted Humphrey. "All the same, a man sticks his neck out. I reckon the fact is, and I reckon this is the reason why I've been so annoyed with her — I knew I was going to marry the girl; and it annoyed me to think she was such an ass."

Isabel, all doubts set at rest, kissed her nephew warmly on both cheeks and advised him to propose to Jacqueline at once, so that they could leave Chipping Lodge together to visit Jacqueline's family, and have the wedding before they came back. In any matter pertaining to courtship or marriage Isabel could show great dash and decision; she was a fearless and successful promoter of matrimony, and Humphrey found himself considerably startled by the speed with which his plans were taking shape. "What about *my* family?" he enquired, almost stubbornly. "They'll be delighted," said Isabel; and added that Ruth thought Jacky a very nice girl.

Humphrey, in the act of lighting a cigarette, let the match burn his fingers.

"And would you mind telling me," he enquired, "how you know?"

Isabel looked remarkably ingenuous.

"My dear boy, I write to your mother once a fortnight. And I naturally mentioned Jacky, and when Ruth wrote back she said she thought Jacky sounded a very nice girl."

"And would you mind telling me what you said?"

"About Jacky, dear? Just how pretty she was, and how nice her father was, and how brave she'd been in the war, and what a help she was in the house. I just mentioned her," said Mrs. Brocken casually.

If the suspicion that his courtship had been subject to a running commentary did not give Humphrey much pleasure, at least it cleared the ground; he was parentally blessed in advance; he had nothing to do but put the question.

2

A man may be genuinely in love, absolutely eager for matrimony, sanguine of success—and yet find it extraordinarily difficult to propose. He is after all, in most cases, tying himself up for life. Some male inhibition operates—not on his emotions, but on his tongue. It is probably for this reason that so many proposals take place as it were sketchily, in unsuitable circumstances—under wet umbrellas, at the end of an evening instead of at its beginning: when the moment comes it must be seized, or perhaps lost forever. Mark Brocken, with all the resources of two large houses at his disposal — two houses, two gardens, two conservatories — proposed to Isabel Massey at the corner of the Ridge and Hill Road, with Dora Tremayne rapidly bearing down on them. Since Isabel then refused him, he had further opportunities, and was finally accepted in the Brockens' summer-house. Simon Brocken, whose lips the fatal words had never passed, very nearly uttered them on meeting his dark siren unexpectedly in Knightsbridge during the General Strike. She was shopping, on foot, looking harassed and preoccupied: Simon carried some of her parcels the short distance to her door; and there on the step the moment presented itself, and he very nearly cooked his goose.

So Humphrey Garrett, throughout two fine days, sat with Jacqueline on the terrace, or strolled with her in the garden, and gave her a detailed account of his experiences with the Eighth Army. Jacqueline listened willingly but inattentively; it was a return to the early period of their relationship, and she was both surprised and pleased to find such a return possible; but she was also preoccupied, for to her the immediate future presented an ambiguous face. She would go home, she supposed, to the Midlands, and there look for another job; her family would be pleased to see her, and probably not expect her to stay long. "I need some one to tell me what to do," thought Jacqueline. "The Army got me into bad habits . . ."

It was a pity, but in her care for her dignity she had taught herself to be, not suspicious, but simply incredulous. One can age very rapidly in the three months before one's twenty-fifth birthday: Jacqueline looked back on her three-months-younger self as on a wide-eyed simpleton. From this new standpoint she also saw her recent behaviour as ill-tempered and unmannerly, admired Humphrey's tacit forgiveness of it, and welcomed his efforts to make the last days of their companionship as pleasant as the first; but her spirit was not now tuned to receive anything more. She smiled, and listened, and thought about jobs.

Humphrey continued to talk about Mersa Matruh.

Perhaps the ground had been cleared too well. Perhaps, at the back of his mind (reinforcing the male inhibition), was a notion that his aunt and his mother between them had somehow forced his hand. Perhaps the damage done by Tilly Cuff had gone too deep. Certainly the peaceful, inevitable flow of intimacy had been interrupted: three months ago they could have turned to each other in the dell, and by a look, a touch, made all clear. But now Humphrey was aware that he must propose in form, and Jacqueline gave him no help.

So the moment did not come; and the moment when Isabel and Tilly were to leave approached; and Humphrey would have been as glad as any one to get the matter settled. He had an uneasy feeling that he was behaving badly; he also felt it to be unjustified; he would have welcomed some compelling incident, and yet could not contrive one, because it must come from without. The result of this frame of mind was unexpected; receiving one morning a letter from a late comrade-in-arms, now engaged in the dress-making trade, Humphrey abruptly announced that he was going to Paris.

"To Paris!" repeated Isabel blankly. "Why Paris, dear?"

"I never got there," said Humphrey.

It seemed to him a compelling reason. Because he had spoken, and spoken without thinking, a decision had been made for him, and he was very glad. That it was completely irrelevant to the situation did not trouble him at all; it had, so to speak, removed the situation; a door is opened, and the draught puffs down a house of cards; and all three women realized this at once. Of the three Jacqueline showed, and indeed felt, the least surprise; she had accepted the collapse of that card-house already, and perhaps too soon. There was a moment's silence, then Tilly began to describe the Champs-Elysées, and Jacqueline said she believed French hats took six yards of material; Isabel said nothing — or said nothing then. Later in the morning she took Humphrey aside for a short and business-like talk.

"If you're not getting married, Humphrey — and I don't ask any questions — and you may be quite sure I shall say the right thing to your mother — but if you aren't getting married, do you still want this house?"

"Yes," said Humphrey. "Anyway, don't sell it."

"I don't want to sell it. But if you're not going to use it — "

"I might."

"Humphrey," said Isabel—quite forgetting her promise—"what *has* gone wrong between you and Jacky?"

"I don't know," said Humphrey.

These things happen; and when they happen, there is nothing more to be said. That same afternoon Jacqueline told Mrs. Brocken that she would like to go home at the end of the week.

"Because if you don't mind," said Jacqueline, "I'd like to leave before you do—the day before, so that I can get you packed. I've had a very happy time here, and I don't want to spoil it; and an empty house is always depressing."

"Then you shall go on Friday," said Isabel. She was very sorry for Jacqueline, but she knew when an egg was addled; she also knew that least said was soonest mended. Such tags of proverbial wisdom, unnecessary to her intellectual superiors, Mrs. Brocken often found very helpful. So (in their effects) did Jacqueline; the parting with her kind employer was greatly eased by their common assumption that there was nothing at all to be said.

So Jacqueline packed her bags. Like Tilly, she had been unlucky. Because of Tilly? It was possible. Least said, soonest mended.

3

How often is the reasonable solution of a dilemma accompanied by a sense of anticlimax! The collapse of a love-affair, unresolved into matrimony, is hardly less flat.

When Isabel sat down to write to her sister, the difference between the letter she might have written, and the letter she had actually to write, struck her so forcibly that for some minutes she sat gazing at the paper, and let the ink dry on her pen, absolutely unable to achieve more than the first line: "*My dearest Ruth.*"

Isabel had thought about this letter a good deal: it should have announced, in modest yet unmistakable terms, the full extent of her sacrifice. As yet Isabel had said no more than that Tilly was staying at the Lodge. ("*Darling, aren't you being a little too charitable?*" wrote back Ruth.) She had waited till the confession of her shabbiness could be gilded by the magnitude of her restitution: looked forward, not without pleasure, to Ruth's underlined astonishment and approval in return. For she knew Ruth would approve, as soon as Ruth understood; she knew that Ruth would have acted in exactly the same way—could Ruth, in the first place, have ever been so base. Now what was there to tell? Nothing; nothing but a change of plan which Ruth would probably attribute to sheer weak-mindedness.

"*My dearest Ruth,*" wrote Isabel:

> *Just a line*—[just a line, instead of eight pages!] *to say that I am going back to Bath. In fact, it is quite an Exodus, as Humphrey is going to Paris to see a friend.*

Isabel paused again. She had told Ruth a good deal more about Humphrey and Jacqueline than she had ever admitted to Humphrey; so much, in fact, that Humphrey's father had scribbled a congratulatory note in the margin of his wife's last letter. . . . Isabel sighed, and went on.

Jacky goes home on Friday, to her people, and so we leave Simon in possession till he gets a new roof. This is just a line, dear, to give you my new address. It's the old one, Browning's Hotel.

With fondest love,
Your loving sister,
ISABEL.

P.S. *I am taking Tilly to Bath with me, which is why I don't need J.*

When she had finished, Isabel contemplated the note in something like amazement. Was this all it had come to, her anguish, her distress of mind, her high resolve and noble intentions? Bravely confronting penury, she found herself instead simply going back to Bath, to a nice hotel, with Tilly instead of Jacqueline. What had happened? She really couldn't tell; but somehow it had all . . . dwindled. With deep regret Isabel contemplated for the last time a mental picture, long cherished in secret, of her own plump figure, decently but suitably clad, performing menial tasks in some grateful and astonished household. Such employment would have been no penance to her, though she had hoped it might count as such: weary but happy would she have returned each night to her frugal supper and a good gossip with Dora Tremayne. It was not to be. Tilly, who in this matter deputized for Fate, had decided otherwise. It was not to be: not only (it seemed) was Fate exacting no penance, Fate simply wouldn't accept it when offered—for Isabel honestly admitted that much as she regretted life with Dora, she also quite looked forward to life at Bath.

She had done her best; and yet her sister might well write back, a little amused, a little impatient, on the assumption that she hadn't, all summer, done *anything*. . . .

"I can't help it," thought Isabel regretfully. "Perhaps Simon is right about me. Perhaps I'm too foolish to be taken seriously." (By whom? Isabel did not explore the question.) But as always cheerfulness broke in; no doubt Mark too, she thought, was smiling at the collapse of her high intentions; and Mark wouldn't really have liked her to go out charing.

4

Though sincerely distressed on Jacqueline's account, and sadly deflated on her own, Isabel soon recovered sufficient spirits to liken Chipping Lodge to a nest from which the chicks are taking wing. Humphrey was the first to go; he could indeed pack up and move off with something of a bird's, or a warrior's, nonchalance; he telephoned another ex-comrade-in-arms at an aerodrome, packed a suitcase in half an hour, kissed his aunt, and was ready. "Been posted?" asked Jacqueline, meeting him in the hall. Humphrey grinned; and then, more soberly, put an arm round her shoulders and kissed her lightly on the cheek. He did not know quite what to say, but Jacqueline did. "Well, it's been nice meeting you," said Jacqueline cheerfully. "God bless!" — and ran upstairs before he was out of the door. Mr. Brocken was waiting for him on the step — furious because he had missed his usual train, but determined to get in a necessary word. "When do you expect to be back?" asked Mr. Brocken. "Lord knows," said Humphrey, with great readiness. "Do you realize," panted Mr. Brocken — for they were walking at great speed — "that your aunt is making this house over to you? What do you intend to do with it?" "Can't we hop a lorry?" asked Humphrey — and actually stepped into the road to halt an approaching van. It drew up; the driver, between whom and Humphrey a peculiar freemasonry seemed at once to establish itself, was going to London. "Come on," said Humphrey. "Certainly not!" cried Mr. Brocken, laying his hand on the vehicle's door — he had a fantastic notion, which he afterwards discounted, but which at the time was peremptory, that he might never see his nephew again. "What do you intend to do with Chipping Lodge? — We should have discussed this in the train!" cried Mr. Brocken. "Do you intend to live in it? Do you even intend to remain in England? Am I to approach the headmaster of Broxbury?"

The two young men — for Humphrey was now seated beside the driver — leaned towards him with the same gently amused expressions. Mr. Brocken, forced to look up, felt himself at a disadvantage; saw himself, suddenly, as even a little ridiculous; could his hand on the door stay the vehicle's progress? Obviously not; it was even then in motion.

"You look after it for me, Uncle Simon," called Humphrey, "then I shan't have to worry. So long, you old bastard!"

This at least was what Mr. Brocken thought he said. The van was gathering speed. Simon had to stand several moments longer on the curb, recovering composure, before he walked on; and so missed a second train.

The departure of Jacqueline was by comparison extremely decorous; she made proper farewells at the breakfast table, and Isabel hired a taxi to take her to the station later in the morning. "I trust," said Simon, almost benevolently, "that you will first enjoy a holiday, and then find another congenial post. Your references from this one will, I know, be excellent." Isabel said very little, but wrote Jacqueline's address carefully in her address book. She felt certain Jacky would get married some day (this was really Isabel's only idea of a congenial occupation) and wanted to be asked to the wedding; tact forbidding her to mention the subject at that moment, she simply kissed Jacqueline warmly and put an extra five-pound note into her bag. (Tilly gave Jacqueline a hair tidy, to remember her by.) Thus only two birds were left to flit; and Simon, observing the immense amount of Isabel's and Tilly's luggage assembling in the hall, cautiously absented himself from what would inevitably be a painful scene.

He said good-bye to Isabel on the Friday night — "As I have to leave unusually early," said Simon. "I have, as it happens, an appointment at nine." "Don't work too hard, dear," said Isabel affectionately. "What should we all do, if you broke down?"

Simon had often wondered this himself. He wondered what the country would do, if persons like himself failed in their duty. But it was no time for ethical discussion. He said merely that he hoped Isabel would keep accounts.

"Of course, dear," said Isabel.

"And if you get into difficulties — " Simon brought out the words reluctantly, but he brought them out — "let me know at once."

"Of course, dear," repeated Isabel. "Don't I always turn to you? You're a dear, good friend, Simon; and always the greatest help to me; and I love you very much."

Tilly Cuff said nothing so irrational. She had never been more than civil to Simon since the night he called her a detestable woman. But she felt they had better part on decently good terms, in case he subsequently found out some way of injuring her. She gave him a small wooden box, with "A present from Berne" on it; and so she and Isabel too left Chipping Lodge.

Chapter 24

They were all gone. Mr. Brocken, returning next day, which was Saturday, rather earlier than usual, returned to an empty house. All were gone, except the Pooles; and Simon slipped the catch into place on the lock of the front-door.

This in itself was a satisfaction to him. Isabel had been used to leave it on the latch, for the typical reason that she could never remember to get the single key copied. There being no one to answer the bell, it was a convenience to the household (and also to Dora Tremayne) to be able to walk in and out at will; and this had lent the establishment an oddly countrified flavour, which every one except Mr. Brocken liked. Mr. Brocken considered the practice an invitation to burglars; perversely, no burglar had yet accepted it; but he felt, as the catch snapped into place, a certain satisfaction.

There was no one, naturally, upstairs, and no one in the drawing-room. Simon passed out on to the terrace: he had the terrace to himself. With a book in his pocket, he postponed the pleasant moment when he should sit to read secure from interruption; it was pleasure enough to pace the deserted flags, glancing now and then towards the deserted garden. Sometimes Mr. Brocken paused, savouring his solitude as his father would have savoured a glass of wine; after the varied emotions, after the varied company of the last few months, he found it inexpressibly grateful. "I am rid—" thought Mr. Brocken; and carried the phrase no further—which was just as well. He had seen Isabel off the premises, and Tilly; Humphrey and Miss Brown; but he had forgotten Dora Tremayne, who at that moment joined him. She came striding round the northern end of the terrace, evidently by way of the stables; Mr. Brocken made a mental note to see that the gates were in future kept fastened.

Mr. Brocken stood still and let her come up to him.

"Well?" said Dora. "Enjoying yourself?"

"Yes," said Mr. Brocken.

Dora nodded.

"I thought you would be. Isabel made me promise to come and cheer you up in case you were lonely. Are you lonely?"

"No," replied Mr. Brocken.

"Good," said Dora. "Then I needn't stay. I'll just rest my feet." She sat down on one iron chair and crossed her ankles on another, and surveyed Mr. Brocken impartially. "Alexander Selkirk, minus goats," said Dora.

Simon said nothing. He believed Dora to be telling the truth about her promise to Isabel; but he also suspected that she would have walked up in any case, prompted by her own interfering disposition; and he did not mean to encourage her.

Dora, transferring her attention from Mr. Brocken to the house, said suddenly,

"Is Humphrey really going to live here?"

"He imagines so," replied Mr. Brocken. "I don't. I imagine that he will return to New Zealand, and that I shall again be left with the task of either letting the place or selling it, on his behalf instead of on my sister-in-law's."

"Cheer up," said Dora. "It may be requisitioned. And at least you've got Isabel off your hands."

"For the moment," said Mr. Brocken — as though determined to keep the conversation gloomy. "She has taken that animal with her. Will any decent hotel tolerate Bogey for more than a week?"

"My dear Simon, the same decent hotel tolerated him for nearly five years. What you don't allow for, and what you never have allowed for, is Isabel's likeableness."

Mr. Brocken stared at her in genuine amazement.

"*Likeable?*" he repeated. "You consider Isabel likeable?"

"Of course she is. And don't tell me she's a fool, because that has nothing to do with it. *You* aren't a fool; but are you likeable? No," said Dora, before Simon had time to speak. "People laugh at Isabel, and I dare say make fun of her behind her back; but at the same time they get fond of her. You're fond of her yourself."

Simon, about to answer with a flat denial, paused. He was a fair-minded man, if irascible: he was perfectly ready to do Isabel justice. What were, after all, his feelings towards his sister-in-law? In the first place, he had resented her; and was honest enough to admit that he would have resented whatever woman his brother married. But in the second place Isabel's character was so utterly different from his own ("Thank heaven!" thought Mr. Brocken) that without this connection he would simply have had nothing to do with her. She was a trouble to him. She was incurably foolish. At the same time, after three months of her society, Mr. Brocken was forced to acknowledge that Isabel was also scrupulous, unpretentious, and diligent in a house.

"I don't dislike her," he said at last.

Dora swung her feet to the ground and stood up.

"Praise from Sir Hubert," she said. "Well, I've done my duty; now I'm away. I dare say I shall see you in Station Road."

"I dare say," admitted Simon.

"But you needn't speak to me," added Dora reassuringly; and with that strode off.

Mr. Brocken resumed his pacing; presently descended the terrace steps and made a circuit of the garden — beating the bounds, as it were, of his solitary domain. Not a creature disputed it with him; all was quiet. He went into the tumble-down grotto, that smelt of damp and ivy, and took a look at it, and on to the strip of kitchen garden, where a row of lettuces was going to seed, and took a look at that; then up again towards the dell, now extremely boggy, to take a look at that too. All was quiet, all was still

— except that at that moment Mr. Brocken heard, coming from somewhere overhead, a most peculiar sound.

It was what he could only describe as a *streeling* sound: reeling, metallic, rhythmical, yet subject to sudden pauses; altogether impossible to identify, and yet vaguely familiar. Mr. Brocken walked to the foot of the staircase, and looking up saw that the winter-garden door was for once open. He mounted, and the mystery was solved. Round and round the tiled floor, in long expert swoops, Greta was roller-skating.

The child did not notice him; her small intent face wore a look of the most utter concentration. At each end of the course she bent one knee and made the half-circle on one foot: round the fountain she executed a sort of double-turn, finishing backwards: sometimes she pirouetted, sometimes jumped. It was a most accomplished performance.

"Doesn't Greta skate lovely?" asked Mrs. Poole.

2

She had come up the steps behind Simon's back; as Greta was too absorbed to notice him, so he had been too much absorbed to notice Greta's mother. But the child was aware at once, and waved a hand; seeing Mr. Brocken also, waved again, and executed a particularly showy leap.

"Humph," said Simon. "So that's why you wanted the use of the winter garden. Why didn't you say so?"

Mrs. Poole waved back to her daughter.

"Well, you never know," she said. "You can't tell. There might have been objections. And kiddies like a secret . . . Greta mostly gave it up these last months, but we didn't think you'd mind."

"No," said Simon, "I don't mind. I realize that your privacy has been seriously invaded."

The Pooles could always get the sense of what Mr. Brocken said to them, however baffling the sound: Mrs. Poole nodded. But she was not resentful.

"After all," said Mrs. Poole fairly, "it was *her* house. Mrs. Brocken had a right to live here if she wanted. And you and Captain G. being relations, and that Miss Brown I will say very easy to get on with, of course you had a right." (Simon noted an omission from this catalogue.) "But I must say it's a treat to be quiet again. *You*'ll be no bother," said Mrs. Poole encouragingly. "You're out all day: we'll give you your breakfast punctual as punctual. Will you go on being out for your supper?"

"It is possible — "

"That's right," said Mrs. Poole cordially. "Just give us a word when you get in, so we'll know to lock up. I can see we'll get on smashing."

Mr. Brocken felt a slight irritation. It seemed to him that the simple Pooles, so defenceless before Tilly Cuff, were adopting towards himself a rather cavalier attitude. It was abundantly plain that they intended to see as little of him as possible — that they intended to be as little as possible put out by his presence. Something besides his dignity was wounded; Simon had believed that the Pooles liked him; he himself had very nearly liked them—or at any rate, he had nearly liked Greta. On their behalf he had undergone considerable distress of mind. He had also tolerated the conversation of Mr. Simmonds, and perambulated Paddington. Looking back over a considerable period of years, he remembered no persons for whom he had so freely (in both senses of the word) exerted himself. Now they expected him to dine at his Club, to save them trouble. . . .

For the first time in his life, in fact, Mr. Brocken was encountering a self-sufficiency to match his own. The Pooles did like him; they thought him a decent old bird, and in their great distress had cast aside their reserve with him. (He hadn't been much help.) They liked him; if he were to fall sick, they would undoubtedly nurse him to the best of their ability. (Only not if he was infectious; Mrs. Poole wouldn't let Greta run any risk.) In short, they liked Mr. Brocken quite a lot; only they didn't want to be bothered with him.

"I trust you realize," said Simon rather stiffly, "that the present arrangement, however desirable, is only temporary. You may soon have Captain Garrett to ignore as well."

Again Mrs. Poole picked up his meaning very adroitly; and added an implication of her own.

"*If* he comes back. But will he?"

"This house," said Simon, "is now his property."

"But he won't live in it," said Mrs. Poole confidently. "He'll go back to his Down Under." (This was exactly what Simon expected, but he was surprised by the woman's assurance.) "A young fellow like him," said Mrs. Poole, "don't tell me he's going to settle down like you might. And I dare say *you*'ll be off before long, and then it'll be just like it was before."

"I shall endeavour," said Simon, "if Captain Garrett does not live here himself, to let or sell the place as soon as possible."

Mrs. Poole looked up, past the winter-garden wall, at the bulk of the house beyond.

"Big, ain't it?" she observed. "Still, you can but try . . . There's Greta had about enough."

The child's speed was indeed slackening; catching her mother's eyes, she executed a last twirl and sped towards the baize door; with a friendly nod to Mr. Brocken — for he was a decent old bird really — Mrs. Poole went in through the winter garden and followed her daughter.

3

Simon returned to the terrace; the afternoon was warm, warm enough for him to sit awhile in the pleasant stillness. He glanced doubtfully at the swing seat; it was covered, and the cover fastened; a last act of piety on the part of Humphrey Garrett. Simon took an iron chair and placed it so that he could lodge his feet between the pillars of the balustrade. Thus he turned his back on the house, and deliberately: the white façade, the fan-shaped pediments, the classic statues, had worked a spell on him once, but would never do so again. Racine, and the classic theatre; a premonition of tragedy, crossing a first wooing into equally foundationless security—"Bah!" thought Mr. Brocken. "What moonshine! I must have been dreaming, overtired, asleep and dreaming, to be foxed into such lunacy!"

And yet it was curious: to set one's foot on a tragic stage, and find that the part thrust into one's hand belonged to domestic comedy: to read on, and perceive in prospect a crisis after all potentially tragic: turn the last page upon anticlimax. How inartistic, and yet how lifelike! "I was right all along," thought Mr. Brocken. "Isabel's no heroine. Nor is she a saint. My sister-in-law Isabel is a fool. And since there is a providence that looks after fools, she may consider herself fortunate."

And yet—and yet—what was it Miss Brown had said? Something about integrity. "The fact that your aunt is a silly ass doesn't alter the case; in fact, it isolates it." Very well, then; give Isabel credit for the virtue of probity; admit that she had made restitution; not quite as she had meant to do (this also was like life) but as thoroughly as she could; *that* didn't alter the case either. Isabel was a fool; and he, Simon, had been right all along the line. . . .

It was very peaceful on the terrace. The knowledge that the house behind him was completely empty (for he no longer counted the Pooles) was deeply satisfying. Until Humphrey returned, if he ever did return, Mr. Brocken could look forward to a period of perfect peace. The attitude of the Pooles no longer hurt him, he was rather grateful for their good sense: the child Greta, in time, might have engaged his affections. Mr. Brocken acknowledged it freely: he had been growing quite fond of the child Greta. And as he admitted to Dora Tremayne, he had ceased to dislike his sister-in-law. There had been a moment when Humphrey and Miss Brown, lying side by side in the dell, positively appealed to his aesthetic sense. Humphrey, Miss Brown, the Pooles, Isabel — with no less than five persons had Mr. Brocken narrowly escaped, if not intimacy, a degree of acquaintance that would have allowed any one of them to become a nuisance to him. Now Isabel was at Bath, Humphrey in Paris, Jacqueline somewhere in the Midlands, and the Pooles safely withdrawn behind their customary defences. "I've been fortunate," thought Simon.

When he looked back over the last four months, Mr. Brocken saw himself as a man who had passed unscathed through very great danger.